THE NIGHT LADY

DEBRA CASTANEDA

SECOND RODEO BOOKS

ISBN: 978-1-7353420-8-5
Edited by: Lyndsey Smith, Horrorsmith Editing
Cover design by: James, GoOnWrite.com

To my grandmother, Fidencia (Chata) Morones.

Chapter 1

Jane Acevedo, on the lookout for the boogeyman, crept along the fence of her front yard, using the vines as cover. It was getting dark, and her mother had said she couldn't play with the other kids down the street. Not unless she wanted El Cucuy to snatch her away and drink her blood.

So far, all she'd seen with her pretend binoculars were her neighbors coming and going, but then she spotted Catalina Montez, the beautiful lady who lived down the road. Jane got to see her plenty at the empty lot across the street where Catalina grew plants for her cures. Her remedies were famous—even better than Vick's VapoRub.

Jane stood on an overturned washtub so she could get a better view. Blood dripped down Catalina's face. It made Jane feel all wobbly, but she couldn't stop watching, like a scary movie at The Brooklyn—she had to know what happened next. Besides, she'd been so bored having to stay in the front yard with nobody to talk to, and nothing much ever happened in Palo Verde.

And just like a movie, the door of the house next to the garden banged open, and Espy Gaten gave a dramatic cry, then ran down the steps. Espy, with her hair tied up in a scarf, didn't resemble a movie star like Catalina, but she was pretty too, just taller and skinnier. Espy helped Catalina into the house.

Jane would have loved to find out what was going on, but her mother didn't allow her to step foot past the gate. Not unless Jane wanted a swat on the *nalgas*. But Catalina with blood all over her face was even better than the gorilla girl matinee she'd seen. And besides, she was only going across the street. Jane checked for her mother to make sure she was still hanging laundry in the backyard, and she was.

Jane dashed across the dirt road and around the side of Espy's house, skirted the wild roses and thorns, then flattened herself against the fence so the *nopales* cactus wouldn't scratch her. Luckily, the kitchen window was open, and that's where the two women were, huddled together. She could hear Catalina crying, and when she managed a peek inside, standing on her tiptoes, she saw Catalina's torn dress, busted lip, and blood coming from an ugly cut above her eyebrow.

Jane couldn't picture Catalina getting into a fight like Uncle Beto. Maybe she'd fallen, or maybe someone got mad at her for one of her cures going wrong. But that was also hard to imagine—Catalina Montez was the most famous *curandera* around.

Keeping one eye on the front door of her house to make sure her mother didn't appear—in which case she planned to make straight for the back alley, jump a fence or two, and end up in her own backyard—Jane peered through the window again. Espy was walking back and forth in front of the stove as Catalina sat, looking as miserable as a kid on the first day of school.

"We should call the police," Espy said, in the same tone of voice Jane's mother used to threaten Uncle Beto.

"No, no, no," Catalina moaned.

The healer muttered something Jane couldn't hear, then the two women switched to Spanish, which Jane understood well enough to know they were having a secret conversation.

Espy asked if Catalina couldn't hex the man who had done that to her, and Catalina said he deserved the worst magic she could summon, even if it meant she had to call on Santa Muerte herself. At this, Jane shivered because her mother would not even allow her to mention the saint of death with the face of a skeleton. But Jane's thoughts were spinning elsewhere.

Magic. *Magia.*

The two women talked about magic as if it were real, and Jane remembered something her mother had said about Catalina, that she wasn't just a healer but a *bruja*, a witch. Jane's father said there was no such thing, which had surprised Jane because if he believed in *El Cucuy* and *La Llorona*—and he did because he always said if Jane didn't behave, they'd get her— then how could he not believe in brujas?

"But we can't just let him get away with it," Espy said in a loud voice.

Catalina stood, slowly enough for Jane to hunker down so they wouldn't see her. "I'll figure out a way, Espy, and he'll be sorry he ever touched me. Can you help me home?"

"Why don't you stay here? You shouldn't be alone. Not after everything you've been through."

"I just want to take a bath. In my own place."

"Then I'll go with you," Espy said firmly.

A chair scraped against wood, and Jane knew it was time to get going. By the time the two ladies left the little house, Jane was standing on her own front porch. She watched them walk down the street.

When they disappeared from view, Jane put on her pretend binoculars, searching for the bad man who hurt Catalina.

Chapter 2

Angel Ramirez didn't remember how he ended up stretched out and facedown on a cot. Through the mental fatigue, he thought maybe it had something to do with a lady he met and the promises she made. Then the fog cleared a little, and he could feel her staring at him from somewhere behind, just barely moving in the darkness. But he couldn't move, powerless to lift his head or roll over.

The smelly, worn blanket beneath him was wet with drool. His. And he was naked—he could feel the warm summer air caress his skin.

Light flickered in between the slats of the rough wooden planks, and in the distance, he could hear men talking, a cat meowing. He was in a cabin, a tiny one because the wall was close to his face. Somehow, he'd ended up in one of the rickety shacks where the old white bachelors, *los viejitos*, lived on the slope of La Loma.

He'd taken the dirt path past the shacks plenty of times on his way to Solano Street to visit a buddy, but he didn't know any of the men who lived there, not enough to stop by and visit. Los viejitos were mostly loners, men looking for work in need of a cheap place to live—some of them drunks. He'd been surprised to see a few of them on the movie set where he'd been lucky enough to find work as an extra, but he hardly recognized them because they were all cleaned up and sober.

Then he remembered.

He had been drinking with someone, probably the lady behind him. She was moving now, and it made his stomach go tight and the backs of his legs tingle. Someone had lured him there, tricked him, and probably poisoned him because his insides felt all wrong.

If he screamed for help, someone would hear him because the shacks were crammed close together on the hill. The trouble was, he couldn't make a sound.

Or move at all.

Angel was scared. More scared than he had ever been before. More than when that *pendejo* Beto from Palo Verde tried to stab him after drinking too much. Because now, he was stuck to a damn cot, and whoever was behind him was creeping closer.

He could hear breathing now, someone whispering his name.

It *was* a woman. Even in his condition, he knew what she was up to—trying to disguise her voice by keeping it low—and he wanted to shout, "Get away from me," and run away.

How had he ended up like that?

He opened his mouth, but no sound came out—just more drool—and he felt his eyes water. From fear. From desperation. Nothing good was going to come from his nalgas facing the ceiling, his *pito* mashed against the filthy blanket.

Naked. In the presence of a strange woman.

And then, just like that, he knew who to blame for the situation he was in.

That no good Louie Bonda, the guy from Loma he helped get a job as a movie extra—which had turned out to be a big mistake. Every time they had a second to spare, Louie wouldn't shut up. *You have a girlfriend, Angel? No? Why not? Have you ever done it? Oh yeah? With who?* And then Louie called him a virgin, to his face, and blabbed it around until all the other guys on the crew were laughing at him.

So, when Louie said he knew how to fix his problem, Angel had refused at first. But Louie said the lady liked that kind of thing, liked it rough—he knew this firsthand. Angel recognized the lady. She was older. Experienced, is what Louie said.

It was coming back to him now: his clothes coming off, him ripping at hers, her head smacking the wooden boards as he pushed her up against the wall in his excitement.

And now this.

Helpless as a baby, and his pito as soft as a baby too.

A finger touched his ankle. Angel flinched, more like a shudder, because that's all he could manage in his condition. Silently, slowly, the finger moved along his calf until it reached his thigh, then the top part of his thigh—slightly inward where the flesh was tender—then stopped. The finger tapped the spot, a playful tap as if to say, "Just wait until what's next."

Angel tried to take a deep breath, but it caught in his throat. Was it possible to choke and die on your own spit? He was trying hard not to panic, but what the hell was the woman up to? Was it just a part of her game—the rough stuff Louie had promised? Because if it was, Angel didn't like it, and when he saw the guy, he was going to knock his head off.

Something touched his other leg at the back of his knee. Normally, it would make him giggle like a girl because he was ticklish. Instead, he felt his insides flip over, and he heard himself moan.

"There you are," the woman whispered. "Is this what you like?"

No. No, he didn't. He hated it, and he hated whatever that hard little thing was poking at the soft spot in the back of his knee.

The woman was beside him now, bent so low her long hair hung over both sides of his face like a curtain, and she was breathing into his ear. He could smell the liquor—wine, sweet and musty. Then two hands pushed into his lower back, and he could feel the weight of her as she settled on him, the floorboards groaning beneath them.

Something scraped the side of his face, brushed across his nose. A rose. The strong and unmistakable scent of a rose, and like most roses, that one had thorns, and he could feel them scratch his skin. The stem raked its way down the side of his neck, his shoulder, his arm, then his hip.

He was whimpering now.

Something soft slipped around his neck. The woman sitting on his back reared up, her knees pressing into his sides, and the material tightened.

Chapter 3

Robert Cleary arrived for his third day on the job with a story to pitch to his editor, one he thought had real potential.

His new boss said he'd give him a few weeks to settle in, make contacts and all that, but Robert hated showing up to a meeting without a story in his pocket, so he'd spent his afternoon the day before nosing around Los Angeles City Hall. And sure enough, he'd gotten lucky. In fact, he'd been so excited he'd called his editor from a phone booth and let him know he was on his way with a decent story.

Harry Barkin looked up when Robert strolled into his office. Harry had a lot of hair for a man his age—mid-fifties—and hadn't turned fat, either. His eyes needed help, though, so he wore black-framed glasses.

Glancing at the clock on the wall, Harry said, "Good, you're early. I've got something for you. Don't even bother sitting down. I'm sending you straight out."

Robert leaned against the doorway and flipped open his reporter's notebook. "Yeah, sure. Whatcha got?"

Harry exhaled and flapped his lips like a horse. "Murder of a young man. Mexican. It's got all the detectives talking, let me tell you."

"Was he in a fight?"

"I'm sure he wished he had been. Nope. They found him naked, with roses stuffed up every opening the human body has. And did I mention he was strangled?"

"Jesus H Christ," Robert murmured. He looked around the newsroom. It was mostly empty in the morning, just a couple of guys on the phone. Harry didn't like reporters sitting around. He wanted them out on the streets, covering their beats. "You sure you don't want to assign one of the other guys, someone who's been around a little longer?"

Harry frowned. "Why? You got a problem covering stories like these?"

Robert knew exactly what kinds of stories Harry was talking about—the ones involving mutilated and brutalized bodies. He wasn't the overly sensitive type; it was just that nothing like that happened in his hometown of Denver where he'd last worked. He knew he'd been lucky in his short career, landing a reporting job in Salt Lake City straight out of college. After two years, he'd ended up back in Denver, the star reporter at the top newspaper.

Moving back in with his family had been the only thing he regretted, but once he'd done it—with all the ready hot meals and clean laundry—he'd lacked the will to look for his own place. His mother had been full of understanding for his long hours on the job but had made it clear she wouldn't tolerate "any funny business," which included booze and women. And that was how he'd arrived in Los Angeles, with impressive work skills but sadly lacking in romantic matters, which he hoped to remedy now that he had his own place and a double bed.

"No, no problem," he said firmly, then tipped his head in the general direction of the newsroom. "I just don't want to ruffle any feathers. You know, getting a good story so early in the game."

Harry pointed his finger at Robert and pulled the trigger. "That's for me to worry about. Not you. And besides, any fucking monkey can cover a crime story. They practically write themselves. This happened. That happened. The police say they don't know. Blah blah blah. It's perfect for the new kid." He paused. "But just don't fuck it up, because who knows what we're dealing with here. This could be the next Black Dahlia case if we're lucky."

Robert sighed. At thirty years old, he was hardly a kid but knew he looked young for his age, and he used it to his advantage, along with his big blue eyes. "Where am I going?" he asked, pencil hovering above the notepad.

"Northeast hills. A neighborhood the locals call La Loma. More like a village from days of yore. They don't even have sidewalks up there, so I hear. They found the dead kid in a shack. There's a row of them up on a hill. I thought it was just a bunch of drunks who lived there, but since the kid was found without any clothes, maybe someone started using the shacks for a little red-light business. Maybe the kid couldn't pay up, and a pimp had to teach him a lesson and send a warning to the other customers that this could be you, too, if you mess around."

Robert frowned at the mention of La Loma because he was pretty sure he heard it mentioned just the day before at city hall.

"Is that near Palo Verde?"

Harry shrugged. "Think so. Ask Gary, the redhead jabbering on the phone. He's been up there before. He'll tell you how to find it. Now quit asking me questions and get out of here."

Robert gave a salute with his pencil, bumping the eraser against his forehead.

He was turning on his heel when Harry said, "Hold on. Didn't you call while I was eating my morning donut and say you had a story for me? What was it?"

11

"I heard at city hall they're delivering eviction notices to some Mexican neighborhoods," he replied, taking off his hat and straightening the brim. "Trying to clear them out to build a housing project. But what I thought was interesting is that not all the suits are happy with the idea. Apparently, there are a few who are having second thoughts about uprooting so many people."

Harry nodded. "Well, son, that's exactly where you're heading. That's the same place where they found the poor bastard, but the eviction story is getting bumped by the kid who got bumped off. I don't have enough reporters to cover both, and I can guess which story is going to sell more papers." Then Harry brightened and snapped his fingers. "Wait a minute. If you want to play Superman and impress the big boys around here, then grab both stories. But you know which one takes priority, and if you've got to let one slip, don't bother calling and asking which one because you already know the answer."

"Understood," Robert said, then shut the door behind him before his boss could change his mind.

Robert knew a good story when he got one.

Robert parked on Solano Street just like Gary, the redheaded reporter back in the newsroom, had advised. Across the road, he could see a dirt path, a row of shacks snaking up the hill, and at the top, a cluster of people, but nowhere near the number he expected for a crime scene. There was plenty of parking, too, which didn't bode well. Maybe the police had already come and gone.

Notebook and pencil in pocket where they always were, camera hanging from a leather strap around his neck, Robert climbed the slope, heart pounding in his chest, nervous he'd missed his chance for an interview. At least it was early enough in the day that it was still cool out.

A neatly dressed man sat on the stoop of his cabin, petting a black cat, gave a friendly wave when he spotted Robert. Robert waved back and made straight for the group at the top of the hill. To his great relief, he saw police officers among them. No other reporters, though, which meant they'd either beat him to it and left, or hadn't arrived yet.

"Oh look, an early bird," an officer said when Robert walked up.

The other four men made chirping noises. Robert ignored them as he pulled out his notebook and flipped it open.

"I take it that means I'm the first one here?" he asked.

The officer smirked. "A genius, this one." He was tall, with black hair and an oddly dainty turned-up nose.

Robert may have worked in a town considered small by Los Angeles standards, but he was used to dealing with wise-ass police officers, and a stone face usually did the trick. He stared with unblinking eyes at the man, and sure enough, it worked like a charm because the officer turned serious.

"I'm Detective Dan Cagle. Which paper are you with?"

"*The Express*, sir," Robert said. He always made a point to be polite.

Detective Cagle's green eyes narrowed. "I haven't seen you around before, which means Harry sent me a new guy. Not sure how I feel about that."

So, that's how it happened. Cagle called Harry directly, which meant Harry had some pretty good connections, or the detective owed Harry a favor.

Robert straightened his shoulders. "You should feel fine, sir." He gave his best disarming smile. "So, if you can please fill me in?"

It was just as his boss said. A Mexican male, aged twenty-two, found dead in a shack, the victim of strangulation, his body violated.

"In what way?" Robert asked.

Cagle scratched his neck so hard it left a red mark on his skin. "Well, for one thing, he had a rose stem jammed into the place where the sun doesn't shine. A stem with thorns. He got the rose treatment elsewhere, too, but that's all off the record until I tell you it's not." He waited until Robert nodded, then continued. "The victim had been drinking heavily, but there are indications he was drugged. Just don't ask me what with because I don't know." Then he held up his hands. "And that's pretty much all we know at this time."

"Has the victim been identified?"

"I didn't mention that?" Detective Cagle rubbed a hand over his face.

"No, sir."

"Angel Ramirez. Place of residence, one village over in Palo Verde. He was working as an extra on that Western they're making up near the police academy. And yes, you can print his name. His parents have already been notified." The detective's expression softened. "I feel awfully sorry for that family—hard-working, good people. He was their only son. Their pride and joy."

Robert looked up in surprise. He wouldn't have thought the detective had a sentimental bone in his body, but he liked the man slightly better for it. "You said he was strangled. Any idea what with?"

Detective Cagle raised his eyebrows. "I guess I didn't have enough coffee this morning because I could swear I said." He paused and shot an inquiring glance at his officers, who pursed their lips and shook their heads. The detective cleared his throat.

"We found a scarf. Floral. With roses, no less. Not sure if that was coordinated, or unintentional."

"Any suspects?"

"No. We do not have a suspect at this time."

Robert tried another way. "Any indication that he was killed because he was a Mexican?"

"I'll give you a pass on that one," Detective Cagle said. "This is mostly a Mexican neighborhood. So, if you mean did we find something like 'Greaser Go Home' in red paint somewhere, no. Nothing of the sort."

"Any idea whether the killer was a man or a woman?"

"Now that's an interesting question," Detective Cagle said, "with the scarf and all, but since I don't know of many women who go around killing men, especially in the aforementioned way, I have to think it's a man trying to throw us off, or he just used whatever he could get his hands on. Who knows? Maybe the scarf belonged to his wife or girlfriend."

"Could be a homosexual," an officer suggested.

Detective Cagle snapped his fingers. "Could be."

"Women have killed before," said another officer—the oldest one in the group with iron gray hair. "There was that lady who ran a nursing home…in Connecticut, I believe. She killed dozens of people by poisoning them with arsenic."

Cagle looked like he was trying hard not to roll his eyes. "I read about that case. She did it for the insurance money. The old folks made the mistake of naming her as the beneficiary, so she bumped them off. This is different. This is the work of a sadist." Turning to Robert, he scowled. "That's also off the record."

Robert nodded, then looked around. Most of the shacks were close together, and some even seemed to share common walls. If someone was alive while being tortured—because the detective didn't have to spell it out for Robert to understand that—surely, someone would have heard the screams. Or something.

"Any witnesses?" he asked.

Detective Cagle shoved his hands in his pockets and frowned. "Not a one. Which isn't a complete surprise because most of the men who live here are drunks just a cut above skid row, so they were probably too liquored up to pay much attention. And besides, it happened over there…" He paused long enough to point at the tiniest shack with a peaked roof that stood the furthest away from the others. "You're not allowed to go in, by the way. You can take a few exterior shots, but just so you know, we've already taken the body away, so you can save yourself the trouble of trying to sneak inside."

Robert's heart sank. He'd been counting on getting some good shots of the victim. Not that they'd print the whole thing—given the graphic nature of his death—but a shot of the feet, maybe. The lack of a suggestive photo would sorely disappoint his new boss, which reminded him: there was still a question he needed to ask.

"Any chance prostitutes used that shack for business?"

"That's not something we've been able to determine," Detective Cagle said with a shrug. "But who knows what goes on here at night. It might be a den of prostitution for all we know, but it's not come to our attention because who's going to call it in?"

Robert glanced down the dirt path toward Solano. Not a fancy neighborhood, but respectable enough. The families living there would certainly have noticed if they'd seen women of the night coming and going. He'd have to ask around later.

"Last question, sir. When can we expect more information?"

Detective Cagle met his gaze. "When we get it, and not a second before." Then he turned his back, signaling the interview was over, and began speaking to his officers in hushed tones.

Robert said, "Thank you, detective," to the back of the man's head, then retraced his steps down the path, intending to interview the residents who lived in the neighborhood below, but the man with the black cat waved him over.

"You a reporter?" He was nearly bald with a hooked nose, his vest and pants clean but threadbare.

"I am. My name is Robert Cleary with *The Express*." He nodded in the direction of the police officers still gathered at the top of the hill. "You know anything I should know?" Which was the fastest and most direct way of getting straight to the matter. No use beating around the bush, he'd learned the hard way.

"I'm not sure about *knowing* anything," the man said, a sly look coming to his face. "But I *have* something that might interest you. It depends on how much money you have to spend."

Robert felt his shoulders tingle. "Oh yeah? You want to show me what you have?"

The man's chin jutted out. "I'll show you mine when you show me yours."

Robert sighed. "Look, I'll be honest with you, mister...?"

"Doesn't matter what my name is," he snapped. "I don't want my name in the paper. This is purely a cash transaction."

"That's fine, sir. Your name isn't necessary. As I was saying, I'll be honest with you. I don't have much money on me, but that's not a problem. I just need to check with my boss. Of course, he'll want to know what he's buying, whether he's getting value for the money, because he's got reports to fill out. So, you need to give me a better idea of what we're talking about here."

17

The man picked up the black cat and set it down on his lap. "Well, since you're being honest, so will I. I can't be completely sure about the value because I haven't used that old camera of mine for a long time. But it had film in it, and the flashbulb was still working, so I took some pictures of that young man—a sight I'll never forget by the way—except I haven't had the film developed yet, so's I can't tell you how good the pictures are. But they gotta be worth something."

Robert's mind raced. He had to get that film, and he had to make sure no other papers had it because an exclusive was the only way to go in that business. Working in Denver was one thing, but Los Angeles was a big city, and he had a lot to prove. Usually, *The Express* hired reporters from other smaller papers in town and sometimes cities like San Francisco. But Robert had taken the initiative to drive all the way to Los Angeles during his hard-earned vacation and had shown up, looking for work, at any newspaper that would let him past the front desk. Harry had agreed to meet him. Robert still couldn't believe his luck. A reporter had recently quit for a job in New York, and Harry hadn't filled the job yet. He'd liked Robert's pluck.

"I could use more of that around here," Harry had said. "Just don't disappoint me, or you'll be out on your ear in two weeks."

Robert knew some of the reporters who'd been at the paper a long time had placed bets on how long he'd last in the cutthroat newsroom, mistaking his affable demeanor and baby blue eyes for the naivety of a small-town journalist. He was determined to make them all lose.

A car door slammed on the street, then another. Reporters were beginning to arrive, which just added to the urgency of striking a deal.

"Listen," he said, forcing himself to stay calm. "I'm sure we can work something out. I just need to get to a phone and

18

call my boss and get the money. But do me a favor. Please keep this to yourself until I can come back and pay you. Will you do that?"

The man's eyes followed the progress of the advancing reporters with interest. "Maybe one of them will have cash money on them," he said hopefully, more to himself than to Robert.

Robert took a couple of steps toward the seated man, hoping to block his view and regain his attention. "No one carries around that kind of cash. Not the kind I'm talking about, anyway."

At this, the man's eyebrows shot up, a pleased expression lighting his face. "Now we're talking." He shoved the cat off his lap and got to his feet. Then he gave Robert a little push. "Off you go, then. I'll be waiting right here. I ain't going nowhere, and I won't say a thing. My lips are sealed."

Robert shook his hand, surprised at the strength of the man's grip. He tipped his hat and headed down the path, but he hadn't got far when the man called after him. "Where you going, kid?"

Robert stopped and stared at him. Maybe the man wasn't all there. "To find a phone booth."

The man shook his head. "The closest phone is in the ravine. If you go to Duran Market, they'll tell you where it is."

Robert only half heard him because he spotted a man from city hall walking up the dirt path. Standing at least six-foot-five, with a gaunt face and grim expression, it was like the grim reaper had exchanged his black robe for a custom-order gray suit, the black leather briefcase he carried instead of a scythe probably full of eviction letters. He hoped someone would warn the man not to knock on the door of the dead kid's house. The Ramirez family already had enough bad news for the day.

Chapter 4

By the time Robert walked from La Loma to Palo Verde, his head was throbbing, and he wished he'd worn more comfortable shoes. Unlike other parts of Los Angeles, the neighborhoods didn't have sidewalks and the dirt roads were uneven and rocky. He felt out of place, wearing a sport coat and tie, which happened to match his blue eyes.

After leaving the shacks, he'd descended into a valley the locals called La Loma. It was filled with houses—some ramshackle with rickety fences, others more substantial. There were power poles but few telephone wires. He continued walking as the temperature ticked up. By the time he reached Palo Verde, he could feel a blister forming on the back of a heel.

It was the middle of summer, so there were plenty of kids around, some of them without shoes. Again, the neighborhood was mixed, with a few houses veering toward the dilapidated, some just needing a new roof or a fresh coat of paint, and others clearly nicely tended. But it was no slum, as one city official had described it the day before. He wondered where, exactly, the tall man with the briefcase planned to hand out his eviction notices and if he was the only one. Maybe there would be an entire team of gray suited men arriving later in the day to deliver the bad news.

When he spotted two little boys working on a go-cart, he stopped and asked directions to Duran Market.

"It's around the block, mister," one said. He had an accent, but only a slight one. The boy sat up on his knees and regarded him with interest. "Are you a movie star?"

Robert laughed. He was of average height, average build, forgettable, an average Joe if there ever was one, except for his lake-blue eyes and long dark lashes. "Me? Nah. I'm not good-looking enough. How about you? Are you a movie star?"

The boy's big brown eyes got even wider. "No!"

The other child, wearing a blue and white striped shirt, said, "There's a lady on my street who looks like a movie star. Her name is Catalina. Everybody says she looks like Katy Jurado."

"Then she must be very beautiful," Robert said, smiling. "Maybe I'll get lucky and see her around."

"My mom says she's a witch," the boy in stripes said, then began tinkering with a wheel.

Robert blinked, taken aback by the certainty in the boy's voice. "Well, I'll have to be careful, then."

Just as the boys directed, he found Duran Market in the middle of the next block, elevated above the road by a flight of stairs. Inside, he found a wiry middle-aged man with a thick shock of silver hair behind the counter.

"I understand you can tell me where I can find a phone," Robert said without preamble, more out of courtesy to let the shopkeeper know he didn't intend to buy much.

The man stood up, a look of alarm setting his jaw tight. "Is it an emergency?"

"No, no, nothing like that. I'm a reporter out on a story, and I just need to check in with my boss."

The man scowled. "You mean what happened to Angel? Because that's a damned shame if there ever was one. That was a fine young man. I can't imagine who'd want to hurt the kid."

Robert raised his eyebrows. "You knew him?"

The man snorted. "Of course, I did. I've lived here all my life. I know everybody. My name is Salvio Duran."

Robert approached the counter, holding out his hand. "Robert Cleary. With *The Express.*"

After they'd shaken hands, Salvio said, "Rose Delgado has a phone at her house. She lives around the block. You can't miss it. She's got a big, fancy car parked out front. But be ready to spend a nickel. You need change?"

Robert dug around in his pocket just to make sure. "Nah, I got one, thank you. I'd like to buy some aspirin. You have any?"

With an exasperated look, Salvio came around the counter. "Of course, I have aspirin, and that's about all I've been selling lately, with those movie people around. That and Cokes, like they're going out of style."

The shopkeeper grabbed a bottle of aspirin from a shelf and held it up to Robert's nose for inspection. "I only carry the one brand. This one fine with you?"

Robert rubbed his temple. "With this headache? I'd take anything." Seeing Salvio's displeased expression, he quickly added, "It's great. That's the kind I always use," and finished paying. "Mr. Duran. Any chance I can interview you about Angel Ramirez? Just your recollections of him. I need a few quotes for my story."

Salvio looked as shocked as if Robert had just suggested something obscene. "*Ai*, no," he muttered. "That doesn't seem right."

Robert knew a "no" when he heard it, so he thanked the shopkeeper and left.

Around the block, he spotted the big car, and when he knocked on the door of the freshly painted house, a petite older woman with a towering silver bouffant answered, dressed in a white blouse, black skirt, and heels.

"Mrs. Delgado? Mr. Duran said you had a phone I could use for a nickel. Robert Cleary with *The Express*."

"Miss, not missus. You're lucky I'm starting work a bit late today. Wait here. I'll bring it out."

Robert waited on the porch while the woman went inside. Moments later, she returned and shoved the phone at him. "You can talk out here. For privacy." She then held her hand out for the coin, which Robert deposited in her palm. Her fingers, with long red nails, closed around the nickel.

The phone cord was long enough Robert could sit on the bench against the front windows, and it felt good to get off his feet. He swallowed two aspirins dry, then called his boss. Luckily, he was there, and the operator put him right through.

"Nice work, son," Harry said, sounding both pleased and surprised at the prospect of landing an exclusive photo. "I tell you what, I'm going to send someone over with an envelope of cash, so you don't have to come all the way back here. Just hightail it back to the old man with the camera and tell him not to get any funny ideas."

After working out the amount to be paid and the meeting place, Robert hung up. Rose must have been listening because she appeared in the doorway, that time wearing a baby blue jacket. She took the phone from him without comment, then joined him on the porch.

"Do you know of a shortcut to La Loma?" he asked hopefully.

Rose looked him up and down and then seemed to decide something. "You're not wearing the right shoes for the one I know of, and it wouldn't save you much time, anyway." Then she clicked down the steps and wiggled her fingers over her shoulders. "Come on. I'll give you a ride."

Robert climbed inside the big Ford Tudor after taking a moment to admire the whitewall tires. He'd seen the sedans on the road, but he'd never been inside one, and it was spacious and stylish—and expensive. Which made him wonder how the lady behind the wheel could afford it.

"What kind of work do you do, ma'am?" he asked, curious.

"I work at the court downtown as a translator, sometimes at city hall," she said as they pulled into the road. "And just call me Rose, please."

As much as Robert was in a hurry to get back to La Loma, there was something he had to mention, even if it meant a slight delay. "I think you forgot to lock the front door, Rose."

The woman sniffed. "I didn't forget. I just don't bother. We watch out for each other around here. And besides, someone might need to use the phone while I'm gone."

Robert shifted in his seat, remembering the eviction notices. "How long have you lived here?"

"All my life. This was my parent's house. My dad built it. My brothers got married. One lives in Bishop with his family, and the other lives in Loma. They let me live in the house, but if I ever decide to move and sell, they'll want their cut."

Robert cleared his throat. That time might come sooner than Rose expected, but he said nothing. "Did you know Angel Ramirez?"

A long silence followed. Rose stared straight ahead, biting her lip. Finally, she said, "He was a wonderful kid. Not like some of the hoodlums around here. I can't imagine why anyone would want to hurt that boy." She paused, frowning. "Those old gringo bachelors who live in the shacks don't bother anyone, but maybe a new man moved in. A bad man."

"The detective I talked to this morning said Angel was strangled with a scarf. A woman's scarf, so maybe it wasn't a man."

Rose's eyes snapped open. "Is that right?" she said, her voice unsteady. "You going to write about that in your story?"

"Yes, ma'am. I mean, Rose."

As the sedan bounced over the dirt road, the woman glanced over at him, eyebrows knit together. "Do us all a favor. When you write about Angel Ramirez, remember that he has parents and a family and friends who love him, and while you're at it, call him by his name and not just the Mexican."

"Of course," he murmured, wiping his brow where beads of sweat had gathered. He hoped the aspirin would work soon, his head still ached, and the day was heating up fast.

Luckily, they were nearing their destination—Solano Street—because Rose looked like she was winding up to continue her lecture.

"You can just drop me off here," Robert announced.

Rose slammed on the brakes, and they came to an abrupt stop. He jumped out, offered his profuse thanks, then waved at the long black car as it sped off, his thoughts drifting back to the eviction letters. He squeezed his eyes shut, trying not to think of the woman returning home after work to discover it tacked to her door.

He didn't have to wait long before a car pulled up, one driven by Gary, the redheaded reporter, who handed over an envelope through the open window. "I'll wait for the film and take it back, but hurry. I've got a story to get back to," he snapped.

Robert raced up the hill, once again wishing he'd worn more comfortable shoes. He waited impatiently while the man with the black cat counted the money, slowly and carefully, then sprinted back to the car, clutching the tin film container and hoping whatever was on it was worth all the effort.

After Gary had left, he spent the next hour knocking on doors and leaning on fences, talking to residents of the Solano neighborhood. But no one had seen anything suspicious, and each looked scandalized at his question about prostitutes working out of the shacks.

"*Ai*, no," said one man, scowling. "It's just a place where some down-and-out men live. It's not a red-light district." He'd been so offended he'd slammed the door in Robert's face.

Robert's stomach grumbled, a reminder he'd skipped breakfast that morning, which probably accounted for his headache. He needed to eat soon before he started getting light-headed, but he still had to get a few quotes about the victim. Hoping to find some people to interview and, hopefully, something to eat, he headed back to the ravine. That time, he drove up through the Bishop neighborhood and into Palo Verde, parking on the same block as Duran Market and Liquor. Salvio Duran, the shopkeeper, looked surprised to see him, even more surprised when Robert asked if there was a diner around.

"You came to the wrong place for that. No diners around here." Salvio walked to the plate-glass window at the front of the market, then pointed down the street. "See that big house down there? It belongs to Bertita. She serves up lunch and dinner to the movie people, so if you want something to eat, that's your best bet, but don't expect hamburgers and fries."

Robert thanked the man, then headed to the end of the block where it intersected with another street. From that vantage point, he could see a large group of people headed his way, some of them dressed like cowboys—the movie people Salvio had mentioned. Not wanting to find himself at the back of a long line for food, Robert made a beeline for the front door, which opened before he could even knock.

Cigar smoke greeted him, along with a stern looking angular woman wearing a brimmed cap. She was old and had a cane, which she smacked against the side of the door. "I wasn't expecting any new ones today," she said. "They told me they were starting Monday."

Robert hastened to explain. "I'm not with the film. I'm a reporter covering a story. There aren't any restaurants around, so Mr. Duran told me I might get something to eat here. Are you Bertita?"

She nodded. A colorful scarf covered her hair beneath the cap, which sat at a jaunty angle on her head. "I am. Sure. Come on in." She pulled him inside, leaving the door open behind them.

He followed her through the living room, which was large and simply furnished but comfortable looking, then into a long kitchen, where a few teenage girls bustled between the stove and counter. One of them dished up food and handed him a plate. Robert recognized nothing on it—he'd never had Mexican food before—then went into the backyard as instructed. He was one of the first to sit on the picnic tables covered in tablecloths made from stitched-together flour sacks. Soon, he was joined by a noisy group of men and women. Movie extras, he guessed, and people with bit parts.

A woman sat across from him. She was dressed like an Indian maiden, wearing a wig of long dark hair and lots of makeup. Watching him with amused amber eyes while he tackled his rice and beans, she tapped her fork against his plate. "You need to take the corn husk off the tamale before you eat it," she said, a smile playing around the corners of her wide and sensuous mouth, her voice low and husky.

Robert studied his plate, and sure enough, the red-tinted rectangle on his plate she'd called a tamale had a stiff outer covering, which he removed and set aside. When he cut into the soft dough, he saw it was filled with meat and tasted it, tentatively at first. It was a little spicy but delicious. He finished it in a few bites, then started on the second one.

A girl from the kitchen appeared at his side and set two more onto his plate. When he thanked her, she gave a delighted laugh and patted him on the shoulder.

"What part did you get?" the woman across from him asked.

Robert swallowed and shook his head. "I'm not with the movie."

She shot him a look of surprise. "With those eyes of yours? That's hard to believe."

Robert tried hard not to stare at her mouth as she licked her lips. He didn't know how to respond to the obvious flirtation, so he just shrugged instead. The sun was straight overhead and hot. The picnic tables sat beneath the trees, but there weren't enough leaves on them to provide much shade. Despite his now full stomach, his headache wasn't any better, and in fact, it was getting worse. He wished he hadn't left his sunglasses at home.

The woman kicked him under the table. "Oops," she said, then winked.

Since she was being so friendly, he decided he might as well make the most of it.

"I'm Robert Cleary with *The Express,* on an assignment. I hear Angel Ramirez worked as an extra on your movie." He took out his notebook and set it on the table. "I'm sure you've heard by now he was found murdered in La Loma. Did you know him?"

The woman twitched her nose. "Only just. He seemed like a sweet boy"—she emphasized boy—"but I hardly knew him, so I can't be of much help." She paused. "As much as I'd like to. My name is Darla, by the way. Darla Diamond."

Robert looked around. The yard had filled up with movie extras, and there wasn't an empty table. "Nice to meet you, Darla," he said, distracted by all the work still ahead of him and the headache that was going to make it a miserable business. Then he made his excuses, got up, and went around the tables until he finally met a few extras all too glad to talk about Angel in exchange for getting their names in the paper. Two of them even agreed to pose for a picture. All the while, he felt Darla continue to watch him, her back now resting against the picnic table, legs crossed. He couldn't help but notice she had nice legs. Long and shapely.

Robert retrieved his plate, nodded at Darla, then headed straight back to the kitchen. He thanked Bertita and paid her seventy-five cents for the excellent lunch. While they were making small talk near the front door, someone began screaming up the street. A man was shouting for help, and it was a voice he recognized.

"*Madre mia de Dios*," Bertita cried, clutching his sleeve. "It's Salvio."

Robert leapt off the porch and raced across the yard and up the street, his camera thumping against his chest. He could hear footsteps pounding behind him. Salvio Duran wasn't at the market where Robert expected to find him. Instead, he was on the porch of a house a couple doors up, waving his hands in the air.

When Robert skidded up, panting, Salvio began rattling off in Spanish to the person behind him—one of the girls from Bertita's kitchen. He couldn't understand a word the man was saying, but whatever it was, he was distraught. Salvio wasn't alone on the porch. The excessively tall man from the city he'd spotted earlier in the day was standing in the far corner, twisting his hat in his hands, a briefcase on the ground next to him.

The kitchen girl shouted instructions at someone who fled down the street. For what purpose, Robert didn't know.

When Bertita hobbled up with her cane, she and another woman helped Salvio into the house, and the door closed behind them.

"What happened?" Robert asked the man, whose pale, gaunt face looked nearly skeletal up close.

The man raked a hand through his hair. "The lady inside got sick. She might have had a stroke. I don't know."

"Are you from the city?" Robert asked. He sounded accusing, even to his own ears.

The man stiffened. "I might be," he replied warily, frowning now. "Who are you?"

"Robert Cleary with *The Express*. Did you just serve one of those eviction notices I've been hearing about?"

"I'm not authorized to talk to the press."

After the man picked up his briefcase and walked down the steps of the house, Robert pointed his camera at him and took a few photos. They'd come in handy when he got around to writing that story. When Robert turned around, a woman was walking toward him. She wore a simple white dress. He didn't know much about fashion, but he couldn't imagine anything that suited her better, with her dark hair, smooth brown skin, and slightly hooded eyes. It must have been the woman the go-cart boy had mentioned, the one who looked like a movie star.

Robert felt himself blushing as she noticed him staring. She returned his gaze, with a look so sultry it was worthy of a close-up in a major motion picture, and gave him a tight nod as she brushed past him.

When she reached the top of the steps leading to Salvio Duran's house, he lifted the camera to his face and called after her. "Catalina?"

She whirled around to face him—her perfect red mouth slightly open in surprise. He noted the swelling of her lower lip, the cut above an eyebrow, and a bruise on a high cheekbone.

31

Framing her in the viewfinder, he thought he couldn't remember seeing a more striking woman, at least not in real life. He snapped a picture, then another.

Chapter 5

While the sun finished its business of rising, Espy Gaten did a vigorous one hundred jumping jacks, drank a cup of coffee, then swept the house, imagining the broom brushing away her troublesome thoughts. That day, her thoughts were especially worrying, following the shocking news that had haunted her through the night.

Angel Ramirez was dead. Murdered.

She was going to lose her home. Evicted.

Evicted from the home she and her husband, Felix, had saved for and bought in the second year of their brief marriage, which ended abruptly with his death in the Battle of the Bulge. Since then, Espy had lived alone and made her living as a seamstress. She'd lucked out when a designer at the clothing factory became a costume designer for a movie studio, and he offered her a job, luckier still when his latest film went on location in the hills above her home in Palo Verde and nearby Elysian Park. Espy had agreed to work on the costumes from home, doing the fittings and fixing the damage that came along with making an action-packed Western.

The filming had recently begun, and from what Espy had been told, there would be a break in the fall, restarting early the next year, to give the lead star time to perform in a play.

Though she hadn't received her eviction notice yet, she expected it any time. She just hoped she could hang on to her house long enough to keep her deal with the movie studio going, along with the nice little bonus they gave her for using her place as a costume shop. Racks of garments—mostly of her making—filled her second bedroom and small dining room.

Espy, a practical woman, didn't think she—or anybody else—stood a chance of fighting the eviction notices, and she had no intention of living in the housing project the city planned to build, where she'd have to rent an apartment. No, thank you. Not after owning her own home. And if that didn't hurt enough, there was the matter of what the city was saying about the neighborhood she'd grown up in: a slum that needed clearing. It upset her so much she didn't look where she was going and stubbed her bare toe on the iron foot pedal of her sewing machine.

Another thing had nagged at her throughout the long night. Something to do with Catalina—someone she considered a friend, although it was impossible to know the woman. Catalina was quiet and secretive, especially about the men in her life. Once, Espy had to learn from neighborhood gossip that Catalina had lost her head over a younger man from La Loma, a handsome devil who'd broken her heart. Espy—the same age as Catalina, thirty-one—couldn't imagine getting involved with a twenty-four-year-old, and it still stung to know her friend had not confided in her.

Hours after Angel was found dead—*was it just yesterday?*—Espy had been on her hands and knees, pinning a hem, when she heard two actresses whispering. They'd seen Angel talking to Catalina a few days before while he was waiting around to be called for his scene, and the two had looked awfully cozy. Espy was so taken aback she'd stuck a pin in the actress's leg instead of the fabric. Catalina had never mentioned she'd visited the set, or that she had more than a passing familiarity with Angel. Come to think of it, he bore a striking resemblance to Catalina's former lover. Even if she found him too young, Espy couldn't deny

Angel was good-looking and smart as a whip—two reasons he landed a bit part with three lines of dialogue.

When Espy had asked Catalina why she'd gone to the set, she explained she'd been asked to deliver fresh flowers from her garden. Espy thought it strange her friend hadn't mentioned the arrangement before. And stranger still that the young production assistant named Don Lange had shown up at Catalina's shed—where she did her curandera work—with cash in an envelope as payment and a special request for bouquets of roses in different colors.

Then, she'd found Catalina, beaten up, and the curandera had refused to name her attacker. Her sexual attacker. And later that night, someone had killed Angel.

The connection between the events had popped into Espy's mind unbidden, and no matter how many times she tried to visualize the dark thought as a dust ball banished by her broom, it immediately reformed, layering guilt on top of anxiety, until it felt like she'd wrapped a three-inch length of elastic around her chest and sewed the ends tight.

Espy pulled on a yellow jumpsuit of her own design, stuffed some coins in a pocket, and put on a sweater against the morning chill. It wasn't even 6:30 yet.

She was passing the lot next door, the one Catalina used to grow all the plants, herbs, and flowers she used for her remedies, when she spotted the curandera among the red summer roses she sold for extra money.

"Good morning, Catalina," she called.

The woman's long dark hair was piled on top of her head, making it easier to see her face and the damage inflicted upon it.

Catalina waved and gave her a tired smile. "The truck from the flower market is late this morning," she replied, picking up a bundle of roses and carrying them to the fence where Espy stood. Catalina was dressed in a checked shirt and dungarees.

No matter what she wore, her beautiful friend made it look intentional, like a costume.

The scent of the roses was overpowering, even in the open air. Espy wondered if Catalina added any of her magic powders to the soil to make them grow so long and fragrant.

"Do you think we'll get our eviction letters today?" Espy asked.

Catalina nodded. "Yes. I read my cards this morning. You will too, I'm sure."

Espy sighed. She knew Catalina often consulted her colorful deck of tarot cards, but she was asking as one neighbor to another, not as a neighbor asking her friend to use her special gifts.

"Will you sell up?" asked Espy.

Catalina's eyes narrowed. "Not if I can help it." Her voice held a sharpness that surprised Espy, for Catalina was rarely perturbed.

Espy leaned on the fence. "But what can you do?"

The cut above Catalina's eye was healing fast. Faster than normal. Probably because of one of the curandera's legendary remedies. The edges had pulled closer together, and it looked less red and puffy, but it still looked like it hurt.

Catalina rubbed her hands against her dungarees. "Fight. Fight the bastards. I talked to Rose last night. She got her notice. She and some other ladies are going to get organized and give the city a run for its money, and I'll be right there with them."

"But you might get arrested," Espy cried in alarm. She'd never heard Catalina talk like that before, and the idea of resisting the authorities made her knees feel wobbly.

Catalina shrugged and said, "So be it."

Espy swallowed, then cleared her throat. "Have you seen Petra?" Salvio Duran's wife had collapsed minutes after the family had received its eviction notice.

36

Catalina sighed, looking troubled. "She's not good. Dr. Eng was there all night, so I didn't stay. He wanted to take her to the hospital, but he was afraid the move might kill her, so they left her at home." She paused long enough to cross herself, and Espy did the same. "I'm going to check on her after I get cleaned up."

"I'm going into town to buy the paper," Espy said. "You still haven't told me what happened, but I want you to know that you can trust me. I won't tell anyone. Not if you don't want me to, but you shouldn't keep stuff like that a secret." She paused, struggling to come up with the right words. "It's not good for you. It's like the *limpia* you did with me after Felix died, and you said I was suffering from a spiritual sickness. It fixed me up, but you also made me talk about how I was feeling, and that made me feel better too. So, the same goes for you, Catalina. You need to talk about your problems, too, and when you're ready, I want you to know you can come see me. Anytime."

Catalina reached over the fence, took Espy's hand, and squeezed it. "You're a good friend, Espy," she whispered, tears coming to her eyes. She swiped at them with the back of her hand and sniffed. "If Petra dies, it'll be the city's fault," she added, her voice turning hard. "For upsetting her so much. The *poracita* had a stroke."

Espy remembered what she heard about Catalina and Angel but decided it wasn't the time to ask about it, with the woman in such a dark mood. She said goodbye and hurried away. When she walked through Bishop, she saw small groups of people gathered, some waving pieces of paper in the air. Even without joining them, she knew what they were talking about. The evictions. She returned a few waves but kept moving. She had a lot to do before she started work at nine, when she expected the first of the fittings to arrive.

Espy made straight for the newsstand closest to Bishop, paid five cents for *The Express*—*The Examiner* cost double that—then ducked into a coffee shop, sat at the counter, and paid another nickel for a cup of coffee—nice and strong, just how she liked it. She opened the paper on the counter and gasped at the front-page headline, then gasped again at the photo, the bare feet and calves—scratched and bloody—laying on what appeared to be a cot.

KILLER SOUGHT IN GRISLY SLAYING OF MOVIE EXTRA

LOS ANGELES - A 23-year-old man, a movie extra, was found slain Monday morning in a small cabin on a hill above the Solano Canyon neighborhood at the southern end of Elysian Park. There are no suspects at this time. An unidentified man told authorities he entered the cabin at about 5:00 a.m. after noticing the door wide open. He found Angel Ramirez's naked body inside. Police Detective Dan Cagle said Ramirez had died from strangulation—pending confirmation by pathologists—and that a woman's floral scarf was found at the scene. Ramirez was believed to have been intoxicated at the time of his death and possibly drugged, also according to Detective Cagle, who refused to describe the nature of his wounds. The city crime laboratory was called to the cabin where evidence was collected.

Nothing in her many years of reading Agatha Christie's murder mysteries prepared her for learning Angel Ramirez had been found naked in, of all places, the shacks of Los Viejitos, drunk to boot. This was not the Angel she knew. She couldn't imagine how his parents were going to react when they read the newspaper and saw the picture of his poor, bloody feet.

What had happened in that cabin?

Angel wasn't like some of the other young men who got into fights or drank away their hard-earned money. When he'd gotten the job as an extra, then the bit part, not even that had gone to his head. Some men working on the movie flirted with Espy when they came for their fittings, and occasionally, she'd slap away a hand when someone got too fresh. Like that darned Louie Bonda from Loma who stuck his hand up her skirt while she was on a ladder reaching for a box of material. But Angel wasn't like them at all.

And then there was the part about his wounds.

Even she could guess that meant lots of wounds, bad ones, and since he didn't have any clothes on, his private parts must have been involved. As she sat staring into her coffee—still hot because the waitress kept refilling her cup and she kept drinking it—her thoughts flickered back to Catalina sitting in her kitchen, her dress hiked up to her thighs, high enough to reveal the bruises. When Catalina had noticed her staring, she'd pushed down the dress and closed her legs. Even if Catalina wouldn't say the words aloud, Espy could guess what happened. This morning, Catalina had appeared changed, filled with a steely-eyed anger. At first, Espy had blamed it on the eviction notices, but maybe there was more to it than that.

All those troubling thoughts made it impossible for Espy to concentrate on her first fitting. She accidentally poked the actress with a pin at least twice, but the lady was too busy flirting with the prop master to react. The prop man's name was Bruce Knox, and he was just as dreamy as the actor Montgomery Clift with his moody good looks, except Bruce was cheerful and laughed a lot.

Espy needed to take in the dress by an inch and a half because the director wanted it tighter, even though the woman could hardly breathe as it was. The director didn't care what the costume designer had in mind. He would not be happy until every woman in the film appeared with their shoulders bared, their bosoms heaving, or their corsets cinched tight. So tight a young lady playing a saloon girl had passed out between scenes.

"I'm supposed to be a teacher," the actress was telling Bruce, tugging at the waist of the dress. "Does this look like something a schoolmarm would wear?"

Bruce didn't respond. Instead, he turned his attention to Espy. "I'm just a man here to borrow another kerosene lamp from Miss Gaten's shed. Let's ask the real expert. Espy, what do you think? Is that dress too tight?"

Espy was so startled her mouth opened, and three pins fell to the ground. People from the movie rarely talked to her. At the studio, she was just a seamstress tucked away in a back room. She'd hoped that there, on location, the actors and actresses would not only see her, but see her differently, as part of the crew, the way they saw Bruce and the production assistant, Don, and all the others who helped bring the movie to life. But that hadn't happened.

At first, she told herself it was because she was Mexican, but then she'd seen the way Angel and then Louie had been welcomed into the group, and the difference rankled. She sat behind her trusty Singer sewing machine, surrounded by extras lounging around her house during a break, and she realized they saw her as a lowly seamstress with no potential like Angel or Louie. One day, she vowed, she wouldn't be just the invisible woman with a measuring tape around her neck and a pin cushion in her apron. She'd find a way to work her way up. She'd get the courage to show her boss her notebook of ideas and designs for the films they were scheduled to work on. Maybe he'd give her a chance, promote her from seamstress to his design assistant.

But for now, the actors and actresses she worked alongside everyday took little notice of her, and once again, she felt like an outsider. Bruce was the first person to ask for her opinion.

"A little," she conceded. "I guess the point is to show her figure off to its best advantage," she added, pleased with herself, because it sounded like something a character in one of Agatha Christie's novels might say.

Bruce grinned. "She speaks! Thank you, Espy, I've just won my bet. Your boss said I couldn't get you to talk to me, and he was wrong."

The actress scowled. Espy's hand trembled slightly as she wove a needle through the striped fabric and pulled it taught.

Bruce walked through the living room, into the kitchen, and out the back door. Usually, the prop man didn't come inside. Instead, he'd go around to the shed in back, which was full of old stuff. He'd called it a treasure trove when he'd first poked through it, but maybe there was another reason he liked to come by. Just the morning before, while he was walking past her house, he'd stopped and said hello. Espy had been too tongue-tied to say much, so she'd retreated inside, leaving him to stare after her. And now this. She didn't know what to make of it.

The schoolmarm and the saloon ladies trooped out, and a half-dozen men and women playing Indians walked in wearing moccasins. Their costumes were so filthy Espy asked what they'd got up to, and one of them explained they'd just finished a scene involving crawling on their stomachs. Now Espy was tasked with stitching up the rips, which was easier if they took off their costumes. They changed into robes in her spare bedroom.

"We're going to the Mexican lady's house for lunch," they called over their shoulders.

Two extras remained: Darla, who had unusual yellow-brown eyes; and that wise guy Louie Bonda. Darla was still wearing full makeup and a wig of long black hair. She sat on the sofa, reading the newspaper, while Louie stared at her shapely bare legs.

Darla shook out the newspaper so hard it snapped. Espy looked up just in time to see the woman cross her legs, causing Espy to blink and catching Louie so off-guard he nearly choked on the water he was drinking. There was no question about it; Darla wasn't wearing panties.

Espy was eyeing the woman nervously, when Darla shook out the paper again, this time revealing a headline Espy had missed in her hurry to read the story about Angel Ramirez.

CITY TO EVICT RESIDENTS OF BLIGHTED AREA

Darla stood, tossing the newspaper aside and retying the belt of her robe. "I think I'll go get lunch," she said in her low, husky voice, then walked toward the front door, where she paused and looked over her shoulder at Louie. "You coming too, kid, or what?"

When the screen door had slammed behind them, Espy sank into the closest chair, one shaky hand fluttering to her head. The thick elastic band was back around her chest, her heart thumping against it. It felt like someone was pulling it tight, and then she was trembling all over. She felt herself pitch forward onto her hands and knees, gasping for breath. A voice was calling her name.

"Espy? Espy, what's wrong? Should I call a doctor?"

Strong hands lifted her to the couch, and then someone was sitting beside her, pushing her hair away from her face. It was Bruce Knox. Of all people, he had to see her like that, and she felt a blush of shame that burned her neck and cheeks.

"No, no," she moaned, shaking her head. "I'll be fine."

Bruce threw aside the newspaper and sat next to her, taking her hands between his and rubbing them as if to warm them. A knock on the door interrupted them.

"You stay there," Bruce said firmly. "I'll get it."

Moments later, he returned with a stern-looking man so tall his head nearly scraped the ceiling. "Are you Mrs. Gaten?" he asked.

Now that the moment she'd been dreading had finally arrived, Espy felt numb. "I am," she said. "And I know why you're here." Then she pointed with a shaking finger. "You can leave it there on the table, and then, please, just go."

The man stared at her for a moment with unfathomable eyes set deep in his skeletal face. "Don't you have any questions?" he asked.

"Don't you have any heart?" she replied. Then she buried her face in her hands and cried.

Chapter 6

Jane sat, waiting for her lunch. She wished her mother would hurry because she was hungry, and she also needed to get back to the front yard to watch Catalina. The curandera was working in her garden, where things grew so wild there were plenty of places to hide if you were a bad man trying to hurt Catalina.

But instead of making her a quesadilla as she'd promised, Jane's mother stood, staring out the screen door into the backyard. She was shaking all over, as bad as the time Jane's big brother got sick and died.

Jane wondered if her mother was sick too. "Mama?" she whispered.

Instead of answering, her mother put her hands over her eyes as if she'd seen something scary. Mouth dry, Jane slid off her chair, crept toward the screen door, and peered outside. There was nothing unusual out there. Just the clothes drying on the line in the midday sun.

Her mother crumpled to the floor and screamed, her mouth open so wide Jane could see the space where two teeth should be.

Heart thudding in her chest, Jane dropped to her knees. "Mama, mama," she cried. "What hurts?"

It was as if her mother could not hear her. The screams got louder, and then her body jerked, like a monster had given her a giant shake, and she yelled, "Get away from me," in Spanish.

Jane's face was all wet, and she realized she was crying. She stared helplessly at her mother, wondering what to do. Her father was far from home, working at the place where he made tiles. She could get Dr. Eng. He could help, but he worked in Chinatown, and she'd have to call him. They didn't have a phone, and she didn't want to leave her mother to walk to Rose's house. And anyway, her parents didn't allow her to leave without permission. But this was an emergency. At that time of day, Rose was probably not at home because she worked downtown, but everyone knew Rose left the door open, so she could just go inside. She'd never made a telephone call before, so she'd have to ask someone to help her.

Jane was so busy thinking things through she hadn't noticed she was no longer alone with her mother in the kitchen. Something made a noise behind her. When she whirled around, she saw it was Catalina, wearing dungarees and her hair up in a scarf with red roses.

Jane had never been so glad to see anyone. "Something's wrong with Mama," she gasped, then burst into tears.

Catalina put both hands on Jane's shoulders, then gently but firmly moved her aside. "She's going to be fine, Jane," she said in a calm, reassuring voice. "It's an *attaque de nervios*."

Jane wasn't sure what that was, but she hoped it wasn't the same thing that killed Esther Duran, the nice lady who worked at the market and gave her a free candy on their shopping days.

"But Señora Duran…," she whispered.

Catalina bit her lip and shook her head. "*Ai*, no, Jane. Petra had a stroke. This is different." She paused and looked down at Jane's mother, who was thrashing on the floor, the heels of her shoes pounding the linoleum. "Now listen, Jane. Can you go get me a washcloth, get it nice and wet, and bring it to me? Yes? Good."

46

Jane's heart leaped with relief, and she ran to the bathroom to do as she was told. When she came back, Catalina was kneeling, her mother's head on her lap as the curandera stroked her hair. Her mother was panting, staring up at Catalina with blank eyes. The curandera ran the washcloth over her mother's neck, then placed it on her forehead.

Jane wondered if her mother had been hexed. She'd heard about such things happening. Like when Rose Delgado, her mother's old friend who lived nearby, fell down for no reason three times in three days, she'd gone to the other curandera—the one who lived in La Loma. She'd made the hex go away, and Rose stopped falling down.

"Is she hexed?" Jane asked.

Catalina glanced up and blinked. A lock of dark hair escaped the scarf and curled down the side of her face. Jane thought she was much prettier than the actresses from the cowboy movie she'd seen walking around.

"It's not a hex, Jane," she said. Then she reached out and took Jane's hand. It was rougher than Jane expected.

Catalina said, "A man came to your house yesterday. To deliver a letter to your parents?"

"Yes," said Jane. Her parents had sent her to her room after the tall man with the scary face came, but she'd stood listening in the hallway. The man said the city was taking away their house to build new apartments. They could live there if they wanted. Jane's father said no, they didn't want to live in them. Jane hoped they could move in with her cousins in Boyle Heights because there was no boogeyman there, and her cousins could play in the streets.

"That letter upset your mom real bad, Jane," Catalina said, sounding angry. "It was more than she could take."

Jane stared at Catalina uncertainly. Other people got the letter too. Like Rose. She'd come over to see her parents after

47

dinner to talk about it. Rose had been so mad her hair seemed to quiver on her head. Her dad's friend Martin had driven over from Loma. He'd cursed a lot, talking about the letter as he and her father sat on the porch, drinking a beer. Jane had gone with her mother to see Espy at her house. Jane loved going to Espy's house because it was filled with costumes from the movie, and Espy let her look through a tin of buttons and ribbons while she and her mother talked. Rose and Espy had been upset, but they didn't scream like a baby having a tantrum. Jane didn't say that though because it sounded mean.

"What should we do?" Jane asked.

Catalina gave her a sad smile. "Can you help me get your mother into the bedroom?"

Jane was small but strong, and she was happy to be given a chance to prove it. She helped Catalina lift her mother off the floor, then half carried, half dragged her to bed. Catalina took off her mom's shoes while Jane pulled the curtains shut. Even though it was warm in the room, Catalina covered her mother with the quilt, then sat beside her on the bed and began talking to her in such a low voice Jane couldn't hear what she was saying. Eventually, her mother's eyes closed, and by the way she was breathing, Jane knew she had fallen asleep.

"She just needs some rest," Catalina said. She put an arm around Jane as they went into the living room.

"Are you going?" Jane asked nervously. Before her brother died, her mother would leave them alone for an hour or so to do her shopping and visit friends who lived in Bishop, but she didn't go out anymore, and Jane couldn't remember the last time she'd been alone in the house.

Catalina smiled. "I'll be just across the street. I have some work to do, but I'll come back to check on your mama, and if she wakes up, just holler at me, and I'll run over."

Jane's heart sank. "My mother says I'm not supposed to be by myself. She says the cucuy will get me."

Catalina scowled, and Jane wondered if she'd done something wrong by telling her about the cucuy, so she hurried to explain. "It's not just the cucuy. My dad says the llorona is out there too."

Catalina put her hands on her hips. "Do you want me to give you something to protect you from them?"

Jane looked at Catalina, who looked angry, her dark eyes flashing. Jane didn't understand why, but the idea of something that would keep the boogeyman from grabbing her and pulling her into a bush or carrying her away made her gasp in relief.

"Oh yes!" she cried.

"Wait on the porch for me, and I'll be right back," said Catalina.

Jane stood, her pretend binoculars pressed against her eyes, and watched as the woman crossed the dirt road, banged through the front gate, and disappeared into the shed at the back of the lot. Minutes later, she was back, carrying a small cardboard box which she set on the porch railing.

Catalina took out a bowl and placed a gray stick in it, then lit one end with a match, releasing a sharp scent into the air. It smelled nice, not bad. Catalina pulled a thick red string from a pocket of her dungarees, then waved it through the smoke.

When she'd done this a few times, she tied the string around Jane's wrist and smiled. "There you go, Jane. This is a charm bracelet. It will protect you from the cucuy and from other danger too." She paused, then rummaged through the box. "And because your mama scared you so bad, I'm going to give you these. They're *bolsitas*. Some people call them *amuletos*." Catalina took out two safety pins and attached one cloth bag to the inside of Jane's shirt and the other to the inside of her overalls.

"Do they work against ghosts?" Jane asked hopefully, thinking of La Llorona, the crying lady who'd killed her children.

"They do," Catalina said solemnly. "And they work really good if you believe they work. Do you understand?"

Jane didn't know what to think. If the charms were magic, why would she need to believe in magic for them to work? It didn't make sense, but she was ready to believe in anything that would keep her safe from the things that terrified her in the darkness of night, when she was alone in her bed.

"Yes," she whispered. "I understand."

Catalina sighed, then kissed her on the forehead. "You're a good girl, Jane. If I ever have a little girl, I hope she's just like you."

Jane's heart soared as she leaned against the porch railing, watching Catalina walk down the steps, the little box under one arm.

Fingering the knots in the red bracelet, she thought how lucky she was to have a nice witch so close by.

Chapter 7

Robert sat in his boss's office and reveled in the rare and fleeting approval that came with landing a story on the front page, although he knew Harry's good mood had more to do with the sensational murder scene photo than the article itself. He wished he could fully enjoy the moment. Despite all the aspirin he'd taken, his head still throbbed. Was it normal for a headache to last that long? He hoped he didn't have a brain tumor or a blood clot. In his line of work, he heard about all kinds of things that could kill a person.

"That exclusive photo sure as hell sold lots of newspapers," Harry was saying. "Worth every penny. In fact, we got a deal." He drummed his fingers on his enormous desk. "That movie that's being filmed where the kid was killed. What's it called?"

"*Beyond the Passage*," answered Robert. "It's a Western."

"What's it about?" Harry asked, then snapped his fingers and pointed. "Don't bother answering. I don't care. I want you back up there for a twofer. Do a nice profile on the movie and tell us how upset and worried everyone is that an extra got killed nearby. You know. Turmoil on the set."

Robert nodded, dutifully taking notes. But it was mostly for show—the assignment was straightforward enough. "I can make it a threefer," he said, getting to his feet.

Harry took off his glasses and cleaned them with a handkerchief. "How's that?"

"I can follow up on the eviction notices. Some locals are organizing, gearing up for a fight."

"Maybe," Harry said with a noncommittal face scrunch. "I'm not sure that's the kind of story we need to follow closely, but if something big happens, let me know about it." He paused, frowning as he scraped a hand through his thick hair. "Since it's a Western, see if you can get a nice shot of an actress in a corset or something. The bosses say our paper doesn't have enough sex appeal, and I've got another meeting coming up. I'd sure like to avoid hearing that again. Think you can do that?"

"I'll do my best," Robert said, thinking of Darla Diamond, the extra with the shapely legs. If he couldn't get a lady in a corset, a shot of her gams might do.

On his way out, he couldn't help but whistle as he walked through the bullpen, slapping the latest edition of the paper against his leg. A little gloating never hurt.

"Yeah, yeah, yeah, Cleary. We get it," one of the guys grumbled. "Beginner's luck."

"The honeymoon phase will be over soon enough," another shouted after him.

Grinning, Robert made a rude gesture over his shoulder and was rewarded with a ball of paper smacking the back of his head.

The drive to Palo Verde was less than four miles, but it felt worlds away from the bustle of the city; the place had a rural feel to it, with all the hills and dirt roads. When Robert parked near Bertita's house, he took off his shiny shoes and put on worn, comfortable ones he'd stashed in the trunk of his car, just in case. He left his tie on but took off his jacket and threw it in the jalopy he'd driven from Denver. Someday, he'd buy a new car, but on his salary, it was going to take a while to save up.

He trekked up a dirt road in the general direction of the movie set. The morning sun beat down on his head—he should

52

have worn his hat, but he'd left it in the car. When he reached the top of a hill, he was sweating, and his head was throbbing worse than ever. He stopped and surveyed the valley below and gave a low whistle.

An entire Wild West town rose out of the dirt: a general store at one end, a hotel and saloon in the middle, and a saddle shop and jail at the far end. How long had it taken to build all that? And what would happen to the set once they'd finished filming? He knew next to nothing about the movie business, and he felt a flicker of excitement at getting to cover something new.

He made his way down the slope. When he reached the bottom, no one paid him any attention. The film crew was sitting around at card tables, eating sandwiches, while women in long dresses sat in chairs, getting their makeup done. His heart sank when he noticed there wasn't a scantily clad woman in sight.

He walked up to the first person who looked his way, a woman about his own age, wearing a white shirt and aqua blue calf-length trousers. She sat in a chair, sewing, a pair of pants in brown suede draped across her lap.

"I'm Robert Cleary," he said, forcing himself to smile despite his headache. "From *The Express.*"

At this, her eyes snapped open. She had an oval face with bangs and a mass of brown hair held back with a headband. "You're that reporter," she said. "The one who wrote the story about Angel."

Robert looked at her with equal surprise. People might remember an article but rarely who wrote it, unless they were a cop or a politician who wanted to give him a knuckle sandwich. "You recognize my name?"

She nodded. "Of course," she said, needle poised mid-air. "I'm Espy. Esperanza Gaten," she said shyly. Her first name rolled off her tongue, and her last name she pronounced Gah-

TAWN. She had pale skin, and even sitting down, he could tell she was tall.

"What do you do here, Espy?"

She blinked. "Oh, I'm a nobody." She gave a little shrug. "I just work on the costumes." She paused and looked around the set, then smiled. "It's a real fun job."

"Too bad about the kid who got killed," he said, then waited.

A shadow crossed her face, and she cleared her throat. "Whoever did that to him is going straight to hell."

"Did you know him? Angel Ramirez?"

"Yeah, sure. I know most everyone who lives around here."

He took out his notebook. "Can I ask you a few questions about him?"

Espy shifted in her chair and frowned. "What do you want to know? I read your story. You already talked to a few people about him."

Robert considered her for a moment. She was quick, that one, and not easily misled. "They worked with him, but they hadn't known him long," he said. Espy looked around nervously, and he realized he was interrupting her at work. "I promise this will only take a few minutes. Will you talk with me?"

She bit her lip as she thought it over. Then she straightened her shoulders and set her sewing aside on the worktable next to her. "All right," she said, but without enthusiasm.

"Did he want to be a movie star?" he asked.

Espy relaxed slightly and chuckled. "He did, even if everybody told him he was just dreaming and he didn't stand a chance. Angel wanted to be the next Pedro Infante." When she noted his blank expression, she said, "You've never heard of him? No? He's an actor and singer from Mexico. A very famous

54

star. My mother says he's the most handsome man in the world, but to tell you the truth, Angel was even better looking. I told him not to pay any attention to the people who said he'd never make it, because you know what? You have to start somewhere. Infante played in an orchestra when he was just a teenager. And Angel was smart. Someone gave him a script of the movie, and he learned every single line by heart, so the actors who couldn't remember their lines would say, 'Hey Angel, what's my line again?' and he'd say it before the script man could."

Robert stared at Espy as she spoke, but he wasn't seeing her. He was seeing the photo of the young man in the shack, violated with a long stem rose, his body scratched and bloodied. A lump formed in his throat. He swallowed hard to get it down. The story she'd told of a kid with dreams of making it big seemed to make his headache worse.

"Did he ever get into trouble?" he asked, then realized his mistake.

Espy's eyes narrowed, and she pursed her lips. "Are you asking if he had this coming?"

Robert winced. It sounded like a line right out of a movie with Edward G. Robinson. He shook his head. "No. It's just a question I always ask. The cops said he was a good kid, but you never know."

Espy cleared her throat. "He was," she said primly. "He was a good kid. You know they gave him a couple of lines in the movie? Well, they did. An extra with lines. You should write that."

"I will," he promised, then stuck his pencil behind an ear. "Who can talk to me about it?"

Espy stood up and looked around, then pointed at a trailer. As he suspected, she was tall. About five-foot-eight, he guessed.

"That man over there. He's the assistant director."

Robert thanked Espy for her time, then wandered over to a man with a white T-shirt stuck into wool pants that looked too hot for summer weather. The man refused to talk to him, but he hurried to a trailer and disappeared inside. Moments later, he came back, followed by a burly man with a bald head and a nose that looked like it had been broken. Not exactly good looking, but a striking figure that commanded attention.

"What's this about?" the new man asked, shoving his hands in his pockets.

It was a good thing Robert had done his homework on *Beyond the Passage*, because he knew exactly who stood before him—the director himself, Mitchell Wood. Robert suppressed a sigh, introduced himself, and explained all over again.

Wood listened without interruption, then gestured at the expansive set behind him. "So, you don't want to know about the movie? Do you know how much this set cost? My workers built thirty buildings in twenty-five days. This thing rivals the Old Tucson studios. And you want to know why we built it here? Because it was better than going all the way to Arizona to film. And you know what else? Everybody who's anybody lives here in Los Angeles, including me. So why travel to Tucson?"

Robert took out his notebook. "That's exactly the kind of thing I'm looking for," he said. "When we're done, if I can ask you a question or two about Angel, I'd appreciate it, but let's focus on the movie." And he would, if he could only find a woman in a corset, and the tighter the better.

With that, the interview began, and Robert spent the next hour following Mitchell Wood around the set, the director kicking aside the occasional tumbleweed, slapping his hand against the side of a wagon filled with hay, and taking a carrot out of a pocket and feeding it to a horse tied up in front of the livery. It was obvious Wood had been surprised and later offended none of the major newspapers had bothered to cover the elaborate set that had gone up in Hollywood's own backyard, which explained why he was so enthusiastic about Robert's appearance.

As they walked past the barbershop, Robert spotted the saloon ahead. There were a few movie extras dressed in their cowboy costumes standing outside.

He was about to ask if they could go inside when Mr. Wood said, "Now, Robert, you've just got to see this because I'm gonna tell you something. The saloon is my favorite, and as a matter of fact, your timing is perfect because we're getting ready to shoot a scene inside, and if you'd like, you can get some good pictures for your paper before we start." Then he turned around and shouted at someone standing near the trailer. "Can you send a few of the saloon gals over here, please?" He turned back to Robert and wiggled his eyebrows. "I'm sure you'll want them in the picture, and if you don't, there's something wrong with you." The director jabbed him in the ribs, which Robert could have done without because the jarring movement sent a sharp pain shooting through his already aching head.

The sight of the women in their corseted dresses cheered him up. It was exactly what his boss had been looking for, and Robert didn't like to disappoint. A woman brushed past him— intentionally, he thought—and when he looked up, he saw a pair of unmistakable legs that belonged to Darla Diamond.

Mr. Wood noticed, too, and couldn't seem to drag his eyes away. "Now that is a fine, fine specimen," he said in a low voice to Robert. "If only the girl could act."

Darla was nearly unrecognizable as a saloon girl, with strawberry blonde corkscrew curls. Leaning against the bar, she regarded Robert with her golden eyes, while her red-painted lips parted, full and soft. He cleared his throat and pretended to scribble some notes, uneasy with the unexpected attention she was aiming his way.

When he glanced up, she was whispering something to the woman next to her, and they looked over at him and giggled.

After the director had shouted directions at the actors, Robert spent the next fifteen minutes taking pictures, getting enough close ups of bare shoulders and come-hither looks certain to make Harry and his bosses happy. He finished his interview with the talkative director, who obligingly gave him a few quotes about Angel, his natural talent, and a promising future cut short.

When they were wrapping up, Robert got up the nerve to ask him about his nose.

Mr. Wood threw his head back and laughed. "The official story? I got it playing football in college. The truth? A jealous husband did it, but if you print that, I'll come after you. Got it?"

Robert nodded. "Got it. It'll stay off the record."

Espy was still sitting in the same spot he'd left her. She looked up when she heard his footsteps. "I see you met the director," she said, then cleared her throat.

"He's a character," Robert replied. He rubbed his temples, which were throbbing.

Espy picked up a pair of scissors and snipped a long thread. "That's one way to put it," she said stiffly.

He lifted his eyebrows in inquiry. "Is that your way of saying the director likes to get fresh?"

"Let's just say he's the reason I wear trousers on the set," she said with a bitter edge. Then her eyes widened. "Oh my gosh, I must be tired or something. Please. Please keep that to yourself. I like my job, and I'm real grateful to have it, and I don't want to get in any trouble."

She looked so worried, nearly panicked, that Robert felt a stab of pity. "Don't worry. It's between us. I promise not to say a thing, and I probably wouldn't remember anyway, the shape I'm in."

"Hangover?" Espy asked, wrinkling her nose.

"No. Just a headache I can't shake."

Espy squinted up at him. "Those are terrible. Whenever I have them, I go to Catalina, and she fixes me something that makes it go away. She's a healer. I bet you she can fix you right up. She's better than anything that comes in a bottle from a drugstore. Plus, she's in Palo Verde, so you don't have to go far."

It sounded too good to be true, but he was willing to give it a try. He'd do anything to make the pain stop, and he was curious about the beautiful woman—the one the little boys had called a witch—the locals had called to help Salvio Duran's sick wife.

He got directions to Catalina's place and then set out again under the relentless summer sun.

Chapter 8

It was a fifteen-minute walk to Catalina's garden in Palo Verde.

Robert found it between a neatly painted house and an empty lot filled with junk, tires, and grazing goats. To the north, he could see the hills of Elysian Park, trees lining the top of a steep, dry hill. As he gazed at the expanse of park in the distance, a movement caught his eye. A little girl with dark hair caught up in a high ponytail stood on the porch of the house across the dirt road. Elbows on the railing, she stared at him intently. He waved. She hesitated, looked back over her shoulder at the house, then gave him a furtive wave.

He reached over the crooked fence and pulled up the rope to undo the latch, then pushed open the gate. Following Espy's instructions, he made his way to the back of the garden where a corrugated metal roof peeked out above the biggest cactus he'd ever seen. At first glance, the garden appeared wild and overgrown. It was no traditional, neatly ordered garden with lilies, tulips, lilacs, paving stones, and carefully placed shade trees. Every bit of dirt had something growing in it: a profusion of bright yellow flowers that looked like a cross between a sunflower and daisy, shrubs with red berries, and bright purple plumes that poked out of grass-like foliage. The only plants he recognized were mint, parsley, and red roses.

Robert stopped and stared at the roses. There were rows of them, some nearly as tall as himself—six feet. Stems thick and covered in thorns and flowers a deep red. He wondered what Detective Cagle would think of that, then recalled the detective hadn't mentioned the color of rose used to assault Angel Ramirez. The photo he'd bought for the newspaper had been in black and white, and he hadn't thought to ask the man who'd taken it what color the roses had been. Red, he'd assumed, but only because they were so common. They could have been yellow or pink. He pulled out his notebook and wrote a reminder to himself to ask.

The lot was bigger than it looked from the road. In fact, all properties on the block appeared to be double lots, deeper than they were wide. He could hear voices coming from the back, and when he got there, head still pounding from the headache he'd been unable to shake, his heart sank when he saw a line of people that snaked into the alley. Catalina the healer was in high demand.

The door to the shed was closed, and there was no sign outside to indicate how long he'd have to wait, but he wasn't about to leave. Not with his head about to explode. Maybe he was making a mistake. Maybe it wasn't just a regular, pesky headache, but something more serious. Something he should see a doctor about, but that would mean getting in his car and finding a doctor. He hadn't needed one since he arrived in Los Angeles. He supposed he could call his boss and explain, ask for a referral, but he hated for Harry to think he'd made a mistake by hiring a hypochondriac. Driving to the nearest phone booth and looking through the directory was another option, but with his luck, he'd get a quack, and then where would he be? Espy Gaten seemed smart and sensible, and there was no reason to doubt her recommendation. So, since he was already there, he might as well stay. And besides, he was curious to speak with the woman.

He was so busy considering his options, he hadn't realized most of the people in line had turned to stare. They were looking him over, from his bare head to his worn, comfortable shoes. Two women wearing aprons over their dresses had their heads bent together, speaking Spanish in quiet voices, as they eyed him with thinly disguised suspicion. The fellow in front of him, not much older than himself, with a white short-sleeved shirt tucked into brown pants, said, "Are you lost or something?"

Robert shook his head. The movement made him wince. "No. Not unless I got the wrong place, and Catalina isn't in there."

"She's in there all right," the man said. His teeth were very white under his black mustache. "What do you want her for?"

Robert gently tapped the side of his temple. "I've got a headache, and I was told Catalina could give me something for the pain."

The man's eyes widened. "Well, that she can do."

"Is there a problem?" Robert asked.

"No. I've just never seen a gringo here before, that's all." He paused, frowning. "I think I know who you are. Salvio Duran said there was some reporter hanging around. Is that you?"

Robert sighed, wondering how many more questions the man planned to ask, and how much longer he'd have to wait to see Catalina. "That's me all right," he admitted. "I'm Robert Cleary. What's your name?"

"Carlos Vasquez," the man said, holding out his hand, then gave him a sheepish grin. "You don't have to worry about me. I'll go quick. I'm just here to pick up some lady stuff for my mom."

Robert glanced at the line and counted at least eight people ahead of them. "Is it usually this busy?"

Carlos made a face. "Not usually, but ever since those agents came around, telling everyone they have to sell up and leave, people are so upset they're making themselves sick with worry. Stomach aches, pains in the neck, you name it. I heard the lady across the street got so riled up after those sons-of-bitches stopped by that she had an attaque de nervios."

"An attack of nerves?" Robert guessed.

"Yeah. Mrs. Acevedo had it real bad, I hear. Catalina had to go over and calm her down, then gave her something to help her sleep. Her poor kid thought she'd had a stroke, like Salvio Duran's wife. Salvio owns the market."

"How's Mrs. Duran doing?" Robert asked. He'd meant to ask Espy, but he'd forgotten.

Carlos grimaced. "She passed away. My mom said she died in the night."

"That's terrible," Robert murmured, shocked.

"It's a crying shame, is what it is," Carlos said bitterly, crossing his arms in front of his chest. The fellow had the well-muscled arms and tight waist of a body builder. "She was a tough lady too. The shock of those evictions must just have been too much. Even for her."

In such a close-knit community, not much could happen without everybody knowing about it. With his head pounding, Robert thought it safer to change the subject. "What kind of work are you in?"

Carlos looked surprised by the question. "Me? I'm a janitor at the French Hospital. The night shift, but my boss said they're going to train me to be an orderly." He paused long enough to smile and flex his arm muscles. "Let me tell you, they can use more help getting people in and out of those wheelchairs and beds. Better pay, so they say, but I'll believe it when I see it. And let me tell you something else, as soon as I start making more money, I'm leaving this place. Find myself a nice little apartment closer to work, so my mother, my grandmother, and my sisters won't be able to nag me anymore."

While they'd been talking, the door to the shed had opened and closed a few times. Robert was relieved to see the line finally getting shorter. Carlos seemed eager to keep the conversation going, so he said, "What's that Spanish word people say to describe what Catalina does? A cura...what?"

Carlos smiled. "Aw, come on. That's easy enough to remember. Curandera."

"That's it. Curandera," Robert said, snapping his fingers, then winced at the sharp sound.

"I think she's a little more than that," said Carlos, a sly look coming over his face.

Robert thought he knew what was going to come next. Something about Catalina's looks. A racy comment maybe. "How so?" he asked. Chickens started clucking on the other side of a fence.

"Well, my mother knew Catalina's mother back when she had this garden, this shed. The old Mrs. Montez was a bruja. A witch. No question about it, and if you'd ask her, she'd tell you right to your face that's exactly what she was, and if you didn't like it, you could go to hell. Now, some people think Catalina's a bruja too, except she won't come out and admit it like her mother did." He paused and took a deep breath, then leaned in a little closer and lowered his voice. "I went to elementary school with her, right here in Palo Verde, and sometimes, she'd act real weird, and the other girls wouldn't play with her and said she could be awfully mean when she wanted to. One girl said Catalina wanted her doll, and when the girl wouldn't give it to her, Catalina put a hex on her and made her tooth ache, then two teeth fell out." Carlos shrugged. "That's the story, at least."

Robert was unsure what to make of the story. "What do you mean she acted weird? Is this something you saw yourself?"

Another shrug. "She used to tell me she could see things. Things that would happen. Mostly bad things. Visions is what

65

she called them, and she'd put her hands over her eyes and shake and cry, and the teacher called her a liar and would hit her with a strap. To be honest, I used to feel sorry for her because she said the same thing would happen at home, with her father whacking her with a belt, saying no daughter of his was going to be a bruja, not if he could help it."

"You seem to know a lot about the family," Robert said.

Carlos swiped a knuckle across his mustache. "Catalina used to live next door to us in Loma. Her no-good father still lives there, but she doesn't come around anymore. Won't visit him. Not after he beat up his wife. Mrs. Montez and Catalina moved to Palo Verde when Catalina was in junior high, and then Mrs. Montez upped and died, and Catalina has been on her own since she was seventeen. Her brothers moved to Arizona or someplace for work, but they were always worse than useless. Never stood up to their dad or anything, so good riddance, I say."

All the gossip about Catalina was making Robert feel uneasy. He was just there to see her as a patient, or whatever she called people who came seeking her help, not to poke around for information on the woman. As promised, Carlos Vasquez was quick. He wasn't inside for longer than several minutes, then emerged clutching a small paper bag. He gave Robert a friendly nod, then sauntered down the alley.

Finally, it was Robert's turn to enter the shed. Catalina's eyes snapped open when he entered. "You…," she said.

He patted the camera hanging around his neck. "Me," he replied. "My apologies. I should have asked your permission before taking your picture. Sometimes I can't help myself."

He looked around, curious. The shed was large, with a tall, cluttered workbench and dried herbs hanging from the ceiling. Just a hard-packed dirt floor, but it had been swept clean. He could still see broom marks etched in the ground. There were a few stools and one chair, a red blanket thrown over one arm. The woman wore a black dress with pink roses, belted at the waist. He thought white suited her better. It could have just been that she was tired, but she had dark circles under her eyes. Her lip was still swollen, and the cut above her eyebrow had begun to crust over. He wondered what had happened to her but, after seeing her stern expression, decided not to ask.

"What do you plan to do with my pictures?" she asked suspiciously, glancing at his camera like it was a snake about to strike.

"Nothing, really," he admitted. "I don't know why I took them." He looked down at his feet. "That's a lie. I took them because I thought you were pretty."

Catalina sat on a stool and regarded him with cold eyes. "I see. You took them because you felt like it." She glanced at a small table shoved against a rough-hewn wall. Robert followed her gaze and noted the newspapers stacked at one end. *The Express* was on the top, folded to reveal the article about the evictions. "It's a shame you didn't spend more time writing that story than you did fooling around taking pictures nobody wants to see."

Robert sighed. It wasn't at all like he'd imagined. He thought he'd walk in, get some sympathy for his headache and something to make it go away, and have a nice little chat. He hadn't expected hostility, and now, he felt like a fool for expecting anything but.

With its metal roof and the sun beating down on it, the shed was hot and stuffy, and after walking around the set, his face felt greasy and in need of a wash. He was also hungry. Something he could easily solve with lunch at Bertita's house, but first, he needed to get what he came for. The curandera's brusque demeanor was at odds with her soft beauty, and he found the incongruity unsettling.

"For the record," he said, perching on a stool, "I did spend a lot of time writing that story. A lot more than you'd think by the number of inches it ended up, but the editor went to town on it. And I'm new. Brand new to the paper, so I'm not in a position to start any fights with anyone."

Catalina stood at her work bench, picked up a stone pestle, and brushed the rounded end off on the apron she wore over her dress. "Did the editor take out the part about how wrong it is for the city to be throwing people out of their homes? Because it's unfair, except none of the newspapers are calling it that. I heard you walked from Loma to Palo Verde. You must have seen how many people live here, and just like that, some busybodies at the city snap their fingers and say, 'go live someplace else because we got other ideas for your land.' We're up here for good reason. Because we can't just move any place we want. When my brothers got married, they couldn't buy the houses they wanted because nobody would sell to a Mexican, so they moved to Arizona. You know how long Rose Delgado and some of the other people around here have been trying to talk the city into putting up sidewalks, streetlights, and real roads? Years. But they haven't done a damn thing, and now, they're calling this place a slum. Look around, mister, does it look like a slum to you?"

"No," he admitted reluctantly, afraid of further agitating the healer.

Catalina smashed the pestle against the stone bowl. Robert jumped at the noise. "That's what I mean," she said, scowling. "Not one newspaper talked about any of that. All you wrote was one side."

Robert studied her profile. Up close, he understood why people thought she looked like a movie star. Not a classic beauty, with enormous, slightly hooded eyes, but captivating, nonetheless. Maybe it was the way she moved that gave her such powerful appeal. Once you started looking at her, it was hard to stop. The woman was mesmerizing.

He cleared his throat. "I interviewed a few of the homeowners. About how they felt about the whole thing. That's still in there." He hated the way he sounded defensive, whiny, like he was explaining to a teacher why he hadn't turned in his homework assignment.

"Well, at least you did good with that," she said. "Because none of the other newspapers even bothered." She sniffed, set down the pestle, and turned to him. "Why are you here?" She held up a hand. "If you're here to ask me about Angel Ramirez, yes, I knew him, but I'm not going to talk about him."

"Nothing like that," he lied. He had planned to ask about him while she was fixing his remedy. Now he'd be lucky to get that. "I met Espy Gaten. She told me you make cures, and I've had a headache that won't go away, and aspirin isn't working, and she said you could help." He paused and held up his hands, palms up. "So here I am," he added with a sheepish expression.

Catalina regarded him silently, pursing her lips. Finally, she said, "What does it feel like? The pain?"

Robert thought for a moment. "It's a dull sort of ache. My forehead feels tight. And it feels like someone has my head in a vice, squeezing, and there's an awful pressure everywhere."

Catalina sniffed, then closed the gap between them in a few brisk steps. She stood in front of him and began rubbing his forehead just above his eyebrows with dry, cool fingers that were surprisingly strong. He closed his eyes. After a few moments of the soothing motion, she ran her hands up both sides of his head, starting just in back of his ears, slowly, until she reached the crown. She repeated it a dozen times.

The effect was almost immediate. The headache was still there, but it didn't hurt nearly as bad, and he felt the tension release from his shoulders. He sensed Catalina move behind him, then put her hands on his shoulders. She dug her fingers into the space just below his collar bones, and he felt himself relax even more. When they slid around to the back of his neck, she tipped his head forward, and starting at where the neck bone attached to the spine, she pressed her fingers into his tender flesh, gently applying pressure in circular motions. He hadn't expected a massage to come with her service, and he wasn't about to protest because he hadn't felt that good in two days.

Catalina carried on with her ministrations for ten minutes, then she softly said into his ear. "You should start feeling better soon."

He was so limp he felt he might topple off the stool. He opened one eye. "Wow. I heard you were magic. Now I believe it."

Catalina shot him an incredulous look as she reached for a dried bundle of herbs hanging from the ceiling of the shed. "That's a *mentira* if I ever heard one. People around here call me a witch, and don't bother denying it." She plucked a small bottle from a shelf above the workbench and poured a viscous pale-gold liquid into a teaspoon.

"Take this," she said, holding the teaspoon inches from his mouth.

Robert opened his mouth like an obedient child and swallowed. It had a mild taste. "What is it?" he asked. Not that it mattered. He would have drunk a bottle of castor oil if it would banish his headache once and for all.

"It's primrose oil," she said, a faint smile coming to her lips. "Usually, it's something I give to the ladies, for their woman problems, but in your case, with the type of headache you have, this should work *muy bien*." When she noted his blank expression, she added, "It should work very well." She gave his shoulder an awkward pat. "You're holding a lot of tension in that head of yours, and I think I made it worse by scolding you."

She turned back to her workbench, poured half the liquid into a smaller bottle, added a sprig of dried herb, plugged it with a cork, then handed it to him. "Take a teaspoon every three to four hours until your headache goes away."

"I will. And by the way, I've been scolded worse by my bosses."

That time, the smile reached her eyes. "I guess I have something to be grateful for then, at least for the time being. The kind of work I do, I don't have anyone to boss me around."

He hesitated because he hated to ruin the truce they'd reached, but he had to know. "What will you do? Are you going to sell up to the city?"

Catalina gripped the workbench. "I'm going to fight it as hard as I can and for as long as I can. My mother and I scraped and saved to buy our house, and I'm not about to let some strangers take it for their *pendejadas*."

He needed no translation. Her meaning was loud and clear. "What about your garden? Do you own that, too?"

She shook her head, dark eyes flashing with anger. "No. I rent it, and before me, my mother did too. So that's another thing I stand to lose. My no-good landlord has already come by. He told me he plans to sell to the city as soon as they let him. He owns a lot of properties in Palo Verde and Bishop, and he wants his payout." She sighed, her shoulders slumping. "Not that I totally blame him. He's getting old, and he says he's sorry, but he needs his money. He lives all the way in Long Beach, so he's hardly ever here. Some of the houses he owns are in real bad shape, but he doesn't fix them up, so the renters do it themselves. But they don't complain because the rent is so cheap. He practically owns this whole block. I just don't know where else I can find an empty lot I can afford, and even if I could, it's going to take a long time to start over, to plant everything I need and give it time to grow." She looked around helplessly. "*If* the plants grow. Just because I can find a lot doesn't mean the soil is any good. My mother used to say there's magic in the dirt here. It's the reason the roses do so good. I make a lot of my money selling them to the flower market."

His heart twisted in his chest at the sight of the woman in such obvious distress. "I'm sorry," he murmured, insufficient words for an insurmountable problem. "How much do I owe you?"

She shrugged, then looked away as if embarrassed by the mention of money. "Fifty cents."

Robert stood up and shoved a hand into a pocket, pulled out a dollar, and set it on the workbench. Maybe she was giving him a break on the price out of guilt for her scolding. Or maybe she didn't have a head for business. Whatever the case, a buck was a bargain for getting rid of the headache, which was finally beginning to fade.

Catalina may or may not have been a witch, but he was sure of one thing. The woman wasn't charging enough because she was a miracle worker.

Chapter 9

Like she always did about everything, Espy had second thoughts. Maybe sending Robert Cleary to Catalina for his headache was a bad idea. He was, after all, an outsider, and what did she really know about him? But he wasn't like a regular stranger. He was a reporter with stories in the newspaper. Besides, he'd seemed like a decent fellow and needed help for his headache, the kind only Catalina could offer.

Still, she wasn't sure how Catalina would feel about treating a gringo, someone who might not believe in the Mexican way of healing. But it was too late now. Robert was long gone, and if Catalina was unhappy, she'd hear about it later.

Catalina hadn't been herself since she'd received her eviction notice. Of course, Espy was upset about her notice too. Very upset. She didn't want to leave her home in Palo Verde. She'd grown up in Bishop, the next community over, where her parents lived. The eviction letter had been a shock, but she knew there was no winning—she might as well throw herself in front of a train hoping to stop it. Maybe it was because Catalina had more to lose. Her home, her garden, and her livelihood, while Espy could find an apartment to rent and keep her job with the movie studio. Catalina's anger over the evictions was not a surprise, but her promise to fight it at all costs was, and Espy knew she was dead serious. She wondered, uneasily, how far Catalina was prepared to go.

Espy was so lost in her thoughts she hadn't noticed she was no longer alone. The actress playing the part of the schoolmarm was standing in front of her, looking hot and cranky. She was holding the patterned blouse Espy had made for a new scene, one where the schoolmarm is romanced by a cowboy with bad intentions.

"The director wants you to fix the neckline," the actress said, dropping the blouse into Espy's lap.

Espy held it up and gave it the once over with a practiced eye. "What's wrong with it?" she asked. All the little buttons she sewed on by hand were still intact, and there weren't any rips or tears.

The young woman flopped into a chair. When she didn't answer, Espy sighed, turned toward her companion, and was surprised to see a tear roll down her cheek. Even though they'd worked together for several weeks, Espy knew nothing about her except her name, Shirley Clark.

"Not a damn thing is wrong with the blouse," came the sullen reply. "It fits real nice, but it's that creep of a director. He says it's too high, and he wants you to take off the buttons and make it open all the way to the top of the belt. I swear that man is obsessed with my breasts. At the rate we're going, he'll be offering them a part of their own, and the audience won't ever see my face."

Shirley looked so irritated—and who could blame her—that Espy covered up the chuckle that escaped her lips with a cough. "He sure does have opinions on what the ladies wear," she said, thinking of her boss, Arnold Feininger, the costume designer, who'd already had several blow-ups with the director about that very matter.

"If this weren't my big chance, and if I didn't need the job so bad, I'd give it the old heave-ho," Shirley said. She pushed the hair away from her face.

Espy noted bright red roots peeking through the actress's bleached blonde hair and wondered if that had been her idea or the director's. Mitchell Wood seemed to prefer women with very light or very dark hair, not much in between.

Espy laid out the blouse on the table and studied it, biting her lip. "How long do I have to work on it?"

"We're shooting in two hours. Is that enough time?" Shirley asked worriedly. "Because Mr. Wood is going to be real mad if it's not done by then."

Espy jumped to her feet and snatched the blouse from the table. "I can do it," she said. "But I'm going to need my sewing machine to do it right, so I'm going back to the house."

Shirley groaned. "All the way up the hill? In this heat?" She rose heavily, then brightened. "Wait. If I go with you, can I take a quick bath? My roommate hogged the bathroom this morning, so I didn't have time, and I'd sure love a wash."

"Of course," Espy said briskly, then strode up the hill toward her house. It might have been small and not much to look at, but at least she didn't have roommates to worry about, and it was all hers. At least for now.

Shirley huffed and puffed behind her all the way. While trim, the woman was clearly not used to walking the hills. Not like Espy, who'd grown up walking the three neighborhoods, up, down and across ravines, without benefit of a car. Getting to work, before the movie began filming up the road, meant walking into Bishop and then into downtown, taking a couple of buses, then walking the final distance. As a result, Espy had easily kept her thin figure, and her legs were strong. She was always a little surprised when people her own age had trouble keeping up.

She reached the house nearly five minutes before Shirley, had already loaded a bobbin and spool with the right colored thread—maroon—and snipped off two of the buttons when Shirley tromped up the steps and flung open the screen door.

"I put out a fresh towel for you," Espy called after her, as she made straight for the little bathroom at the end of the hall.

"You are an angel of mercy," Shirley shouted back. Fifteen minutes later, she emerged wearing a towel wrapped around her midsection, a big grin on her face. Her legs and arms were covered with freckles. With her hair piled high on her head, she looked younger than Espy first thought. Probably closer to twenty-five than thirty. She made straight for the couch and stretched out, eyes closed. "I swear, I could go to sleep right here and now. My roommate snores something awful."

Espy cut a deeper V into the blouse, which was made of a thin stretchy material, perfect for a little artful ruching around the bust. Normally, that decision would be made by Mr. Feininger, but he was back at the Hollywood studio lot, and there was no way to reach him in time. Besides, he'd made it clear from the start that he trusted her to do the right thing. Espy knew she was lucky to have such a good boss.

Espy put her full attention on the alteration. There was only one blouse, and there was no time to start over if she made a mistake. She pinned the tiny pleats into place and began stitching over them to create the pleasing ripple-like effect.

"Didn't you hear what I just said, Espy?" Shirley said from the sofa, her voice sleepy.

Espy didn't answer until she was done sewing. "I didn't. What was it?"

Shirley sighed. "I said, or asked rather, if you know Catalina, the lady who delivers the flowers. The one all the fellows can't stop talking about."

Espy stopped and turned to stare at the actress, who was sitting up and yawning. "Catalina?" she asked in surprise. "Yes.

76

She's my neighbor." She paused, frowning. "Who's talking about her? What are they saying?"

"You know, the usual stuff men say about women who look like that," Shirley said with a bitter edge. "They got a good look at her when she came to the set, and the next thing you know, that's all they could talk about. Even better looking than Jane Russel, some of them said. Although I don't see it myself. Catalina is a little too..." She stopped mid-sentence, gave a sidelong look at Espy, then cleared her throat. "Dusky, if you know what I mean."

Espy gave a tight nod. She knew exactly what Shirley meant. Catalina had a darker complexion than was acceptable in Hollywood. "What was she doing on the set?" Espy asked. She already knew the answer—or at least thought she did—but it was worth double-checking.

Shirley came over and stood next to Espy. "Well, the set decorator wanted roses for the scenes in the hotel, and she caused such a stir with some of the men that the director wanted a look for himself. At least that's what I heard. So, Mr. Wood's assistant asked that extra who got killed to bring Catalina to his trailer so he could meet her."

The scissors slipped from Espy's fingers. That was the first she'd heard of it. "And did they? Meet?"

"I think so," Shirley said, frowning. "At least, I saw her walking to Mr. Wood's trailer, but I didn't see what happened after that. Everyone took a dinner break. We all had to come back for a night scene. But later, I saw her sitting and talking with that extra—"

"Angel Ramirez," Espy interrupted.

Shirley wrinkled her nose. "Who gives a kid a name like that?" She paused, registering Espy's expression. "Never mind. I guess it's not much different than naming your boy Ardy where I come from. But I saw her sitting with Angel around the back of the saloon. There are some benches there, and that's where they were. He had his arm around her, and her head was on his shoulder. I wasn't the only one who noticed because the guys wouldn't stop teasing him about it. I could tell they couldn't understand why someone like her would take an interest in him. He was good-looking but young. One fellow even went up to her and said, 'Hey, if you're interested in a real man, you know where to find me.' "

Espy took all this in. Catalina hadn't mentioned any of it, including her meeting the director, if it really happened. And what had been going on between Catalina and Angel? Something wasn't right.

"And I'll tell you something else," Shirley said, tugging at the towel. "That other Mexican, Louie somebody, he wasn't too happy with all the attention Catalina was giving Angel. When she left, he followed her up the hill, and when he finally came back, he wouldn't stop pestering Angel."

Espy glanced at the clock on the wall. They were wasting time sitting there, gossiping. But she was troubled by what she'd just heard, and she wasn't going to be able to shake the uneasy feeling until she had a chance to talk to Catalina and see what she could find out.

"Let's see how this fits," she said, shaking out the blouse.

In the bedroom, Shirley dropped the towel on the floor and stood, nude, while Espy slid the blouse over her head, careful to avert her eyes. She had no desire to see the woman's nakedness, and not for the first time, she wondered how some of those actresses had become so comfortable walking around without a stitch. Still, she couldn't do the rest of the job without looking, so she dragged her eyes back to the blouse. She was pleased to see the ruching added some nice detail to an otherwise plain blouse, and it gave the impression of more fullness to the bust.

Shirley stood sideways, hands on her bare hips, and surveyed herself in the mirror. "Well, I had my doubts, Espy, but you made this blouse look real nice. Thank you." She puffed out her chest. "And what you've done should make Mr. Wood happy because you've made me look like a thirty-six D."

Espy watched as Shirley pulled on her underpants and long skirt, wishing she would hurry. She wanted to catch Catalina. Shirley was lacing her boots when Espy spotted the young woman's bra draped over a chair.

With thumb and index finger, she plucked it up and dangled it in front of the actresses' nose. "I think you forgot this," she said pointedly. The room was warm and stuffy, but she could see Shirley's nipples pushing against the thin fabric of the blouse.

Shirley gave a hard laugh, snatched the bra from Espy's hand, and shoved it under her arm. "I did not," she said, rising. "I've decided to give that creep of a director exactly what he's looking for. Now he won't have any excuse to cut my scene."

When she'd left, Espy closed up the house and headed straight to Catalina's shed, entering through an alley. There was a line of a half dozen people waiting, all of whom she either knew by name or sight, which included one woman from La Loma. Espy wondered why she chose to walk to Palo Verde when Loma had its own curandera, but she didn't have to wonder for long because the woman began explaining to the lady standing next to her that Lencha had refused to help her, saying what she needed was a bruja.

Which gave Espy something else to think about while she waited.

It was yet another thing Catalina was secretive about. Was she or wasn't she a witch? Everyone had known Mrs. Montez was a bruja, and a proud one, and many people assumed Catalina was one too, but Catalina never would say. Only when she was cruelly teased and pushed to anger—and there had been a lot of that in their school days—she would imply it in that sly way of hers, which was more effective than any boast. Those hints that she was a bruja had just added to her mystery and, eventually, made her tormentors uncertain enough they'd picked the safer choice and just ignored her. Espy had never seen her do witchcraft, but who really knew what went on in the shed, where Catalina often worked late into the night when anybody in their right mind was in bed.

The line wasn't moving, and she couldn't wait around all day. She had a job, and she needed to get back to the set. The door opened, and Catalina appeared. She raised her eyebrows when she spotted Espy and came toward her.

"Are you all right?" Catalina asked worriedly. She looked exhausted, with dark circles under eyes, the skin around her mouth tight.

"I'm fine," Espy said. At that moment, she knew she couldn't ask any of the many questions she had rolling around in her head, questions that now seemed ridiculous. What she'd heard was just gossip. People did it all the time on the set. There was more time waiting around for filming to begin than actual filming.

So what if Catalina had been seen with Angel? So what if she'd met the director? She was a grown woman. She didn't answer to Espy. Catalina didn't like *metiches*, people who interfered in other people's business, and that's exactly how Espy was behaving, like a metiche. Like her own mother, in fact, who was famous as a neighborhood busybody who had no problem sticking her nose where it wasn't wanted. If she dared ask Catalina what was on her mind, Catalina would probably say, "Oh, look who's acting like her mama now," and she'd deserve it.

Catalina rubbed her hands on her apron. Rust-colored smears appeared on the white cloth, releasing the unmistakable scent of cinnamon into the air. "Then why are you here?" she asked, frowning slightly.

"To see if you wanted to come over later," she said hurriedly. "Have dinner with me." She had no idea what she'd make, but she'd figure out something.

Catalina shook her head. "I'm sorry, Espy, but when I'm done, I'm going home and straight to bed. I haven't been sleeping so good." There was no mistaking her meaning. She was still recovering from whatever had happened to her, the thing she refused to talk about or explain. The cut above her eyebrow was still there, scabbed over now, and the bruise on her cheek had turned purple.

"You don't want company?" Espy asked, unable to keep the hurt from seeping into her voice.

"Not tonight. But maybe tomorrow?" she said over her shoulder, walking back toward the shed.

"Tomorrow would be nice." With that, Espy turned on her heel and hurried back toward the set, exiting through the garden instead of the alley. It was so overgrown she took the wrong path and ended up near the towering rose bushes. Not for the first time, she wondered how Catalina got them to grow so tall, so sturdy, with thorns so sharp she shuddered just looking at them.

Chapter 10

Espy woke up with the sun shining in her eyes, a pounding headache, and the uneasy feeling she'd done something wrong, if only she could remember what it was.

Glancing over at the other side of her bed, she saw it was still made up. She hadn't yet gotten over the habit of crawling in and leaving the spot where her husband, Felix, used to sleep undisturbed. To take the whole bed to herself seemed disrespectful of his memory, but that would have paled compared to what she had contemplated the night before when she'd had the second glass of red wine from the bottle Bruce Knox had brought over, along with his handsome self.

She'd been surprised to see him on her doorstep. So surprised she'd invited him in for dinner, and then they were talking, and then they were on the old sofa on the back porch. They were kissing when her mother began pounding on the front door, so that had put a stop to things. Otherwise, she might have rolled over to see Bruce Knox in her bed. In fact, she was sure of it. Bruce might not have made it under the sheets, but he'd made it into her dreams, and now there was a delightful warmth between her legs.

She swung out of bed and stared down at her feet. Maybe she'd paint her toes red, like Shirley and Darla. The change in position made her head hurt even more. Had she drunk that much? Just two glasses of wine. And then she remembered the Tequila Bruce had found on top of the refrigerator—the bottle she kept for her father's visits. He liked to have a small glass sitting out on the porch when he came over, which wasn't often because his knees were getting bad, and her parents lived down the hill in Bishop. She'd sipped from the same small glass as her father, and then she remembered Bruce pouring a second glass, and she gave a little moan.

After that, things were a little less clear. Some petting on the sofa on the back porch, the moonlight shining on the prickly pear cactus, his hand beneath her blouse, her hand on his strong, lean thigh—more than she'd ever done with her husband before they got married—and she was thinking it wasn't like she was a virgin anymore. Not that they'd had a chance to reach that stage, not with her mother at the front door, shouting her name.

So why did she feel so guilty now?

She'd pushed Bruce in front of her as she buttoned her blouse, and he tucked his shirt back in his pants, then he'd grabbed her by the waist and pulled her to him and kissed her on the mouth, left through the back gate and disappeared into the alley. No, it wasn't anything that happened with him that was making her uncomfortable. She walked into the bathroom, turned on the faucet, and watched the water pour into the basin. She immersed her head into the water, and then she remembered and came up sputtering.

She'd told her mother about Catalina. About her suspicion that Catalina had been sneaking around with Angel Ramirez. As soon as it had escaped her lips, she knew she'd made a mistake. A big mistake. Espy had learned when she was a little girl her mother repeated everything she was told. It didn't matter if it was something small and unimportant—like overhearing someone ask Salvio Duran for credit at his store—to big and important—like a neighbor in Bishop saying he planned to sell up to the city without a fight.

Espy groaned as she reached for the towel, remembering the way her mother had clapped her hands and said, "That girl was always trouble." Then she'd rushed off, eager to get home.

When she went into the kitchen to make a cup of coffee, she saw it was only 6:00. She was a firm believer in exercise, but that day, her head was in no shape for jumping jacks, so she decided a walk in the fresh air would do, and it might even be good for her aching head. She wondered when she'd see Bruce, then frowned as she grabbed the broom and gave the floors a quick sweep.

Probably, he would pretend like nothing had happened between them. He was awfully handsome. She knew Shirley and Darla both had their eyes on him, and she was just a nobody. Not even a two-bit actress with stars in her eyes. A seamstress, and a Mexican American to boot, who was about to lose the only thing she ever had: her home. At least she had her Singer sewing machine. They couldn't take that away from her.

She ran a dust cloth over the wood table of her ten-year-old sewing machine, then went back into the bedroom and dressed. She pulled on a pair of blue tapered pants and a black and white checked shirt, comfortable shoes, then headed out.

There was no sign of Catalina in the garden, which was unusual for that time of the morning when the curandera usually did the weeding. Mrs. Acevedo was in a corner of her front yard, near the chicken coop. When she spotted Espy, she hurried over the fence and leaned on the railing. Espy sighed and stopped.

"Are you feeling better?" Espy asked briskly, adopting a tone that would give the woman a hint she didn't have time for a long chat.

Mrs. Acevedo—a soft doughy woman with brown hair scraped back from her face, caught in a tight bun—flapped a hand at her "Yes, yes. Catalina fixed me right up. But you know, I just might start going to see Lencha, even if she is in Loma."

She lifted her chin and raised her eyebrows. "After what your mother told me last night," she added in a sharp tone.

Espy's heart sank. It was just as she'd feared. Her mother had already started spreading the story Espy had confided the night before.

"My mother likes to talk," she said sternly. "And you can't believe everything you hear."

Mrs. Acevedo gasped, her hand fluttering to her throat. "*Ai*, listen to you, Espy Gaten, talking about your own flesh and blood like that. Your mother is a good woman, and don't you forget it. And here's another thing. Something your mother didn't even have to tell me." She pointed at Catalina's garden. "That woman sneaks out at all hours of the night, and who knows what she's up to. No good, is what I think. A woman that age should be married and not fooling around. But like mother, like daughter is what I say because Mrs. Montez was nothing but a hussy."

Espy blinked. Mrs. Acevedo was a high strung, nervous sort of woman, so she wasn't surprised to hear she'd suffered an attaque de nervios after receiving the city's eviction letter, but she'd never known her to be mean.

"If you see Catalina go out, it's probably because someone asked for her help." Espy cleared her throat and looked Mrs. Acevedo straight in the eye. "Like she came to help you," she added pointedly.

"Yes, she did help me, but no one called her," Mrs. Acevedo replied stiffly. "She walked right into my house and put a spell on me because I couldn't wake up for a whole night and day." Mrs. Acevedo wagged a finger at her. "You better watch out because she might do the same to you some day, especially if she decides she wants that good-looking gringo who came over to your house last night."

Espy clutched the fence so hard her knuckles turned white. She'd hoped that with so many movie people coming and going no one would notice Bruce Knox paying a later than usual visit. But it was a tight-knit community, and she'd clearly been fooling herself. Still, she wasn't a kid anymore. She was a grown woman with a good job, and she wasn't about to let Mrs. Acevedo treat her like she was a teenager.

"I need to hurry if I'm going to get to work on time," she said, then waved goodbye, leaving a sour-faced Mrs. Acevedo staring after her.

She walked across the dirt roads, not stopping to talk to anyone. She passed by Duran Market & Liquor, which was still closed after the death of Petra Duran, then hung a left at the end of the block and followed a dirt path over the hill toward La Loma. At the top, she stopped and surveyed the little valley of houses below. Even at that early hour of the morning, she could tell it was going to be a hot one. The sun warmed the top of her head, and there wasn't a hint of a breeze. She walked down into Loma, waved hello at the lady who sold *nopalitos*, then paused to watch a few men walk into the tortilla factory at the end of a street. Louie Bonda had worked there before he'd lucked into the job with the movie.

Espy stuck to the main road and headed up a steep hill. She didn't have a specific destination in mind, but the walk was doing her good. Somewhere between Palo Verde and La Loma, she'd lost the headache, and her thoughts returned to Bruce. She remembered the feel of his hands on her hot skin and felt herself blushing. She couldn't remember feeling like that before she got married. Sexy feelings. When she was a teenager, she was convinced the flames of hell would consume her for such thoughts, but she was a woman now, and she no longer believed it was a sin to want a man, not at her age, a widow and all. She deserved a little happiness after years of loneliness and misery.

She'd reached the top of another hill, the one with a well on a bare patch of ground. Something was sticking out of it. It was far enough in the distance she couldn't quite make it out. She stepped forward, squinting. A giant sack of flour, maybe, or beans. One of those hundred-pound bags they sold at Duran Market. It was half-in, half-out of the well. A stick protruded from it, and at the end, a red globe against the blue sky. But why would anybody put that there?

She walked toward the well. Her mouth opened and closed in wordless protest as the horror took shape. It wasn't an enormous sack of beans.

It was a body.

A man's body, bent over the rough wood of the well—naked, scratched, and bloody—a red rose protruding from the buttocks at a nearly horizontal angle. Her head spun. Somehow, her feet kept moving as if drawn to the defiled figure, and then she was standing next to it, and she could see who it was.

Louie Bonda.

Chapter 11

The phone rang for the first time in Robert's new apartment in the Hollywood flatlands. He picked it up on the second ring, guessing it would be someone at *The Express* because he hadn't yet called his parents and given them his new number. And at 7:30 in the morning, something was up, something that couldn't wait for him to get to the office.

"Hello?" he said into the receiver. Sun streamed in through a gap in the blinds. He grabbed his sunglasses from the nightstand and shoved them on his face.

"Oh good, I got you before you left." It was a relieved-sounding Harry Barkin on the other end of the line. "I just got a call from Detective Cagle. They found another dead guy up near where they found the last one. Why don't you head straight up there?"

Robert sat up so fast his sunglasses fell off. "Was it the same sort of situation?" he asked, then winced at the imprecise wording. He wished he hadn't slept in. If he'd gotten up at his usual time, he'd have had coffee and would be thinking straight.

Harry cleared his throat. "If you mean he was a Mexican kid, yes. And if you mean he got the special rose treatment, also yes. But that's about all I know, so hightail it up there. Cagle says you can find them on a hill in…" He paused, and Robert could hear shuffling papers. "In Loma. Correction. Make that La Loma. There's a well near the reservoir on city-owned property. That's where they'll be. And Robert, get there as fast as you can.

Cagle says he's giving an exclusive shot to the first reporter who gets there, and he gave us a fifteen-minute head start."

"I'm on it," Robert said. He was already pulling clothes out of the closet. He had more questions, but they were better saved for the detective.

"Drive fast, kid. I'll pay for the tickets." Harry slammed down the phone.

There was no time for a shower, coffee, or breakfast. Just time to go to the bathroom and splash water on his face, then he was out the door, wearing his most comfortable shoes and the lightest-weight trousers he could find. He could tell from the heat of the sun in his apartment it was going to be a scorcher.

He still couldn't believe his luck at finding such a nice place on his salary. Working as a reporter for *The Express* had its perks, he'd discovered. The landlady had been impressed and was even happier to rent to him when he explained he was too busy working to do anything but eat and sleep. She'd even let him park in the driveway in front of her garage, saying she didn't drive anymore because there were too many cars on the road for her liking.

Dew glistened on the roses lining the walkways of the quadruplex. He studiously ignored them. For him, roses were forever destined to be associated with unspeakable violence.

Robert guessed it was about six miles to the murder scene. He took Melrose to the Hollywood Freeway, and that time, he knew his way around enough to enter the neighborhood of La Loma. He drove around until he spotted a few black and white police cars parked near what appeared to be the only streetlight in the area.

When he jumped out of his car, a man approached, carrying a basket on his head.

"You know where the well is around here?" he asked, hoping the man spoke enough English to understand him.

"You mean where they found Louie Bonda?" the man asked. He spoke in accented English, but Robert understood him perfectly.

His heart sank. If the man knew the name of the murder victim, he was probably not the first reporter on the scene, and that meant he lost the photo exclusive the detective had promised.

"Is Louie Bonda from around here?" he asked.

The man nodded. "From right here in Loma. He worked at the place where they make the tortillas until Angel Ramirez got him in a job in that movie they're making near Palo."

Robert glanced at the steep hill behind the man. He could see activity up at the top. That's where he needed to be, and fast, but he could spare a few seconds to see what else he could find out.

"What was this Louie like?"

The man pursed his lips. He had brown wrinkled skin and high cheekbones. "He thought he was king of the hill. And if you want to know the truth, he was mean. All those Bondas are mean, even the mother. Why you asking?"

"I'm a reporter," Robert admitted. "From *The Express*."

The man shrugged, unimpressed. "I only look at the Spanish papers. The funnies are better."

Not much different from Robert's parents, then, who only got the newspaper to read the comics.

"How do you know it was Louie?" he asked, itching to get moving but reluctant to leave the source of information. Who knew how much the detective would be willing to share that time around?

Another shrug. "I don't know. Just everybody is saying it's him." The man took the basket off his head and held it out so Robert could see what was inside. Pastries. Fresh pastries, smelling of raw butter, sugar, and a hint of cinnamon. "You want some *pan dulce*? My wife just made them. A nickel a piece."

Robert smiled, rummaged around for a dime, and reached into the basket to pull out two—one shaped like an ear of corn, the other one round and topped with a crumbly dry chocolate, which made him long for a glass of cold milk. His stomach rumbled, reminding him he hadn't had breakfast or coffee. At least he'd found something to eat to tide him over until he could get lunch at Bertita's. With the story, he'd be in the ravine well into the afternoon.

"Thank you," he said. "I better go. Thank you for talking to me."

The man smiled, pleased, lifted the basket to his head, and walked off whistling.

Robert locked the car, then remembered he'd forgotten his camera, so he retrieved it and hung it around his neck. He ate the pastries as he trekked up the hill, following a path of hard-packed dirt cut into the scraggly brush. The hills were wide open, except for the ridge of trees in the distance, which he'd been told was Elysian Park. As he approached a crest, the area flattened out, then rose again, and it was there he saw the gaggle of police officers. It wasn't quite so barren. A stand of trees stood off to the right of what was presumably the well, hidden from view by a piece of canvas stretched around it.

Two men were crouched on the ground, making a cast of a footprint. Detective Cagle stood nearby, smoking a cigarette, his black hair still damp. No sight of any other reporters though, he noted with relief. He exhaled, brushed the pastry crumbs from his shirt, and wiped his mouth.

If only he'd had time for a shower before he left. He already felt grimy, and his day hadn't even started yet.

Detective Cagle waved him over. "There you are sunshine. I was wondering if you were ever going to make it. Looks like you got the prize after all." He turned and shouted in the direction of the canvas tent. "Hey guys, you got an incoming. Move aside and let him take a picture. And just one, mind you. That's all he gets." To Robert he added, "And that's only because I owe your boss a favor, so don't expect any special treatment in the future." Then he winked to make sure there were no hard feelings. "When you come out, we can have a little chat."

Robert nodded. "Anything I should know going in?" he asked.

The detective looked like he was trying hard not to roll his eyes. "I promise not to tell Harry you just asked the dumbest question I've heard this year. Like I just said, kid, look first, talk later." Then he pointed at the tent.

Robert took a deep breath, then gave a curt nod, silently cursing himself. If only he'd had a cup of coffee. Or better, two.

He'd seen the crime scene photo of Angel Ramirez, so he knew what to expect. Generally. But still, he felt his body stiffen when he approached the canvas, and he had to force his feet to keep moving and resist the ridiculous urge to turn around. When he'd become a reporter, he hadn't given much thought to the kind of stories he wanted to cover. Politics maybe. He'd never angled to become a crime reporter. When he worked in Denver, the paper had two full-time photographers who took the grisly pictures. But *The Daily* only had one, and when Harry had hired him, he'd made it clear he'd have to take his own photos. He'd willingly agreed. So that's what he had to do and do it well because he'd only have one shot at it. It didn't help that his hands were shaking.

He stepped through the canvas, nervously clearing his throat. "So, what we got here…" The words died on his lips.

If he thought what happened to Angel Ramirez was bad, that was horrific, even more obscene due to the positioning of the body.

Louie Bonda—if that's who it was—was bent over the lip of the well, a long stem red rose poking out of his ass. And if that wasn't a statement, Robert didn't know what was. From what he could see of the victim, except for the bloody scratches, the man had been in remarkably good physical shape, with strong legs and a small waist. The police officers parted, silently, and let him approach the well for a better look, which he did warily, not knowing what other horrors awaited. He had a glimpse of broad shoulders and a thatch of shiny black hair before he averted his eyes.

"It looks like he got a rose rammed up his nose, but it must of fell out because it's at the bottom of the well," said one of the officers. He shone a flashlight down the well and waved it around. "See?"

Robert did, reluctantly. "Yes, thank you," he said faintly. "What are you trying to keep out of the paper?"

One of the officers stood back and used his fingers to frame the shot, biting his lip as he moved it around. "I think a shot like the other one you used would do the trick. You know. The back of the legs, but not too high up. And the rose is off-limits."

Another officer snickered. "Just count yourself lucky we're not showing you the damage to the front end."

Robert felt his toes curl up. His stomach heaved, and a sour taste filled his mouth. He hid his discomfort by lifting the camera in front of his face. Shielded, he swallowed. Hard.

His hands trembled as he squinted into the viewfinder. The back of the dead man's feet were dusty, but not as dirty as might be expected if he'd been walking around without his shoes.

"Where are his shoes? His clothes?" he asked, the camera still pressed to his face.

"I heard that, Cleary!" the detective shouted on the other side of the tent. "What did I tell you? Look first, ask later. And hurry up, I've got work to do."

Robert sighed. The detective had better ears than his mother, who was famous in the family for her eavesdropping skills. "Yes, sir," he said, chagrined. The detective couldn't have made himself clearer, and at the first opportunity, he'd acted like he hadn't heard a word. A problem he blamed on the lack of coffee.

He focused the camera on the back of the victim's well-muscled calves, wondering what he'd done to earn them. Genetics, or maybe he was one of those guys who liked to run. There certainly was plenty of open space in the ravines for that. The bloody scratches came into focus, stark red against the light brown skin. He snapped a picture, and when he was done, he turned away, glad it was over.

The tent was open at the top, letting in the fresh air, but Robert didn't think he could look at the body bent over the well a moment longer.

Detective Cagle waited for him, puffing away at another cigarette. "Didn't that make your day?" he said flatly. Then he threw the cigarette on the ground and mashed it with his shoe. "I wouldn't wish that on my worst enemy," he added, shaking his head.

Robert took out his notebook. "You have an ID yet?"

"We sure do. His name is Louis Bonda, but everybody called him Louie. Age twenty-four, also an extra on *Beyond the Passage*. Youngest of three sons of Victor and Juana Bonda." The detective nodded in the general direction of the houses dotting the ravine below. "He lived in La Loma with his folks and two brothers who, by the way, are known to us. One of them is a frequent visitor of the joint, and the other one is fast on his way to becoming a dope fiend." He paused and raised a hand. "And before you ask, we don't have any indication, yet, that this has anything to do with our victims being Mexican. It could be that somebody's targeting young men from this area, or movie extras, or guys the ladies call dreamy. Or maybe all of the above. Louie fancied himself the Mexican William Holden from what I heard, and the camera loved him, even if he wasn't the most popular guy around the movie set."

Robert looked up from the notebook. He made it a point not to lose eye contact for long during an interview. "You think it's the same killer?"

The detective dipped his chin and frowned. "What the hell is wrong with you this morning? Of course, we think it's the same killer. Just don't ask me who because we don't have a suspect yet. How many perps do you think go around doing that to a guy? Hopefully just one, and when we get him behind bars, let's hope that's the end of it."

"You said he," Robert pointed out.

Detective Cagle shrugged. "Figure of speech. We still haven't ruled out a woman, except I have no idea how a woman would have the strength necessary to get him into that position." He hesitated. "Unless, of course, he did it willingly, and then she killed him. Or something like that…" His voice drifted off, leaving Robert to fill in the blanks.

"That footprint back there, was it a man's or woman's?"

"Man, probably." The detective gave a heavy sigh. "We think they may belong to the victim."

"Speaking of which—"

Detective Cagle interrupted. "Speaking of which, we haven't found his shoes or, for that matter, any of his clothes. The last time he was seen alive, he was dressed like an Indian warrior. You can print that in your paper. We need people to be on the lookout for those missing items. Before you leave, ask the officer over there with the mustache to give you a full description."

"How about the roses?"

The detective's black eyebrows shot up. "What about 'em?"

"Are you ready to go on the record with them yet?"

Detective Cagle didn't answer for a long time. He lit another cigarette and blew a smoke ring. That gave Robert plenty of time to study the man's profile. Pushing forty, if he ever gained weight, that small dainty nose of his would disappear into his fleshy face, but for now, it suited him. "No," Cagle finally said. "Nothing about the roses. Yet. But I'm not sure how much longer we can keep it to ourselves. We got lucky with Angel. The guy who found him kept his mouth shut. The young lady who found Louie Bonda might start blabbing. I hope not. She seems like a smart girl, but you never know."

"A local?" Robert asked.

"Yes," Cagle said, eyes softening. "From Palo Verde. She was out, minding her own business, taking a nice walk to get some fresh air, and she got the surprise of her life. Two of my guys had to practically carry her to the squad car, she was so shocked. So, she saw that rose, and now she probably won't be able to stop thinking about it, and she'll probably tell someone because who can keep something like that to themselves. She promised to keep quiet, but I'm not counting on it. So, for now, it's off the record. I told my guys to get her a doctor, give her something to calm the poor girl down, so that might buy us a little extra time. But she refused because she couldn't be late for work. She's got a job making costumes for the movie."

Robert looked up sharply. "You mean Espy Gaten?"

The detective tilted his head and stared. "You know her?"

"I met her at the set," Robert replied. "She's one of the people I interviewed about Angel." And now he planned on talking to her again as soon as he was done at the crime scene.

"That's right," Detective Cagle said, snapping his fingers. 'I thought I remembered her name from somewhere."

Robert tapped his pencil on the notepad, thinking. Had he covered all his bases? No, he hadn't. He'd forgotten the critical *when*.

"What time did Espy find him?" he asked.

"Approximately 6:30 a.m. She's an early riser."

"How about the time of death?"

Detective Cagle rubbed a hand across his chin, frowning as it met stubble. "Now that's one I can answer. Sometime between nine o'clock last night, when some teenagers were fooling around up here—it's a popular make out spot—and when Miss Gaten had the misfortune of discovering the body. We'll get a better idea when we have the results of the autopsy."

At the mention of autopsy, Robert slapped the side of his head. He was really off his game that morning because he hadn't thought to follow-up with the obvious. "How about Angel's autopsy? Get anything back yet?"

The detective squinted at him. "I didn't already say?"

"No!" shouted an officer still working on the plaster cast.

"Thank you, mom," Detective Cagle said, smirking in the direction of his officer, who flapped his hand and went back to his work. Turning to Robert, he said, "It's as we suspected. Angel Ramirez was strangled to death. We haven't got the toxicology report back yet, but like I said, we believe Angel was drugged."

"How about Louie? You think he was drugged too?"

"We do," Cagle replied, distracted by the sound of voices coming up the hill. "I think we're done here, Robert. I just hope your boss appreciates the return favor because these other reporters aren't going to be too happy when they find out I gave you an exclusive." He shrugged. "Oh well, what can you do? Debts must be repaid, no matter how odious."

As Robert turned to go, Cagle said, "And I don't want to see a rose in that paper of yours, Cleary, and if you even mention the word flower, you're in trouble. Don't disappoint me."

"Yes, sir," Robert replied. As he fast-walked down the hill, he gave a friendly nod to the three reporters who moaned when they spotted him.

"How the fuck did you get here so fast?" one said.

"How do you think?" another replied, huffing with exertion. "That fucking Cagle is playing favorites."

Neither comment merited a response. Even if he'd known the guys, they were professionals who knew it wasn't personal, so he gave a friendly wave and kept moving. He had to get to Espy Gaten before anybody else learned her name.

Chapter 12

Robert parked at the northern end of Palo Verde and walked over the hill to the movie set in search of Espy Gaten. She wasn't in her usual spot. The chair was empty, the worktable bare. A quote or two from her was just the ticket to punch up his story: the shock of discovering the body of a co-worker, just days after the murder of Angel Ramirez.

A group of people standing around in front of the jail at the far end of the set caught his attention, and he hurried toward them.

There was no sign of the director, Mitchell Wood, but Bruno, the assistant director, was standing in front of the actors and actresses, who formed a circle around him. They all looked worried.

"Now, listen, everyone," Bruno said. "If you want my honest opinion, I don't think anyone is in danger, and I don't think anyone is targeting people working on this production. Louie and Angel had one thing in common. They were both Mexicans, so it's probably someone who has a beef with Mexicans."

Robert hung back and listened. Bruno wore his usual uniform of white T-shirt and dark trousers. What Bruno was saying didn't mesh with Detective Cagle's version of events, so he wondered if the assistant director was getting his information elsewhere, or just making it up to calm everyone down.

Several actresses dressed in saloon outfits whispered among themselves. Robert recognized one of them—Darla Diamond, one foot set on a crate, skirt splitting at her thigh, revealing a garter belt. She must have felt him staring because she turned toward him, then snapped the garter with a nod of acknowledgment. Robert hastily looked away, embarrassed by the effect the woman had on him. She made him feel like an awkward, inexperienced teenager. If he asked her out, he was sure she'd say yes. If he could only get up the nerve. And if only he didn't find her so inexplicably unnerving.

Bruno continued. "Now listen, just to be safe, until they find out who did these horrible things, this is not the time to be going out anywhere alone. Use common sense and stick together. When you leave the set, make sure you walk with someone else to your car, to your bus, however you get home. Take the shortest route possible. There are lots of isolated places around here, and you'll want to avoid them."

An actor dressed as a cowboy raised his hand. "What about some extra security on the set?"

"We're hiring someone," Bruno said. "But the guys weren't found anywhere near here, so again, I'll be honest. I'm not sure what good security is going to do."

Darla waved a hand overhead. "Hey Bruno. What about Angel and Louie? We all knew 'em. They were nice kids. Don't they deserve a memorial or something?" This was met with murmurs and nods of approval.

Bruno blinked and shoved his hands into pockets. "Yeah, sure. We can do that. Let me see what I can do, and I'll let you all know." He paused. "That's a real nice idea, Darla."

Darla gave a little shrug, then gave Robert a sidelong look. Suddenly, he felt like his whole face was on fire.

Bruno clapped his hands. "All right, everybody, we're all very sorry about what happened to Louie and Angel, but we've got a movie to finish and a scene to get through this afternoon. So, let's get back to work."

Robert waited until all the actors had wandered off, including Darla who pouted at him over a bare shoulder before he approached Bruno.

"Back again?" the assistant director asked.

"Just a quick question. Is Espy Gaten around?"

Bruno grimaced and shook his head. "Sorry, no. I sent her home. She was in no shape to work today, but I give her credit for coming in. I wish everyone had the same work ethic she has."

The summer sun was beating down on Robert's head. He sidestepped into a spot of shade. "I heard you tell people that Angel and Louie were killed because they were Mexican, but that's not something I'm hearing. You have a source on that I should know about?"

Bruno spread his hands wide. "You think I need someone to tell me what's as plain as the nose on your face? My dad's a cop. Retired. He was around for the Zoot Suit Riots. He says some people have it out for Mexicans and Negroes. Saw it for himself firsthand. In my humble opinion, the only one who needs extra protection around here is Espy Gaten."

"But she's a woman," Robert said, frowning. "And both victims have been male."

Bruno shook his head. "So far. Maybe somebody doesn't like us employing Mexicans. Taking work from whites. For all I know, Espy could be next."

It was a thought. A dark one, but not totally unreasonable either. If this was something Detective Cagle had entertained, he wasn't ready to talk about it on the record.

"Why do you?" Robert asked.

"Do what?" Bruno cocked his head.

"Hire Mexicans."

"Oh. They work hard," Bruno said. Then, almost an afterthought, "And they work cheap." As Robert turned to leave, Bruno reached out and clapped his shoulder. "That story you did put a smile on Mitch's face. It was a real nice spread. And it finally drummed up some interest because now the other papers are calling the studio, wanting to do their own stories and asking why they'd never heard about the new set."

Robert gave a curt nod but said nothing. It wasn't his job to publicize the movie, so he was reluctant to accept the thanks. Besides, the interest in the set might have more to do with the murders than the movie itself.

After Bruno had given him directions to Espy's house, he said goodbye and set out for the neighboring ravine. His stomach grumbled, but food would have to wait.

He took the steep steps to the porch two at a time. Voices drifted through the screen door. He was about to knock when he heard Espy say, "Where were you last night, Catalina?"

Espy sounded tired and distressed. There was a long silence.

Heart beating faster, Robert stepped to the side where he couldn't easily be seen. He felt a brief pang of guilt for eavesdropping, but it wouldn't be the first time he'd done it in his line of work.

"Catalina," Espy said sharply. "Mercy Acevedo said you weren't home last night. She said you go out a lot. Where? Where do you go?"

Robert heard feet pacing just inside the door, and for a moment, he thought Catalina would come out and catch him standing there. Instead, she stopped and said, "Wherever I feel like it. Sometimes, I go to the Avadon Bar. Sometimes, I go dancing downtown."

"Dancing!" Espy cried.

Catalina scoffed. "Yes, dancing. It's not a sin, Espy. And it's none of Mercy's business where I go. She should give her daughter a little more attention, instead of watching me all the time."

"She said you put a hex on her," Espy said uncertainly.

Catalina gave a bitter laugh. "Maybe I did. Maybe I did something that put her to sleep for a while so she'd quit spying on me, and so she'd give poor Jane a break from all her nagging."

"Catalina!" Espy gasped.

Robert's heart pounded in his chest. It didn't sound like Catalina was joking.

"That woman had it coming," Catalina said. "I would have done it before, but I felt sorry for her, the way she lost her son. But she's only gotten worse since then. She's grown a mean streak a mile wide."

"So, you can do hexes," Espy said.

"And spells, yes," Catalina replied stiffly.

There was a long silence, then Espy said, "Do you go to the bars alone?"

"Sometimes," Catalina answered. "But that's not always a good idea." A pause followed as she began pacing again. "Louie had been going with me. He's a real good dancer."

The sofa springs creaked. Robert imagined Espy sitting bolt upright. "Louie! You went dancing with Louie?" she cried.

Catalina gave a heavy sigh. "Yes, I used to go dancing with him. He was a good-looking guy, and he was fun."

"Fun?" Espy practically shouted. "He's a pervert. He stuck his hand up my skirt. I heard he was following you around like a dog in heat. That's what people are saying."

"Are you jealous?" Catalina asked in a casual, offhand tone.

"No!" Espy cried, her voice rising with indignation. "Of course not."

"You didn't think he was good-looking?" Catalina pressed.

The sofa creaked again. "He was," Espy admitted, reluctantly. "But that's neither here nor there. What was going on between you?"

"What do you think?"

Espy gasped, so loudly it sounded like she was right next to the open window. "You weren't!"

"Would that be such a crime?" Catalina laughed. "Come on. Haven't you ever had a little fun?"

"No! No, not like that."

"You haven't had sex since Felix died?" Catalina said, voice softening. "Now that's a crying shame, Espy. You're too young to dry up. You need to enjoy life, live a little."

"So, you were having sex with Louie Bonda?" Espy whispered, but loudly enough for Robert to hear her every word.

"Yes, Espy," Catalina replied with exaggerated patience.

"Then why don't you sound sad?" Espy demanded.

More footsteps across the room. "I think I must be in shock. I can't believe it because I just saw him. He came to see me in the shed after work." She paused. "Quit looking at me like that. He came over for a quick little visit, if you know what I mean, and then he left. I don't know where he went after that."

"You have to tell the police."

Catalina gave a harsh laugh. "No, thank you. After how they treated my brothers? Arrested them for nothing. And what me and Louie were up to has nothing to do with what happened to him."

Robert's heart was pounding so hard he was afraid the two women inside might hear it. A trickle of sweat ran down his forehead as he pressed himself against the space between the windows. He was in a ridiculous position—out in the open for all to see, eavesdropping. It was just a matter of time before someone came by and caught him. He had to make his presence known.

Before he could decide what to do, Espy said, "Some of the movie people saw you with Angel. Were you doing it with him too?"

Something struck wood. Maybe Catalina's hand slapping a table, or a door jam. "So now you're saying I'm a slut?" she nearly shouted.

"No," Espie said, sounding uncertain. "Well, you're so casual about these things, Catalina, and Angel was good-looking, too, so you can't blame me for thinking that maybe, yes, you were doing it with him too."

"I wasn't," Catalina said, then sniffed. "We were just friends."

"I heard you were at the set," Espy asked, voice dripping with suspicion. "What were you doing there?" Another long silence.

Robert wiped his brow. He was as anxious to make himself known as he was eager to hear the answer.

"Bringing flowers to the set decorator," Catalina said.

"You're lying," Espy said. "About something. When I found you hurt, did Louie do that to you? Because he's a rough guy. Is that what happened? He roughed you up, and you told Angel?"

"Louie could get a little overexcited sometimes, but no, to answer your question," Catalina said.

So that explained the cut above her eye and the bruised face. Someone had messed her about, and that someone was probably Louie Bonda, victim number two. He was no expert, but he could swear Catalina was lying, and she sounded strangely casual about describing Louie as "overexcited."

"Maybe you like it rough," Espy said.

"Maybe I do," Catalina replied hotly. "I don't see how it's any of your business, Espy. And by the way, I think you're being a bit of a hypocrite because I've seen that guy from the set hanging around at all hours." There was a long pause. "Why didn't you tell me about him?" she asked in a small voice.

"Why didn't you tell me about Louie?" Espy snapped.

"Because sometimes, Espy, you're such a goody two shoes, that's why. I wanted to tell you because we're best friends, but then I thought, no, I better not because you wouldn't understand."

The sofa gave another creak. He could hear Espy come off the sofa, her two feet hitting the floor. "I'm your best friend?"

Catalina's sigh drifted through the screen. "Yes, Espy. Of course, you're my best friend." She gave a brittle laugh. "Who else around here has ever given me the time of day?"

As Espy's shoes brushed across the wooden floor, Robert knew it was his chance to make a move. He jumped over the rail of the porch, landed on the ground, then raced around to the front steps, calling, "Hello? Anyone home?"

Two figures appeared behind the screen door. Espy pushed it open, her eyes red, face swollen. "Robert," she said in surprise. Catalina stood just behind her, lips pressed into a straight line. She said nothing to him. Instead, she gave Espy a tight hug, whispered something in her ear, gave him a nod, then walked down the steps.

As she passed him, he noticed scratches on her hands and arms. They looked fresh. Had they been there when he'd visited her shed for a headache cure? Surely not. If they'd been there, he would have noticed them. He was *trained* to notice things.

Espy motioned for him to enter. It was hot and stuffy inside the small house, but at least the sun wasn't beating down on his head. She went into the kitchen, returned a few moments later with two glasses of water, and handed him one. He drank it down gratefully, not realizing how thirsty he'd been.

"I hear you found Louie's body," he said. "I'm sorry."

Espy sank down onto the sofa and squeezed her eyes shut. "Me too. I wish I never went up there. I hardly ever go to Loma. That poor guy. I can't believe it. I just can't believe it."

"I saw the body," he said. "So, I know how you feel. It's awful."

Her eyes flew open. "They let you see him? Like that?"

Robert nodded. "Yes," he said, then fell silent. After a while, he said, "Can I ask you a few questions? For the paper? I think it's important for…"

She bit her lip and shook her head so violently her dark hair whipped around her face. "No," she cried. "I don't want to talk about it. I can't."

He nodded, disappointed. He should have guessed as much. He probably wouldn't want to talk about it either, and no matter how she felt about Louie Bonda, the way he'd been left to die was truly shocking. Espy had begun to shiver.

He jumped to his feet. "You should lie down," he said in alarm.

She allowed him to settle her back onto the sofa. Grabbing a pillow, he put it under her head, then looked around helplessly, wondering if he should fetch Catalina. She would know what to do. Espy stared at the ceiling, her dark hair trailing off the side of the sofa, eyes wide and frightened. That did it. She needed help, help he couldn't give. He was walking toward the front door when he heard footsteps on the porch. Maybe it was Catalina.

Instead, it was a tall man on the other side of the screen door. When Robert opened it, the man frowned slightly and said, "Is Espy home?" He was holding a vase of enormous long-stemmed red roses.

Chapter 13

Robert stepped aside and nodded toward the couch.

The man took one look at her, set the vase on the closest table, and knelt next to her. "Espy, I heard what happened." Then he leaned over and kissed her forehead. "Are you all right?"

Espy struggled to sit up, and the man gently pushed her back down. "No, no, just stay there. You've had a shock. You can tell me all about it in a minute." He turned to Robert and said, "And who are you?"

"Robert Cleary. Reporter from *The Express*. I just stopped by to see if I could get Espy to give me another interview." When he saw the man open his mouth in protest, he held up a hand. "She declined, and I was just on my way out."

The man, who bore a striking resemblance to that actor Montgomery Somebody, nodded. "I'm Bruce Knox," he said. "I'm the prop master for the movie and a friend of Espy's."

Robert guessed he was more than that by his proprietary and protective air.

"Don't get up," Bruce instructed Espy, who closed her eyes and nodded.

Bruce got to his feet, grabbed the vase, and went into the kitchen. Robert followed, close on his heels. At the sink, the prop master dumped out the water, turned on the tap, and filled the vase with fresh water. As Robert stared at the flowers, an electric tingle raced up his spine. Roses. Long stem red roses.

The kind he saw sticking out of Louie Bonda. He didn't know much about the flowers, but those were unusual. Long, stiff, straight stems covered in thorns, with bright, proud heads in the deepest of reds. He couldn't drag his eyes away, as much as he wanted to.

"Where did you get those?" he asked in a quiet voice.

Bruce gave him an odd look before replying. "I got them from the woman who lives down the street."

"Just now?" Robert asked. Because Catalina had just left, and not enough time had passed for such a transaction to take place.

"No, early this morning," Bruce replied, confused. "I came by to see Espy, see if she wanted to walk with me to the set, but she wasn't here, and then I saw a delivery man picking up flowers from the garden down the street, so I went over there to see if she'd sell some to me. For Espy, you know. So, I paid the woman, then hid the vase on the side of the house until I could give them to Espy. Why are you asking?"

Robert shook his head. "They're just real nice," he lied.

"They are." Bruce picked up the vase and went back into the living room where Espy was sitting up.

When she saw the roses, she gave a little cry and clapped a hand over her mouth.

"What's wrong?" Bruce asked in alarm.

Espy shook her head and squeezed her eyes shut. Bruce glanced at Robert, chin jutting out. "Is there something you should be telling me?" he demanded.

Robert's attention wandered toward the roses. He'd seen their type in three places: the back ends of Angel and Louie, and the garden belonging to Catalina Montez. It was obvious Espy had made a similar connection. If anyone was going to explain it to the prop master, it wouldn't be him. He needed to get away. To think.

"I'm sure you two want to be alone," he said, then with a quick wave at Espy, he bounded out the door, down the steps, and ran to his car. When he was almost there, he doubled back to Catalina's garden, unlatched the gate, and made straight for the red roses. There was no sight of Catalina. The curandera was probably in her shed. He could hear voices in the distance. Probably people gathered in the alley, waiting for their turn to see her.

Nervously, keeping one eye at the back of the property, he looked around for something to cut one of the stems. He didn't dare do it with his bare hands. The thorns were plentiful and sharp, and the stem was too thick to simply snap in two. His foot hit something with a clang, and when he looked down, he saw he'd nearly tripped over a rusted metal bucket filled with gardening tools. He grabbed a pair of shears, went to the closest rose bush, took out a handkerchief, and carefully wrapped it around a section with the fewest thorns, then cut the stem.

After dropping the shears back into the bucket, he hurried through the garden, looking over his shoulder. Catalina was nowhere to be found. If she was a witch, at least she wasn't the type in children's fairy tales, the kind who surprised and captured trespassers.

He made it to his car without anyone shouting after him, demanding to know why he had taken a rose. If they had, he wouldn't have known what to answer because only the vaguest of plans had begun to form among his many conflicting thoughts.

That part of Palo Verde was short on trees and shade. The sun had baked the inside of the car, and he was forced to take the handkerchief from the flower stem and wind it around the steering wheel. As he passed by Bertita's house, he saw members of the movie crew trickling in for lunch. His stomach grumbled in protest, and he thought longingly of a plate of tamales, rice, and beans. He was hungry and sweaty and desperate for a shower, but that would have to wait too.

Detective Cagle had mentioned he worked at Central Division, and without thinking about where he was headed, that's where Robert ended up, sitting in his car, looking out at the building while the red rose wilted on the seat next to him.

If he went inside, what exactly would he say? And if he finally uttered the words, Detective Cagle would have questions. Lots of questions. And he still had a deadline to meet. Harry would be none too happy to get a phone call saying he was stuck at the police department, sticking his neck out, and there was no telling how long Cagle would keep him. He couldn't just drop off the rose and leave.

His obligation, first and foremost, was to make sure he kept his new job. Cagle could wait. And the truth of the matter was, he felt awful thinking about casting suspicion on Catalina Montez. What evidence did he have? Not much. Just that she grew long stem roses and had been seeing Louie Bonda and maybe Angel Ramirez. But that didn't make her a killer. She was, after all, a healer. It didn't make sense she'd want to hurt anyone. Then again, what did he really know about her? And he hadn't been imagining Espy's shocked expression when she'd seen the red roses in the vase.

But didn't he have another obligation? To the truth? Passing along information was a neutral act. It wasn't his job to investigate it or prove it. That was up to Cagle and his officers. He merely had to walk in, say what he'd heard, and leave. The rest would be out of his hands, and he would have done his part.

The hell if he knew what to do.

On his way to *The Express*, he stopped for a quick lunch at Philippes on Alameda Street. He ate his French Dip sandwich, macaroni salad, dill pickles, and potato chips, sitting at a counter, and washed it all down with two cups of coffee. Since he still wasn't quite full, he ordered a slice of chocolate cake and ate that too.

As he drove across town, he turned on the radio and listened to a breathless report on the murder of Louie Bonda. The radio guys were fast. The story had all the basic information, but it was clear whoever they'd sent didn't know the area that well. The short blip on the radio was no substitute for a big splashy headline and the exclusive photo his paper would run the next day.

When he got to the newspaper office, he left the rose on the front seat, grabbed his camera, and headed inside. He dropped off the film to be developed, swung by Harry's office to let him know what he had, then made straight for his desk. Gary, the redheaded reporter, looked up when Robert flung himself into his hard wooden chair.

"You're on a roll," Gary said dryly, crossing his arms in front of his chest.

Robert stuck a sheet of paper into his typewriter and rolled it into place. "You can say that," he replied easily. "What are you working on?"

"Same damn thing I've been working on since you got here. A series on that new draft law that's supposed to help with the Korean War effort," Gary said.

"You don't sound too excited about it," Robert remarked.

"No one's fault but my own," Gary said with a sigh. "The story was my idea, and Harry said yes. I got tired of covering nothing but crime, crime, crime, but now that I'm doing this, I'm having second thoughts." He pointed at Robert's gray Remington typewriter. "Now if I was writing your story, I'd be done in an hour and home in plenty of time for dinner with the wife. But instead, I'll be sitting here trying to make this article sound as exciting as I made it out to be."

"That's rough," Robert said with a sympathetic smile.

Gary shrugged. "Like I said. No one to blame but myself." Then he picked up a notebook and thumbed through it, scowling.

It took Robert a half hour to bang out the story. He ripped out the sheet of paper and made edits in red pencil, referring to his notes to make sure he had all the details correct. Then he retyped it, marched into Harry Barkin's office, and slapped it on his desk.

Harry stuck his elbows out, wiggled his shoulders, then attacked the first sheet with a red pencil, mumbling, "Good. Nice. Passive voice. Fuck. More passive voice. Boring. Oh, now that's good." When he finally looked up, he said, "Nice work, kid. So, we can't say anything about the rose up the ass yet?"

"Not yet." Robert shook his head, then stared at his shoes, which were covered in dust from all the walking he'd done. The mention of the rose reminded him of the decision he'd delayed that was still waiting for him.

Harry's shoulders slumped. "I guess we'll just have to be patient." He looked up and sniffed, nose wrinkling in distaste. "Jesus, Robert. Is that you?"

Robert took a giant step back and rubbed the back of his neck. It was slick with sweat. "Sorry about that, boss," he said sheepishly. "It was hot as the blazes out there."

Harry took his glasses off and wiped them on his tie, then pointed at the door. "Well," he said slowly. "I probably didn't do you any favors by calling you so early and rushing you out the door. Why don't you go home? Get yourself cleaned up. Get a cold beer while you're at it. I have to babysit the story, anyway, make sure we crop the photo."

Before his boss could change his mind, Robert thanked him, but halfway through the newsroom, his footsteps slowed. Was he making a mistake by not telling his boss about Catalina? What if Harry told him to keep his mouth shut? What would he do then? Or what if Harry scolded him for not taking his concerns directly to Detective Cagle? Either way, he wouldn't win. The problem was, he didn't know Harry Barkin well enough, so he couldn't predict how he'd react, and he didn't want to risk damaging their new relationship when things seemed to be going so well.

But he had decided one thing while he wrote his story.

He had to tell Detective Cagle.

There was no question about it. His conscience wouldn't let him do otherwise. Anonymity. That's what he'd ask for, and he'd hope the detective would honor it. He picked up his pace and sprinted the rest of the way to his car.

Chapter 14

Jane's father held her hand tightly as they crossed the dirt road to Catalina's, and she did her best to hide her excitement at getting to spend the day with the pretty curandera. She didn't feel bad about leaving her mother behind in bed, not one little bit. Especially not after Mama yelled at her when she said she didn't mind if the city took their home because then she could live with her cousins and run around the neighborhood like they did. Her mother had pinched the backs of her legs, called her an *ingrata* and a daughter of *El Diablo* himself.

That had scared Jane so bad she'd burst into tears, and she was still crying when her father got home from work. She thought she was in big trouble, but instead, her parents had started arguing, and the next thing she knew, her mother had fallen to the floor and had to be helped to bed.

And there she'd stayed. She was so weak she couldn't get up the rest of the evening. When Jane tiptoed in, carrying a fresh glass of water, Mama had put her hands around her throat and said in a croaky voice that the witch across the street had hexed her. That made Jane's father mad again, and he told her to stop scaring Jane.

Jane wanted to tell him the truth. That she wasn't scared of Catalina, even if she was a witch, but she was afraid of her mother. Mama cried all the time now, complaining about so many things Jane lost track. How somebody was killing Mexican men in their own backyard. How Jane's father would be next.

How Espy Gaten thought she was better than everybody else since getting that job with the movie. How Catalina was a no-good hussy, and that everybody in their right mind should go to Lencha, the curandera in La Loma, instead. Jane didn't know what "hussy" meant, but the way her mother said it, with her face all *chueco*, she knew it was bad.

When her mother didn't get out of bed in the morning, all Jane felt was relief. Her father hadn't known what to do with her. He didn't want to leave her alone, with her mother unable to wake up, and he didn't have time to take her to Boyle Heights to stay with her aunt. So instead, he'd gone across the street and talked to Catalina.

And now he was walking her to the slightly crooked shed in the coolness of the morning, and Catalina was standing in the doorway with a welcoming smile. She looked very pretty, in a red dress and sandals and her shiny hair loose around her shoulders.

"There's my little helper," she said.

Jane felt a big smile come to her face. When her father told her to mind Catalina and not give her any problems, she'd thrown her arms around his waist, grateful to be away from the house and her mother's dark moods.

"I promise, *papá*," she said.

When he left, Catalina tied an apron made from an old flour sack around Jane's waist, pulled her hair up in a ponytail to keep it out of her face, and did the same to herself. Then she dragged over a crate in front of the work bench and told Jane to step up on it. Now Jane could work comfortably next to Catalina, who showed her how to use the *metate*. They had one at home, of course, that her mother used to grind the peppers for enchilada sauce, but this one was longer and flatter, and Catalina showed her how to mash the seeds and dried flowers she used to make her remedies.

Soon, the shed was full of nice smells—some familiar, like cloves, that Jane remembered from the time she had a bad earache, and new ones, like a flower that smelled like honey. Catalina said the dried flowers used in tea helped people sleep, and that a lot of people in Palo Verde, La Loma, and Bishop had trouble sleeping because they were so worried about the city stealing their houses.

"What do you mean, 'stealing'?" she asked worriedly.

Catalina gave her a funny look. "*Ai*, Jane. That's what they're doing, isn't it? The city is taking something that belongs to other people. They can call it an eviction and make up lies about where we live, but to me, those city people are nothing but a bunch of no-good thieves and robbers."

Jane nodded, thinking of the tall man who'd visited their house and gave her dad a piece of paper. He looked more like she imagined the boogeyman appearing than a robber, but if Catalina thought he was a thief, then she believed it.

"Where will you go, Catalina?" she asked.

The curandera bit her lip, then said, "I don't know, Jane. This has always been my home. I can't imagine living anyplace else."

Jane sat patiently on a stool in the corner of the shed while Catalina went about her business. An old man from Bishop showed Catalina a red sore on his arm, and she fixed him a lotion and told him to wash it off when he got home. Two old ladies hobbled in, complaining of arthritis, and Catalina gave them something for that. A young lady came in and said in a real embarrassed way that she couldn't stop peeing, and Catalina had taken her aside so Jane couldn't hear what they were saying. When she left, she clutched a small bottle to her chest and looked happier than when she came in.

The pan dulce man stopped by, too, and delivered some pastries. He wouldn't take any money from Catalina. The man always made her mother pay, so Jane asked why she got them for free.

"It's because I help him and his wife," she said, looking at him sadly as he walked away down the alley. "They don't have much money, and I've known them since I was little."

Jane noticed Catalina's big eyes had filled with tears. Now that she had taken her sweater off, Jane could see there was something wrong with her arms. They were covered in scratches. When Jane asked how she got them, Catalina's face got all funny, her mouth stretched straight.

"*Ai*, Jane, I fell into the rose bushes," she said, then went to the door and opened it to the next customer.

While Catalina was busy talking to a pregnant lady, Jane got so bored she decided to explore. It was bigger than it looked from the outside—two shacks stuck together, attached by a short, skinny hallway made of rough wood planks with gaps so big Jane could see the giant cactus outside. She crept into the second shed and looked around. It had a tiny window, but it didn't let much light in. As she squinted in the dim light, her knees bumped into something. A cot, covered in blankets. Catalina had a house down the street, so she didn't know why she needed a cot too. Maybe she liked to take naps. Jane hated taking naps.

The walls were covered in strange symbols scratched into the wood, and they gave Jane a funny feeling, so she tried to stay in the middle of the room as far away from them as she could get. There was a pack of cigarettes on a little table and a few bottles of a murky-looking oil. Next to it was a small, shallow bowl filled with something. Thin, brittle half-moons. Fingernails. The sight of them made her stomach feel like it was filled with butterflies trying to get out. There was something else in the bowl too. Dark hair. As she backed away, something

122

brushed her face, and she gasped, but it was just a black cloth hanging from a hook in the ceiling.

The air was cooler than the first shed and drier too, the dirt floor covered with an old, faded carpet. A workbench took up an entire wall. Jane stood on her tiptoes and peered inside small wooden boxes filled with all kinds of things: thick red string, nails, seeds, shiny black rocks, and a silver star with numbers and letters. The rest of the table was covered with white candles.

Jane was studying the silver star—she'd made out the letters TE and TRA—when she heard a noise outside. Not from the other shed, where she could still hear Catalina talking quietly to the lady with the bulging stomach, but from outside in the garden. Feet stomping on the ground. Lots of feet. She peeked between a gap in the boards and saw men in black uniforms. The *policía*.

The Police Academy was close by, and once she went swimming in their pool with other kids from Palo Verde as a special treat, and an officer gave them Carnation ice cream sandwiches afterward. She wondered if an officer had gotten sick and needed Catalina's help.

Someone shouted in the distance. Then pounding on a door so hard it made the walls of the shed rattle, and Jane heard Catalina cry out.

Jane's legs went wobbly. Men were talking in loud voices and Catalina was saying, "No! No! No!" She had to go in there, find out what was happening, but she was having a hard time getting her feet to move. When she raised her hand to her temple, something she'd seen her mother do when she was upset, the red bracelet Catalina had given her slid down her wrist. Catalina said it would protect her from the boogeyman, so it might work on the police too. And whatever they were there for, it wasn't for her. She hadn't done anything wrong. They had no reason to take her away and lock her up.

123

Jane took a deep breath, then hurried through the short hallway to the main shed, where she found Catalina bent over as two police officers struggled to put handcuffs on her wrists. The officers didn't look friendly like she remembered from the Police Academy. Their faces were stern, almost angry. Catalina's mouth was twisted, and when she spotted Jane, she said, "Go get Espy, please."

That was all Jane needed to hear. Her head—which felt big and fuzzy—cleared, and energy flowed into her arms and legs.

One of the men tried to grab her arm as she shot past, but she dodged him and sprinted out the door. For one terrible moment, she thought he'd chase her, but he didn't. She didn't dare look over her shoulder. She just kept running, sticking to the alley, around the corner, then up the block to Espy's house.

She threw open the gate, pounded up the steps, and began hammering her fists against the wood of the screen door.

A man loomed into view. Startled, Jane took a step back. Then she recognized him. He worked on the movie with Espy, and he had a very nice, friendly face.

"Are you okay, kid?" he asked, opening the door.

He looked beyond her, and his eyes widened. "What the hell?"

Then Espy was standing at his side, clutching his arm. "Jane!" she cried. She looked down the road, and her voice dropped to a whisper. "*Madre mia de Dios.* What's happening?"

Jane felt dizzy, and her mouth was so dry she could barely talk. She had no words for what she saw happening because it didn't make sense. Catalina was a nice lady. A beautiful one. Why were the officers being so mean? Instead of saying anything, Jane shook her head and began to cry.

Espy and the man were talking in quiet, urgent voices, when a group appeared on the street in front of Catalina's garden. It was the police officers with Catalina walking between them.

When Jane glanced up at Espy, her face was a scary white color, but that didn't stop Espy from dashing down the steps and across the dirt road in her bare feet, the nice man running after her, as an officer pushed Catalina inside the black and white car. It drove off before Espy could get there, the wheels raising a cloud of dust in the dirt.

Chapter 15

Detective Cagle had assured him he'd done the right thing, but Robert wasn't so sure. His doubt increased with every long hour that passed in the night, and by morning, he'd become convinced he'd wronged Catalina Montez by voicing his suspicions to the detective.

Cagle had shown only mild interest at the possibility the woman was having an affair with Louie Bonda and possibly Angel Ramirez, but he'd sat straight up when Robert produced the long stem red rose—limp after hours in the hot car—and had leaned forward, elbows on the desk, as Robert explained her experience as a local medicine woman.

"So, you're saying she had the know-how to drug a man into a stupor," Cagle had said thoughtfully, his fingers forming a steeple.

"Maybe," Robert had replied, suddenly uncertain. Catalina making his headache go away was one thing. Catalina slipping a guy something from her garden to render him unconscious was another. And assuming she had the knowledge to do that, would she? And why? He'd convinced himself that once he'd unburdened himself of his dark thoughts about the woman, his duty would be done. If she was innocent, then Cagle and his men would find out, and all would be well. If she wasn't, then he'd done the right thing, and they could bring a killer to justice.

But that's not how it happened. Maybe because he'd had a long day, and maybe because he was nervous about giving the police a tip about someone he knew—someone who'd *helped* him—he found himself nervously blabbing about Espy's reaction to seeing the red roses. Then he relayed the conversation he'd overheard between the two women, including Espy's questions about where Catalina went at night. Now *that* certainly grabbed Cagle's attention. When he was done answering the man's questions, Robert felt like he'd turned his own sister into the police.

He rolled out of bed, made himself a cup of coffee, then drew the blinds. The southeast-facing kitchen was too bright, even at 6:00 a.m. He picked up the business card and tried calling Cagle at work, but of course, it was too early, and he wasn't in yet. It was just as well because he hadn't planned on what to say. That he was sorry, and he was wrong? That his imagination had gotten away from him? *Please, no, detective, never mind. Ignore everything I said.*

At least if it all went wrong, Cagle had promised not to say a word to his boss, Harry. The clap on the back Cagle had given him as he'd left Central Division, housed within police headquarters on First Street, just added to the feeling he'd crossed a line he had no business crossing as a journalist.

As he drank his second cup of coffee, he became convinced Harry would fire him on the spot if he ever found out. He ate his slightly burnt toast, and a new thought began to form. By the time he'd finished his over-easy eggs, he groaned at his own stupidity. Because no matter what happened next, he was bound to cover it for *The Express*. He'd have a front row seat at a show of his own making. And by the good mood Cagle was in when he last saw him, he had little doubt Catalina Montez was in for a rough time.

Leaving the dishes in the sink, he bathed and dressed quickly, then walked to the nearest news stand, eager to see the murder scene photo he'd taken of Louie Bonda on the front page.

There was a small group of men standing around in front of the stack with *The Express*, so Robert had to reach between them and grab a copy.

Harry Barkin had cropped the photo well. The photo managed to be sensational enough—bare calves covered in scratches with a streak of blood smeared across a heel—without being too offensive.

He was reading the article when a thin, chinless man said, "Another Mexican found in that neighborhood near the police academy."

A short man with jowls standing next to him said, "My sister paints up there where that fellow was found. La Loma, I think it's called. She says it's real picturesque. Like being out in the country or something."

"I wonder who did it?" Chinless said, folding the newspaper and sticking it under his arm.

The man standing behind the green newsstand counter cleared his throat. He had a round face and was wearing sunglasses and a beret. "A Mexican did it. That's who. All you need to do is understand their psychology to figure that out."

Robert lowered the newspaper and turned to the man in surprise. "What's that supposed to mean?"

The newspaper agent drummed his fingers on a stack of magazines. "It means they're not like other people. They got the blood lust, like. From their ancestors in Mexico. The Aztecs. All those Aztecs used to do human sacrifices, and it's still in them. Nothing you can do about it, and now, more of them are coming here, and now we're dealing with the Mexican hoodlum element." When he saw Robert's expression, he hastened to add, "Now, not all of them are like that, of course. Most of them are law abiding citizens. But some of these young Mexicans are prone to violence, and if you doubt my word on this, I'm just repeating what an expert with the sheriff's department said during the Sleepy Lagoon trial of those zoot suiters."

This was the first time Robert had heard of Sleepy Lagoon and vowed to look it up, but he couldn't get away fast enough from the man and his talk of Aztecs and blood lust. If it was true, then half his family would be running amok with axes and shields, while the other half would be wearing kilts and swinging swords. The argument was absurd.

He paid a nickel for the paper, walked back to his car, and drove across town to the newspaper office.

No matter how early he got there, he had yet to beat Harry into the office. The man sure had a hell of a long day. Harry looked up when he walked into the bullpen and waved him over.

"Morning, boss," he said, hanging out near the door.

"And a very good morning it is," Harry said grinning. "I already got a call from Detective Cagle himself. The good fairy just keeps dishing it out."

Robert's chest tightened. "Is that right? How so?"

Harry leaned forward, bringing both hands down on the table, palms down. "Well, we're being given another exclusive, and I'm not one to question a gift horse in the mouth because next week, who knows? The detective will get a crush on some other paper, and then we'll be left out in the cold. But for now, I want you to go to police headquarters and wait. They're bringing in a suspect for questioning in the murder of those two unfortunate boys, and you can get her picture." Harry stopped, then grinned at Robert, whose heart dropped to his stomach like an out-of-control elevator hitting the bottom of a shaft.

Robert sagged against the side of the door. "Her?" he asked weakly.

Harry snapped his fingers. "Exactly! Her. They're eyeing a woman for this, if you can believe it. But that's about all I can tell you. Cagle's being awfully sly about the whole thing. So go on." He flapped his hands in the air. "You're on stakeout. When you've got something, give me a call, so I know if we got a lead story or not."

"Sure, boss," Robert said, then turned to leave. He walked in a daze through the newsroom. In the bathroom, he went into a stall, closed the toilet lid, and sat, sucking air into his lungs. When he could breathe normally again, he went to the sink and splashed water on his face. His blue eyes stared back at him. "Those innocent baby blues," Harry had teased him on his first day.

Well, he wasn't innocent. Far from it. Detective Cagle and his guys were out in Palo Verde, arresting Catalina Montez. They would never have known about her if it wasn't for him. Cagle seemed like a decent man, but what did he know? The detective could harbor the same crazy ideas about Mexicans as the guy at the newspaper stand, except he might just be better at hiding it.

How could he have possibly convinced himself to do such a thing?

He drove toward First Street, wishing he'd never eaten those eggs. His stomach was jittery, and his mouth tasted sour and bitter.

Finding parking wasn't easy. Police cars lined both sides of the road, so he found a place on Hill Street and walked over. Shade was even harder to come by, so after a half hour of standing in the morning sun, he ventured inside to wait. He flashed his press credential at the inquiring officer sitting behind a wide desk, then hung out near the double doors, keeping an eye on the street. After a half hour passed, it occurred to him he might be staking out the wrong doors. Maybe they planned to bring her around the back. The desk officer assured him he was in the right spot, so he continued waiting.

Finally, a black and white Ford pulled up to the front. Detective Cagle was sitting in the passenger seat. When Robert darted out, his stomach lurching, Cagle stuck his hand out the open window and patted the side of the big car, his way of acknowledging Robert's presence. Robert dipped his head, his eyes sliding to the backseat.

A woman sat there. Catalina Montez. When she spotted him, she blinked, confused, and opened her mouth as if to say something. She sat, half-in, half-out of the car, frozen.

Detective Cagle cast a look of exasperation in his direction as if to say, "Take the picture already." Catalina glanced from the detective to Robert, and her eyes narrowed, expression hardening. Right then and there, Robert knew she'd figured it out, that he was the reason she was there, that there was some sort of collusion between himself and the police. Nothing else could explain his presence, at exactly the right moment.

When an officer came around the side of the car, and tried to help her out, she jerked her arm free and shot Robert a venomous glance. He winced, then fumbled with the camera and raised the viewfinder to his face. It acted as a shield against her hostile glare. With his shaking hands, he was having a hard time getting Catalina in the frame because she was intent on getting through the double doors as fast as her sandaled feet would carry her. An officer rushed ahead and pulled her arm to slow her down, and at that moment, she turned, and her eyes landed on Robert, and he snapped the photo.

He closed his eyes, imagining the shot he'd just captured— hooded eyes filled with cold disdain, mouth a defiant sultry pout. One of those people the camera loved. In person, lovely. Caught on film. Stunning. Striking. The high cheekbones, the square jaw. She didn't seem to have a bad angle.

He snapped another picture of her retreating back, the stiff shoulders, the dark hair cascading down her back to her small waist.

Harry was going to love it.

Chapter 16

The next day got off to a miserable start with the discovery Harry Barkin had changed the headline he'd written—the one he'd slaved over for the story about the police questioning Catalina Montez in the deaths of Louie Bonda and Angel Ramirez. He'd awakened early and headed straight to the newsstand and asked for a copy of *The Dispatch* because *The Express* rack was empty.

"They flew out of here this morning," the news agent said. "I'm hoping for another delivery this morning. But you're in luck, young man, because I have one last copy, if you don't mind that it's the one I already read."

"That's fine," Robert replied, setting a nickel on the counter and holding out his hand for the paper.

The man was in no hurry to hand it over. He leaned his elbows on the counter and said, "When I saw that picture, I thought they'd made a mistake. Thought it was Jane Russell. You know, from that Western movie. But then I told myself, no, Dave, you're wrong, that isn't her at all, not that anybody who's buying the paper this morning gave a hoot. Now see that?"

Dave pointed at the cluttered wall behind him. Biting his lip, Robert followed his finger to an illustration of a woman with red hair and a come-hither look, smiling over her bare shoulder, her perfectly rounded bottom in a bathing suit. He was familiar with the pinup calendars. They'd hung in every newsroom he'd ever worked in. Sometimes, it was just a page torn out and tacked up near a desk.

"Now, see what I mean? That witch in the newspaper?" Dave paused and waved the latest edition of *The Express* in the air, just out of Robert's reach. "She's every bit as sexy as those gals on the calendars, but the paper is cheaper."

At the mention of "witch," Robert's eyes snapped open. He reached over the counter and snatched the newspaper from the man.

Catalina stared back at him with reproachful eyes. The headline made his stomach flip over.

SUSPECTED MEXICAN WITCH HELD IN BRUTAL SLAYING OF TWO MEN

Dear God. That's not what he'd written. His headline had been much more straightforward: "Palo Verde Woman Detained in Deaths of Two Men."

The article he'd written contained no mention of "witch," just that she was a respected local healer. Then he remembered mentioning to Harry Barkin some of the locals called her a bruja, a Mexican witch, and squeezed his eyes shut, recalling the way Harry's eyes had lit up.

"Is that right?" Harry had said, his pencil flying across the notepad.

At the time, he hadn't registered the significance of all that note taking, so focused had he been on getting through the edit session with his boss while secretly consumed by guilt.

Harry had changed the copy, of course, using the fascinating little tidbit Robert had dropped without giving it a second thought. And because Harry was the boss, he had final say on such things. Even if Robert had been given the chance to protest, Harry would merely have shrugged and said something like, "That's the way the cookie crumbles, kid."

Damn. Damn. Fuck.

Holding his breath, he sped through the article. He found it in the third paragraph, the addition of, "some locals claim the 31-year-old woman is not only a healer, but a so-called '*bruja*,' or Mexican witch." His eyes flicked up to the cloudless blue sky, and he exhaled. It could have been worse. At least there was some equivocation with the use of "so-called" and "some locals."

The question of whether she was an actual witch wasn't further addressed in the story. It was left to hang there, an implication, an innuendo splashed on the front page of a newspaper for all to read, including her neighbors and everyone in the little town she called home.

At least for now.

Until the city got its way and gave them the boot.

As he walked to his car, he wondered if the city had delivered all its eviction notices and what the next steps were. Maybe he could talk Harry into a follow-up piece. Obviously, he still wasn't thinking clearly because Harry had an assignment ready for him when he walked into the newsroom.

"One live woman with sex appeal sure beats two strangled dead guys," Harry announced cheerfully, setting down the phone. "That Catalina Montez sure can sell papers. We had to do an extra print run just to keep up with demand, and since there's such an interest in our gal, I want you back up there to see what else you can find out about the woman. We need to follow up, see what the neighbors have to say about her."

Robert's heart sank. He couldn't think of anything worse. He opened his mouth, then shut it when he noted the frown coming across Harry's face.

"You got a problem with that?" Harry snapped.

"No, sir," Robert said. "I just thought maybe I could do that story about the residents organizing a protest against the city." When Harry stared at him blankly, he added, "About the evictions. See what the politicians have to say about it."

Harry sat back in his chair, the springs creaking. "Now, why would I want you to do that when we have a much more obvious story to do today. Because that eviction story you keep talking about isn't going anywhere. It's an evergreen for some day when we've got nothing else. But today, we need to keep up the momentum." He paused, picked up a pencil, and tapped it on his desk. "Now, please tell me you have other pictures of the lady we can use."

Robert rubbed the side of his face and sighed. "Yes," he finally said. "I have some."

Harry grinned and clapped his hands. "I knew I could count on you. Now off you go, and don't come back until you have at least three people on the record telling us about her witchy ways."

Chapter 17

By the time Robert was back in Palo Verde, he had the beginnings of another headache. But that time, there would be no Catalina to massage his temples and mix him another batch of her miracle cure because she was still being questioned by the police. He'd managed to reach Detective Cagle on the phone before he'd set out, and all the man would say is that Catalina Montez was not cooperating, and as such, they intended on keeping her until she wised up.

"Does that mean she's under arrest?" he'd asked.

Cagle had refused to answer the question directly. "We're continuing to hold her until we get some answers out of her," he'd snapped, then hung up.

Which meant holding her in a cell, where she'd already been for the better part of twenty-four hours. Could they put someone behind bars without formally charging them? He'd put that to his boss before he left, but Harry was just as vague as Cagle had been and hadn't shown the slightest interest in pursuing it.

"Let one of the socialist newspapers cover it," Harry had said. "Or that Spanish paper. That's right up their alley."

Despite his unease over the assignment, he found it was much easier to get people in Palo Verde to talk about Catalina Montez than he'd imagined. The woman who lived directly across from her, Mercy Acevedo, had readily invited him inside and talked to him, while her daughter hovered in the kitchen doorway, eyes wide.

"Some people might disagree with me," Mrs. Acevedo said with a sniff. "But that woman is a bruja, just like her mother." The small living room had fresh scrubbed floors but not much furniture, just three easy chairs of worn brown leather and a small table covered with a lace doily.

"But how do you *know* that?" Robert asked.

She gripped the sides of the chair and leaned forward. "Because she put a hex on me. I couldn't wake up. It was awful. It was like I was trapped in my body. I wanted to move, but I couldn't, and there I stayed for a whole day and night."

Robert pretended to make a note in his reporter pad. There was no use pressing her for proof because she didn't have any. Didn't need any because she believed Catalina was a witch, and that was enough for her.

"Jane, show the man the *pulsera* that woman gave you," Mrs. Acevedo said to her daughter.

The little girl shuffled over to him and shyly held out her thin wrist. A simple bracelet made of thick red string dangled from it.

"What's that?" he asked, peering at the bracelet, which was knotted in places.

Jane covered it with one hand, as if afraid he might take it from her. "Catalina made it for me," she said in a small voice. "To protect me."

"From what?" he asked, raising his eyebrows.

"From el cucuy and la llorona. I don't want them to take me, so Catalina told me to wear this and promised they'd leave me alone."

When he shot an inquiring look over Jane's shoulder, Mrs. Acevedo shrugged and said, "That's the boogeyman and a lady ghost. A really bad one." She paused long enough to cross her arms in front of her chest and shiver.

Robert cleared his throat and jotted that down. "Just so I'm understanding correctly, what you're saying is that only brujas know how to make these protection bracelets?"

The woman shifted in her chair, nostrils flaring slightly. "Well, Lencha is a curandera, and she doesn't get up to things like that. You can ask her yourself. I saw her going to Bertita's house to help make the lunches for the movie people."

Robert thanked the woman for her time, eager to make his escape. When he looked over his shoulder, Jane was standing on the porch, looking at him with sad eyes. He felt bad for the little girl. She appeared to be the only child living in the house, and Mrs. Acevedo seemed like a high-strung woman with a mean streak. Ten minutes in her home had been enough for him. He gave Jane a friendly wave. She smiled and waved back.

At least he could kill two birds with one stone: get lunch and talk to this Lencha woman.

Bertita answered the door. For a moment, he thought she meant to hit him with her cane—she looked so annoyed—but instead, she took a few steps back and used it to wave him in.

"Back again?" she asked as she led him into the kitchen.

As before, the kitchen was a hive of activity, with three teenage girls sitting at a long table, forming an efficient assembly line, making tamales. An older woman with a long black braid and dark brown skin stood at the stove, stirring something that smelled spicy and delicious.

"Lencha's making her special beans," Bertita said as way of introduction.

So, this was Lencha.

"I've heard you're the curandera from La Loma," he said, proud he hadn't bungled the pronunciation of the foreign word.

Lencha turned to him and looked him over. "I heard you're the man who called Catalina a bruja."

He didn't know what he'd been expecting from a healer named Lencha, but it wasn't that. Not the unnerving, piercing gaze that seemed to look right through him, not the directness of her speech. More like one of those women he occasionally came across at city council meetings who had no trouble speaking their mind, and to hell with anybody who dared disagree with them. He'd have to watch his step.

"Only half guilty," he said sheepishly. "The headline wasn't up to me."

Lencha wiped the spoon on the edge of the pot and set it aside on a chipped pink saucer. "I just don't see what her being a bruja has to do with the murder of those two poor boys."

The woman was full of surprises.

"So, she is a bruja?" he asked, hardly able to believe his ears, or his luck.

"It's not a bad thing if she is," Lencha said disapprovingly, wiping her hands on her apron. "It's a proud tradition where I come from."

Bertita sat on a stool with a little grunt. "Lencha's mother was a bruja." She took a cigar out of her pocket and contemplated it for a moment. As before, she wore a colorful scarf wrapped around her hair, topped with a beret in gray wool. "But Lencha didn't have the knack, did you Lench?"

Lencha came over and plucked the cigar from Bertita's long fingers, nose wrinkled in distaste. "*Ai*, how many times do I have to tell you to smoke this thing outside? And you know as well as I do that my mother died before she had a chance to teach me."

The teenagers at the table smirked.

With another grunt, Bertita grabbed the edge of the counter and pulled herself into a standing position. She snatched the cigar from Lencha, shuffled across the faded red linoleum, and banged out the screen door into the backyard. Moments later, smoke wafted through the open windows. Lencha sighed, leaned over the sink, and shut them.

"Mercy Acevedo says Catalina put a hex on her," he said.

The girls' heads snapped up. "Serves her right," one of the teens muttered.

Lencha wagged a finger at the girl. "Now, now, now. You be nice. Mrs. Acevedo has suffered through a lot. She lost her only son, and she's been real upset by those eviction letters." Then she turned to Robert and said, "There's only one way of knowing if Catalina did such a thing, and that's to ask her yourself, but I don't see how that gets you any closer to knowing what you want to know. Which is did Catalina kill Angel and Louie."

She went to the icebox and rummaged through it. With her back to him, he couldn't see her expression.

The teenagers exchanged glances.

"Do you think she did?" he asked uneasily. That wasn't his intended line of questioning, but now that Lencha had brought it up, he'd be a fool to ignore it.

When the woman turned around, a block of white cheese in her hand, her expression had changed, softened a little. "It doesn't matter what I think. And even if I had an opinion, you'd be the last person I'd tell. My mother and Mrs. Montez were good friends. Very good friends. They grew up together in Mexico. Mrs. Montez came here first, and then later, my mother did too. I used to babysit Catalina when she was little while our mothers went to work in town. Here's the only thing I'm going to tell you, and you're welcome to write that down for your paper. That girl has always had guts. People around here haven't always been nice to her, even when they've needed her help."

When Lencha stopped talking, she stared at him with inquiring eyes. He felt the hairs lift on the back of his neck. It was as if she *knew* what he'd done. Then again, maybe Catalina had told Lencha she'd helped him with his headache, and all Lencha had to do was put two and two together.

Robert gave a tight nod. "Thank you for your time." He made his excuses and turned to leave. Lunch would have to wait. He didn't want to chance a similar lecture from Bertita.

He was walking up the street, wondering if Salvio Duran, the shopkeeper, would agree to speak with him about Catalina, when he heard someone behind him. When he turned around, it was one of the tamale-making teenagers.

"I can tell you something about Catalina," she said.

Robert sighed. As much as he wanted to hear what she had to say, he had no intention of relying on a kid for his story. "How old are you? And the truth now, because I have ways of finding out if you're lying."

"Eighteen," she replied, lifting her chin. "I turned eighteen on June 12th."

He studied her for a moment. She was small and birdlike, so it was hard to tell her age, but she said it with such authority that he believed her.

"Okay," he relented. "What did you want to tell me? But what's your name first?"

She looked over her shoulder, back at Bertita's house, before answering. "Julia Martinez. I just graduated from Lincoln High School. Look, I don't want to say anything bad about Catalina because she's been nice to me. But she was real mean to my sister. My sister used to go with Louie Bonda." When she saw Robert's expression, she shook her head. "This was months ago. My sister was getting real upset because she thought Louie didn't like her anymore, like maybe he was interested in someone else. I tried telling her he wasn't worth it, but she liked

144

him a lot. She was crazy about him. Then my sister heard that Catalina does love spells." When she noted Robert's blank expression, she added, "You know, the kind that helps you find true love."

"If you say so," he said with a little shrug.

She bit her lip while she studied him for a moment. "A lot of girls have tried it," she said stiffly. "Like I was saying, my sister went to Catalina and explained the situation. Catalina said she could help and told her to go home and collect some pee in a jar and bring some hair and fingernails from her boyfriend too. She said to come back real early on Friday morning, before the sun came up. So that's what she did. But when she went, you'll never guess what happened."

She pursed her lips and lifted her eyebrows expectantly, waiting for Robert to respond. He shook his head. To say he was out his element would be the understatement of the year. He only had one sister, and she was a tomboy. It certainly qualified as the most extreme type of girl-talk there was.

"You got me," he admitted.

Julia rolled her eyes. "My sister saw Louie coming out of Catalina's place. At dawn! She knew right then and there what he'd been up to all along. But my sister is such a *tonta* that she didn't even confront him. She went all crying and everything to Catalina and begged her for a spell to keep him. But Catalina just laughed at her. She said no spell would work on someone like Louie and told her to dry her tears and go away." She paused. "Wasn't that mean?"

Robert allowed himself a heavy sigh. "Not really. More like Catalina was doing your sister a favor by telling her the truth."

"Catalina just wanted Louie to herself," Julia replied, scowling.

Robert stuffed his notepad in the pocket of his pants. From what he'd just heard, there wasn't one word worth jotting down.

145

The past five minutes had been an utter waste of time. Still, being rude served no purpose when you were a reporter. He might need to talk to her again—one never knew—so he politely thanked her for the information and went on his way.

Over the next hour, he managed to get ten short but worthwhile interviews from the local inhabitants, all of whom had confirmed that Catalina Montez was considered a bruja who regularly performed works of magic, from cleansing rituals to protection from evil spirits to magic to bring luck and make money.

Walking to his car, he saw a familiar figure sashaying toward him in a green and white checkered dress, and he stopped, feeling his face grow hot. It was Darla Diamond, eying him with her cat-like amber eyes.

"Robert Cleary, if I do declare," she said playfully, batting her eyes.

"What are you doing here?" he stammered.

Darla raised her eyebrows. "I'm going for a fitting at the seamstress's house, but it seems I lost my way." She sniffed. "All these dusty streets look the same." She was still wearing heavy movie makeup, a green scarf that set off her eyes covering her hair. She studied her shoes, then looked up at him from under her long lashes. "You wouldn't care to walk me there, would you?"

He cleared his throat, vowing to get a hold of himself. He was a reporter with a major Los Angeles newspaper and, he'd been told, not a bad-looking guy. Straightening his shoulders and bringing himself to his full height, he said, "My car's right there. I can save you the walk."

Darla fanned herself and smiled prettily. "Thank you."

As soon as they were in the car, he did his best to focus on the short drive, but the sight of Darla's bare legs—somehow her dress had hiked up above her knees—were a serious distraction, and he found himself tongue tied in her presence.

"Working on another story?" she asked as they pulled in front of Espy Gaten's cottage.

"Another day, another story," he said, before jumping out to open her door.

She swung her legs out—those legs!—and looked up at him from under her long lashes. "You have the most fascinating job, Robert." Darla stood closer than was strictly necessary, then gave his tie a playful little tug. "One of these days, I hope you can tell me about it." Heat seemed to radiate off her body, and this close, she smelled faintly of a musky perfume that was as warm as the day.

"One of these days," he said, with far more confidence than he felt.

Her hips swayed as she walked up the path to Espy's house, and when she was halfway there, she turned and gave him a wave full of promise. In the car, her fragrance lingered, lasting all the way to Philippe's. That time, he ordered a lamb sandwich, potato salad, and for dessert, a slice of apple pie a la mode, his appetite fueled by his brief, intoxicating encounter with Darla Diamond and the satisfaction he'd managed to get on record that Catalina Montez practiced witchcraft. It was only after he was back at his desk the sense of accomplishment he'd briefly enjoyed had drained away, and the guilt he felt about portraying Catalina as a witch came flooding back. Somehow, he'd managed to write the story.

Harry Barkin was pleased, except for the grumbling it could use a bit more "spice," like it was a bland dish and not a news article. Robert knew how it turned out the last time, so he gritted his teeth while Harry's red pencil scratched its way through the article. When he went back to his typewriter to make the revisions, it wasn't nearly as bad as he'd expected. That time, Harry had confined himself to basic copy editing.

When he was walking out of the newsroom, Gary invited him for a drink, and he'd happily accepted the invitation, eager for another distraction from his dark thoughts. The drink turned into two, then four, and five. When he finally got home, he stumbled into bed and slept through the night. There was nothing like a couple of dry martinis and several Singapore Slings to see to that.

The phone rang at an hour even early for Harry Barkin, 6:30 a.m.

"We got another body, Robert," Harry announced with a heavy voice.

Robert lay blinking at the ceiling, too stunned to do anything else.

"You there, Robert?" Harry asked, the sound of fingers drumming on a hard surface coming over loud and clear

"Yes, of course," he said, sitting up and feeling his head spin. He was already regretting those drinks, and what was sure to be a long day hadn't even started yet. "Where is it?"

"Just inside Elysian Park, not far from that movie set."

"Same sort of situation?" he asked, then held his breath.

Harry's sigh drifted across the line. "Another day, another guy, another rose."

Now he understood why Harry sounded so gloomy. "Does this mean what I think it means?"

Except for the sound of Harry breathing into the receiver, there was a long silence. Finally, he said, "I don't think there's any getting around it. Someone else must have done it because our pinup girl was still behind bars when it happened. Cagle says they're probably going to release her soon."

Chapter 18

With no specific directions on where to go other than Elysian Park, Robert drove through the eastern entrance along North Broadway. It wasn't long before he discovered the park was much bigger than he'd imagined; endless acres of semi-wild hills and ravines stretched before him. During the middle of the week, that early in the morning, there were few people about. He drove around until he spotted an older gentleman out for a brisk walk and pulled over.

"Excuse me, sir, have you seen any police cars around?" he asked through the open window.

The man's eyebrows shot up in surprise. "Not a one," he said.

Robert quickly thanked him and drove off before the man could start asking questions. He headed up a promising drive lined with eucalyptus trees, but it ended in a dirt parking lot leading to a trail, so he turned around and followed another road, that one leading to a canyon looking like a location for a movie set in an exotic jungle. Again, there were places to park but no signs of police activity.

The enormous park was a maze of footpaths, so the officers could have been anywhere. He wished Detective Cagle had bothered to give Harry some details when he'd tipped him off about the latest murder. Harry said Cagle sounded in a rotten mood. Not that Harry blamed him, what with *The Express* running a front-page picture of Catalina Montez, who'd been sitting in a jail cell at the time of the new death. Fortunately, Cagle had kept his promise and hadn't said a word about Robert sharing his suspicions about Catalina, and for that, Robert would be forever grateful. He just hoped Cagle wouldn't change his mind.

There was no other choice than to keep driving around. At least the weather was in his favor for once. The morning had dawned cloudy and cool, but after another twenty minutes of searching, Robert became more anxious with every minute that passed. Finally, he spotted a black and white police car and, when he got closer, saw it was the last in a long line of police cars parked under a row of fan palms.

He grabbed his camera from the front seat, hung the strap around his neck, then hurried up the path to a small overlook crowded with people. His heart sank when he got closer and saw their faces. Reporters from the other papers. That time, they'd beat him to it.

A stocky man with a thick thatch of blond hair turned to him when he walked up. "We're being corralled up here," he announced. He paused, frowning. "Wait. Are you the guy from *The Express* who got the shot of the Mexican witch?"

Robert nodded stiffly. "That's me," he admitted.

The stocky man grinned. "Last night, my boss was chewing me out for not getting the story or the shot. This morning, he was thanking me." When he saw Robert's expression, he clapped him on the shoulder. "Hey, it happens sometimes. Don't beat yourself up about it." Then he leaned toward Robert and in a low voice added, "But you want to watch out for Cagle. He's in one helluva mood. If you ever get to talk to him because I'm first in line, and it looks like you're last. I'm Jeff by the way. From *The Dispatch*."

"Nice to meet you," Robert said, then walked to the edge and looked down.

A steep brush-covered hill led to a terraced waterfall, stone staircases on either side and a pond at the bottom. A crime scene tent had been erected about halfway down the waterfall. He spotted Detective Cagle talking to two men on a pathway at the bottom of the falls. To his surprise, he saw one of them was Bruno, the assistant director, who wore a dark blue sweater over his usual white T-shirt. The presence of the assistant director of *Beyond the Passage* was unusual. He hadn't turned up at the murder scenes of Angel Ramirez and Louie Bonda.

Bruno must have felt him staring because he glanced up and, when he saw Robert, held up his hand in recognition. Cagle looked up, too, and scowled, keeping his hands in his pockets.

So that's the way it was going to be. The detective's scathing look explained everything he needed to know. It explained why the other reporters were already there, and why Cagle had hung up on his boss without giving him the exact location in the vast park. The detective was unhappy with him, and it didn't take a genius to figure it out. He'd passed along a tip that hadn't panned out, and now Robert was getting the blame for making the department look bad. Because it sure as hell didn't make the department look good to have a suspect behind bars when another murder took place.

"Do you know what that fellow is doing here?" he asked Jeff when he appeared at his side.

Jeff sighed. "The reporter from *The Times* who got here first said they brought him to identify the body. We don't know who it is yet, but he must be from the movie."

Robert lifted the camera to his eyes and took a few shots. "His name is Bruno Jenkins, and you're right. He's from the movie. Assistant director."

When he lowered the camera, Jeff was staring at him in surprise. "Well, thanks, Robert. That's real generous of you."

Robert shrugged. He doubted the other reporter would remember the favor if the shoe was on the other foot, but over the years, he'd found sharing non-critical bits of information with other reporters sometimes paid off.

"What are we waiting for?" Robert asked Jeff.

Jeff snorted. "For Cagle to deign to talk to us. And I wouldn't expect any special treatment today. One of the officers said he'd talk to all of us at the same time, when he got around to it." He paused, looking Robert up and down. "So, you're new in town, right?" When Robert nodded, he continued. "I'll save you some grief then." He pointed at the stretch of park beyond the pond. "You see that building way over there? Well, that's the police academy, so whoever did this sure had some nerve to kill someone in the academy's own backyard."

Robert's eyebrows shot up. "You're kidding?"

"I kid you not," Jeff said, shaking his head. "Either the killer knew about it and was bold as brass or didn't know about it. And if that's the case, that tells us something about the killer. He—or she—isn't from around here."

"Or they could be just plain stupid," Robert offered.

"Could be," Jeff said, rocking back and forth on his heels. "I always thought Bonnie and Clyde were just a pair of dumb kids. This one may take the cake."

After a half hour, an officer yelled at the reporters that Cagle was ready. With no path to ease the way, they had to clamber down the steep hill. Robert, surefooted, took the lead, zigzagging his way down until he'd reached the first of the stone steps, Jeff on his heels. One of the older reporters in shiny black shoes fell and cursed up a storm, while the others were forced to grab onto trees to steady their way. Cagle's face remained impassive as he watched their progress.

When everyone had assembled, notebooks at the ready, Detective Cagle cleared his throat.

"Alright, everyone, here's what we have. At approximately 6:15 this morning, we received a call at Central Division from a resident who lives nearby. This area is part of his regular walk. He found the body of a deceased male, half-in and half-out of the middle tier of the waterfall." He paused, shoved both hands into his pants pockets, and frowned. "The victim was nude, and we did not find his clothing during an extensive search of the area. The victim's name is Donald Lange, twenty-three-years-old. He was employed by the movie studio making *Beyond the Passage* as a production assistant."

He paused to clear his throat.

"Detective Cagle…," two reporters began in unison.

Cagle held up a hand. "Patience, gentlemen. I'm not done yet. Don is a recent graduate of the USC School of Cinematic Arts. He was last seen leaving the set of the movie just after seven o'clock last night, alone. He was wearing a white button down short sleeve shirt and gold-brown trousers. Now, we haven't seen those clothes because the victim wasn't wearing them when he was discovered."

Robert was busy taking notes, but he did manage to glance over at Bruno. His skin looked gray in the cold morning light, and he was staring at Cagle, breathing through gritted teeth. He didn't know for sure, but he got the impression the death of the production assistant had hit Bruno hard in a way the murders of Angel Ramirez and Louie Bonda had not. Which reminded him.

"Just double checking, Detective Cagle," Robert said. "Donald Lange was not Mexican, is that correct?"

The corners of Cagle's mouth twisted up. He shook his head. "No, he was not, as you could probably guess by his name. But by the evidence left near the body, we have every reason to believe the three murders are linked."

He let that sink in for a moment and looked around expectantly as he crossed his arms in front of his chest.

Jeff was the first to ask the question clearly on everyone's mind. "Can you elaborate on the evidence?"

Cagle blinked slowly. "Why yes, Jeff, I can. Now, this is the first you're hearing this, so be sure to get the details straight. At each crime scene, we found three roses. Three very long-stemmed roses."

The reporters exchanged glances. Jeff nudged him in the ribs, hard. Robert said nothing. Mostly because Cagle was now glaring at him.

"And where exactly were these roses found in relation to the body?" asked *The Times* reporter, rubbing his knee where he'd fallen.

"Let's just say in close proximity," Cagle said. His cryptic response wasn't lost on the reporters, who murmured to each other. "But that's all I'm about to say on the matter. At least for now. Any other questions?"

"What about the lady you pulled in for questioning?" Jeff asked.

"Yeah, the so-called Mexican Witch," said *The Times* reporter. This was met with a roar of laughter, which immediately quieted down once the reporters registered Cagle's thunderous expression.

Detective Cagle chewed on his lip for a moment, then said, "Our witness, Catalina Montez, has kindly helped with our investigation and is on her way back home, if she's not there already. My officers will be talking to residents who live in the area and will be conducting interviews with everyone who works on the movie. That's all I have for now, gentlemen."

The reporters exchanged yet another glance because Cagle had forgotten one important thing, except no one wanted to be the one to ask, given the lousy mood he was in. Robert decided to take one for the team since he was already deep in the detective's doghouse.

"How about the cause of death, sir?" he asked, with as much deference as he could manage.

Cagle did a double take. "I didn't say?" he asked with dismay.

The reporters shook their heads. When Cagle glanced at the officer standing closest to him, the man grimaced and said, "No, sir."

Cagle's shoulders slumped. "Okay. The cause of death was strangulation, but that will be confirmed by the autopsy, of course. As with the other two murders, we suspect the victim was drugged. We did get the toxicology reports back on the first victims. The analysis found small amounts of a rare drug called Curare, which is sometimes used with general anesthesia in surgeries." He paused and cleared his throat. "And since you're probably going to look into Curare, I'll save you a few steps. Some tribes in South America use it on poison darts to paralyze animals while hunting. The report also showed that our first two victims had a fair bit to drink. We expect the toxicology reports on our latest victim to come back with similar results. We suspect something was used to strangle him, a scarf perhaps, but we've not found anything like that in the vicinity. Just to reiterate, we have an active search in the park, but it's going to take some time as it's more than five hundred acres."

With that, Cagle turned on his heel, ignoring the shouted questions that followed him.

Robert wandered over to Bruno, the assistant director, and offered his condolences.

Up close, he could see the man's reddened, puffy eyes and the grim set of his lips. It wasn't the best time to ask, but he didn't know when he'd have another chance.

"Detective Cagle said they'd be interviewing everyone working on the movie," he began. When Bruno gave a tight nod, he continued. "Is that the first time they've done that?"

Bruno rubbed the back of his neck. "Yes. It is."

"So, they didn't do that after Angel Ramirez and Louie Bonda, both employees of your film?" Robert pressed.

"No. No they didn't," Bruno said, contemplating his shoes. Robert's pointed questions weren't lost on the assistant director, who said, "I need to get back to the set." He walked quickly away, shoulders hunched.

Robert watched him for a moment, then hiked up the steep hill to the car, remembering the first and second times he'd met Detective Cagle and the other officers. Their entire demeanor had changed from concerned to very serious. The difference was so stark it was palpable, and he was beginning to think it had less to do with Cagle's frustration over bringing in Catalina Montez and more to do with Ramirez and Bonda being Mexican. To be more precise, poor, working-class Mexicans and not a Caucasian from Pasadena who'd gone to a prestigious college.

Such was the way of the world, but suddenly, he felt lost in it.

Chapter 19

Earlier that morning, Espy had blamed the sudden change in weather for all the sniffling and throat clearing happening on the set. One of the actors said he'd heard on the radio driving in that it was just fifty-five degrees out, and it wouldn't even reach sixty-two by the end of the day. It was highly unusual for mid-summer in Los Angeles, and few had dressed for the weather, most not even bothering to bring sweaters. The costumes didn't provide much additional warmth because the scenes they were shooting were all supposed to take place in summer too.

Bruno was looking around for the production assistant, Don, to send him to buy some throat lozenges for the cast and crew, but he was nowhere to be seen. It annoyed the assistant director, who went around shouting the young man's last name and, when there was no response, kicked the side of a cart filled with hay, startling the horses nearby.

Espy had arrived at the set just after 7 o'clock, wearing a sweater and a light coat. No use overdressing when the low clouds could lift, and she'd go from freezing to roasting within an hour. Her presence wasn't absolutely essential, but her boss had asked her to be on standby just in case the actresses ripped their dresses during the scene they were shooting. It involved three women riding on horseback through the middle of town after escaping their captors. Espy had been pleased to learn some bad cowboys had kidnapped the schoolmarm and two other women, and it was some Indians who snuck in and let them go, then gave them horses to get back to town. Her boss was afraid the actresses would pop their buttons or seams with all that riding around because their dresses were so darn tight.

It turned out his prediction had been right because, within the first hour, Espy was standing on an overturned crate next to a horse, stitching two cloth-covered buttons onto Shirley's pretty blue dress. Espy thought the missing buttons made sense for a woman who'd barely escaped with her life, but the buttons in question were located six inches above her waist, so their absence left an awkward gap that looked terrible on camera. Bruno had halted filming while Espy fixed them.

And as soon as she had, Darla Diamond pulled on the reins of her horse so hard the seam connecting a tight sleeve to the even tighter bodice split wide open. Again, Espy thought it made more sense to leave it that way, considering the scene. Her boss was all for leaving it alone, but Bruno had weighed in, and Espy was sent scurrying over to fix it.

Luckily, she could stitch quickly, but it had required Judith getting off the horse and slipping out of the dress, which she did in full view of the cast without blinking. Underneath, Darla wore a corset and slip, so at least that time, she was clothed, but barely. Most of the men stopped whatever they were doing to enjoy the free show, something that didn't seem to bother Darla in the slightest. In fact, Espy suspected she enjoyed the attention and wouldn't have been surprised if she'd manufactured the rip. Mitchell Wood was sitting back in his chair, staring at her over his lowered newspaper.

With a little sniff, Espy handed Darla a robe, which the actress accepted with a roll of the eyes. Shirley glowered as she watched, still astride her horse. When she caught Espy's eye, she stuck her tongue out at the back of Darla's head. Espy suppressed a giggle. As much as she'd grown to like Shirley, it wouldn't do her any good to take sides in a cat fight.

Espy wished she had a sewing machine on set. Instead, she had to make the repairs by hand, which she did expertly. She was walking over to Darla who lounged in a chair, her legs propped up on a crate, when she spotted a man in police uniform talking to Mitchell Wood. The director stood up so suddenly he knocked his chair over backwards. Espy handed Darla the repaired calico dress and continued to watch the two men converse. They were too far away for her to hear anything, but by the way Mr. Wood was gesturing, he was upset. Bruno, the assistant director, joined them, listening intently. In a moment, Bruno went from relaxed, or as relaxed as someone with his job could ever be, to surprise, to disbelief.

He shook his head, and while Espy was no lip reader, it was clear he was saying, "No, no, no."

But whatever he was saying "no" to didn't prevent him from trotting off with the officer, in the direction of the police academy.

Mitchell Wood announced there would be a break until Bruno returned, leaving the crew to exchange nervous glances, trying to guess what could have happened to shut down production, which was unheard of. Not even the deaths of the extras, Angel Ramirez and Louie Bonda, had done that.

An hour or so later, Bruno came back and disappeared inside the director's trailer, where the two remained while everyone nervously milled about. Finally, they walked out, looking so grim Espy's stomach rolled. She looked around for Bruce Knox, suddenly longing for his comforting presence, then remembered he was down at the studio, sorting out props for the next day's shoot.

Calling the cast and crew together wasn't even necessary. When the two men crossed to the center of the large set, people quietly gathered around with wide and wary eyes.

Bruno stood just to the right and slightly behind Mitchell Wood, who cleared his throat, then scraped a hand across his bald head. "Well, I don't know how to say this, so I'll just say it. We just got some very unfortunate news. This has to do with Don." He paused and took a deep breath. "Our production assistant was found dead this morning. Bruno has just returned from identifying his body."

Espy sagged against a cart holding hay and felt it creak against her weight. It was just a prop, barely held together with nails. She recognized the name and remembered the face that had gone along with it. An eager, friendly young man. Espy held her breath as she continued listening, her nails biting into the palm of her hands.

"We don't know much at this point," the director said. "Just that he was found, strangled at a waterfall not far from here. They think the same lunatic who killed Angel and Louie attacked Don too."

"What about that woman they arrested?" one of the cowboys demanded.

"That's right," another actor said. "The one who's supposed to be a witch."

Mitchell Wood shook his head slowly, then turned to Bruno and whispered something.

Bruno nodded tightly, then said, "I was there when the police talked to the reporters. Someone asked that question. Sounds like they'll be letting her go. And the police had something new to share. It's gonna come out in the papers tomorrow, and there's no harm in me telling you now, but they found roses near the bodies. Red roses. Now, don't ask me what it's supposed to mean because if the police know they're not telling me. Here's another thing that's going to come out. Don was found without clothes, and they're missing. They're searching for them around Elysian Park, but everyone please

160

keep your eyes open. If you see a pair of brown pants and a white short-sleeve shirt, don't touch them."

"The police will be here soon, so if you find anything, leave it to them. They'll need to talk to everyone, and until they do, please stay on the set. We're postponing today's shoot until tomorrow, but no one is allowed to leave until the police say so. Got that?"

Everyone nodded, too stunned to do anything else.

Espy wandered back to her table. Someone had dropped another dress on it with a scrap of paper pinned to it. It read: *Fix the hem. Stepped on it. Oops.*

The workers split into two groups: the actors and actresses, who had little else to do but discuss what they'd just heard; and the crew, who still had things to do. As upset as Espy was, she had no choice but to continue working. She surveyed the damage done to the long dress with dismay. Stitching it by hand would take all day, and she had to start on a new costume for the saloon dance scene that would film in a couple days. She needed her sewing machine.

The trouble was, her boss had left to attend a fancy awards luncheon in Hollywood, so she had no choice but to ask the assistant director and hope he'd listen. When she explained she needed her sewing machine to complete the work on time, and she'd be back in a few hours, he'd looked up from making notes on a clipboard and nodded. "Sure. No problem. Take as long as you need, but don't go anywhere else. If the police need to talk to you, I can send them your way since it's not far."

"Thank you," she said gratefully.

She grabbed the torn dress from the table and sped up the hill toward Palo Verde, thinking about Catalina the entire way. The police had to let her go now. They couldn't possibly keep her, not after what happened to Don, because there was no way she could have done it. It was obvious they'd arrested the wrong person.

It was still cool out. The purple morning glories climbing the picket fences were still covered in dew.

She was rummaging around for a bobbin with the right color thread when she heard a car drive by. Cars weren't unusual in Palo Verde, but not many people owned them on her street. This one was driving faster than was typical on the dirt road, so she went to the window, looked out, and saw a police car parking in front of Catalina's house.

A door flew open, and then Catalina rushed up the path to her small house with the flaking white paint and sagging windows. Like many of her neighbors, Catalina didn't make enough money to fix up her house, and while there was no doubt about her skills as a curandera, they didn't extend to carpentry.

Two police officers stood by their car and stared after her, then a moment later got back in and drove off.

Espy was running down the street when she heard someone shout, "Who let that witch out?"

When she stopped and turned, she saw it was Mercy Acevedo standing on her porch, a broom in one hand.

"You better not go in there, Esperanza Gaten. Not if you know what's good for you."

Espy glared at her. The woman was really too much, but everybody knew Mercy had changed from bad to worse ever since her son got sick and died. She'd lost someone too—her own husband—and she found it the saddest of excuses for behaving the way that woman did. She was especially hard on her living child, that poor little Jane, who gave Espy a sad wave.

Ignoring Mercy, she waved back at Jane and said in a loud voice, "Why don't you come over and visit me sometime? I can make a dress for your doll." Jane brightened and nodded enthusiastically, while Mercy, disgusted, flapped a hand at her and went back to sweeping the porch.

She didn't bother knocking. Inside, she found Catalina slumped in a deep easy chair, still wearing the red dress she'd seen her friend in the day before, her hair mussed, dark circles under her eyes. The inside of Catalina's home never failed to surprise her. It could have been the house of a bachelor. Just the old heavy furniture she'd lived with since Espy could remember. No fresh paint on the walls. No pretty curtains in the windows. Espy had offered to make them, but Catalina had merely shaken her head, uninterested. The whole house looked run down and neglected. Catalina never seemed to notice, or care, something Espy always had found at odds with Catalina's careful attention to her clothes, which Espy had sewn for her over the years.

Espy knelt beside her. Up close, she could see the tight set of Catalina's square jaw, and that her friend was shaking.

"I'll make you some coffee," she said, getting to her feet.

Catalina gripped the sides of the chair, taking deep breaths through gritted teeth. "I need something stronger than that," she said, then closed her eyes.

Espy went into the kitchen—which was even more plain and sad than the living room—and saw with relief there were leftovers in the refrigerator. On the top, she found a bottle of Tequila, exactly where she kept hers, the same brand too. Everyone bought their Tequila from Salvio Duran, who refused to stock any other brand.

She poured two inches straight into two glasses—she'd had a shock too—then added another inch for good measure and carried them into the living room where Catalina was still sitting, staring blankly at the wall.

Catalina sipped her Tequila.

Espy perched at the edge of the chair opposite Catalina. "What happened?"

Catalina didn't answer for a long time. Then she set her glass down so abruptly on the little table next to her that the gold liquid splashed over its sides. "That reporter Robert Cleary thought I killed Louie and Angel and told the police, and then they came and got me."

Espy swallowed, thinking back to what had happened at her house the other day when Bruce had brought over the vase of beautiful red roses that could only have come from Catalina's garden. All her old suspicions came rushing back, the ones she could hardly give voice to, the suspicions she had shared with her mother, who'd told Mercy and Lord knows who else about them. Not that she could ever admit that to Catalina. Catalina would never forgive her.

"How do you know it was him?" she asked faintly.

"I saw him cutting one of the roses and taking it," Catalina said, picking up the glass and holding it with both hands. The red dress hung limply from her knees. "He didn't see me. I was out near the shed. I thought he wanted to take it to a girlfriend or something. I don't know. That policeman who talked to me, he didn't tell me it was Robert, but I guessed because he said someone had told him that I grew the kinds of roses they found with Angel and Louie."

Espy stiffened. Since it was coming out in the paper the next day, she didn't see the harm in telling Catalina what she'd seen with her own eyes. "I was the one who found Louie Bonda," she said, then took her first sip of the Tequila, feeling it slide down her throat with a pleasant burn.

Catalina's eyes snapped open. "You did? They didn't tell me."

"You didn't read the paper?"

"I just saw the picture." She gave a bitter laugh. "At least he didn't make me look bad. But that headline that called me a witch? It doesn't sound the same in English, does it? I like bruja better."

"I have a copy of the article at home," Espy said. "I'll bring it over later so you know what it says." She winced thinking of the number of people who talked to Robert Cleary and told him Catalina practiced witchcraft. Some of their names were in the paper. How Catalina would react, she had no idea.

"Thank you," Catalina said in a small voice. "So, you found Louie? How awful." A tear slid down her face. "Espy, what did you see? They only said they found him at a well in Loma. What happened to him?"

Espy cleared her throat and took another swallow of Tequila, a big one this time. "He didn't have any clothes on. I didn't take a real good look, you know, because I was so shocked, and I ran away." She couldn't bring herself to explain the rest of what she saw.

She felt Catalina staring at her, and she looked away.

"What about the rose, then?" Catalina asked in a hard voice, sitting up straighter in the chair.

Draining the rest of her Tequila, Espy stood up and stammered, "I...It...It was sticking out of his bottom."

The glass slipped from Catalina's fingers and crashed to the wooden floor. Instead of breaking, it bounced as if it was made of rubber. They both watched as it rolled under the table.

Catalina made a sign of the cross and Espy quickly did the same. "Whoever did that is pure evil," Catalina said, one hand fluttering to the side of her head.

"They are," Espy said slowly, her thoughts drifting in another direction. She went over to Catalina and put a hand on her shoulder. "You never told me. Who hurt you? That day I found you in the street. Was it Louie?"

Catalina closed her eyes and bit her lip. "No. No, it wasn't."

Espy's thoughts circled back to the set. The set that Catalina had visited to deliver flowers. The set where some men had been talking about her. Her eyes snapped open. "Was it the director? Mitchell Wood?"

Catalina stiffened and clutched the arms of her chair. With her eyes still closed, she whispered, "Yes. Yes, it was him." She opened her eyes and stared up at Espy, eyes pooling with tears. "He said he thought I should be in the movies, and he just wanted to take a few pictures. I told him I wasn't interested, but then he started talking about all the money I could make, and I thought, why not? If I ever have to leave Palo Verde, I'm going to need more money for a new place to live. There wasn't anyone around. Mitchell told me to go into his trailer and change into a cowgirl outfit..."

Espy gasped. She knew exactly the costume Catalina was talking about because she'd made several of them. Not for the movie, but for a special party for the studio bosses. The outfits were tight and showed plenty of leg.

Catalina pressed her lips together, then continued. "He came into the trailer while I was still dressing. Then he threw me on the couch. I tried to fight back, but he was too strong. That's how I got so beat up—fighting—but he won. He forced himself on me, then he tried to give me a couple hundred dollars and told me to keep my mouth shut, and when I wouldn't take the money, he said nobody would believe me if I told them what happened. He said he knew about me and Louie, and that I was just a whore." Catalina buried her face in her hands. "And he was right. Because that's how the police treated me at the station. Like a *puta*."

Espy stared at her old friend, speechless. She knew Mitch Wood liked to see his actresses in the skimpiest possible costumes, and the way he'd stared at the young women on the set—herself included—made her feel mighty uncomfortable, but she hadn't suspected he was a molester. Now that Catalina had told her what had happened, she believed it. Of course, she did. Mitch was a powerfully built man, and she shivered at the thought of him assaulting her friend.

"Oh, Catalina," she cried.

Catalina held up her hand, a cold light coming to her eyes. "Don't. I told you, but I'm not going to talk about it anymore. I don't want to talk about it ever again." She pressed a hand to her mouth. "But I did wrong, Espy. I should have told you. Warned you to stay away from that man." She looked up at Espy, eyes narrowing. "Have you seen that reporter Robert Cleary around?"

Espy knelt and retrieved the glass. She looked up at Catalina in alarm. Her hard tone made her uneasy. "Why?"

"Why do you think? I have a thing or two to say to that man. He's the reason all this happened to me. If they didn't find that other poor fellow, I'd still be there at the damned police station. And by the way some of them acted, it was like they'd never seen a woman before. I was lucky the man with the keys was decent, otherwise who knows what would have happened to me in there at night." Catalina's eyes flashed with anger.

"Are you going to do anything to him?" Espy asked nervously, clutching the empty glasses to her chest.

Catalina pressed her lips together. After a moment, she said, "Maybe. Probably."

Espy couldn't help but shiver as she watched a dark shadow cross the curandera's face.

"Catalina," she said uncertainly.

"Whatever I decide to do, Espy, he deserves it," she said in a cold voice, then took her by the elbow and walked her to the door.

Chapter 20

After a simple dinner, Espy was cutting out a dress pattern at the kitchen table when a sound stopped her. It was a man's voice in the distance, loud and angry. A moment later, she heard shrieks coming from down the street, and then someone banged on the front door. She dropped the scissors and threw open the door. It was Jane Acevedo, breathless, with terror in her eyes. Her mother Mercy was not far behind, running up the path.

Jane threw herself at Espy so hard the little girl nearly knocked her over. "What's happening?" Espy shouted at Mercy over the top of Jane's head.

Mercy doubled over, clutching her side, and gasped. "It's Joe Bonda. I saw him stagger up the street, drunk. When I told him to go home, he got nasty, and said…"

Distant shouts interrupted whatever Mercy was about to say. "You lying bitch," Joe Bonda screamed. "You may have fooled the cops, but you can't fool me!"

The ruckus was coming from Catalina's garden, and without a moment's hesitation—driven by a grim certainty something awful was about to happen—she ordered Mercy to stay with Jane, then ran down the dirt road toward the garden.

She was approaching the shed when Joe Bonda emerged, eyes glassy and wild. It had been some time since she'd last seen him. He was taller and thicker set than she remembered, with a powerful barrel chest, his shirt and face splattered with blood. She was too shocked to feel any fear. Time seemed to slow down, and she watched, one hand over her mouth, as he walked toward her, his jaw hanging open.

All was silent. The screaming had stopped. Not a sound came from the shed.

As Joe Bonda pushed past her, she clutched at his sleeve. "Where's Catalina?" she demanded, a shudder running through her.

He stared at her. Finally, he seemed to register her silent accusation, and he ran, feet pounding on the hard dirt path, stumbling through the gate and onto the road.

Espy wanted to run, to make sure Jane and Mercy were safe, but she had to find Catalina first. She clutched her stomach even though it was her chest that felt funny. Her entire body shaking, breaths coming in ragged gasps, she slowly stumbled the short distance to the shed in the fading twilight.

The door to the shed was off its hinges. She could see a cot inside and an overturned nightstand. Broken glass bottles, the kind Catalina used for her remedies, and bundles of dried herbs scattered everywhere.

And on the floor, a trail of blood.

Espy knew what she would see next. All she had to do was lower her eyes and take it in.

When she finally did, she saw Catalina on her back, wearing a blood-soaked blouse and sweater, her mouth twisted into a permanent scream of fear. And just a few feet away, a bloody tool lay on the ground.

Joe Bonda had killed Catalina with ordinary gardening shears—the ones her friend had used to cut flowers and do the pruning. Joe, the troublemaker and hothead, had murdered Catalina just hours after the police had let her go. He had decided the police had gotten it wrong and showed up in a drunken rage to take care of Catalina himself.

Whether he intended to kill her, she didn't know. The only thing she knew for sure was her old friend, Catalina, was dead. When she finally found her voice, she started screaming.

Chapter 21

Robert, Gary, and two other reporters from *The Express* sat eating dinner in the palatial dining hall of Clifton Cafeteria. He'd been invited to join the group to celebrate Gary's thirty-third birthday and, at first, thought a cafeteria had been an odd choice, but as soon as he'd walked in, gaping, he understood the appeal. He'd never seen anything quite like it. The owner, Clifford Clinton, had transformed the space into a magical woodland that made Robert feel like a little kid again, and since they got to serve themselves, they didn't have to waste time pondering the menu and waiting for the food to arrive. Robert had chosen roast beef, green beans in mushroom sauce, and his favorite, macaroni and cheese.

The atmosphere was both lively and relaxing. The stress of the newsroom and its constant deadlines was far away, and he soon found himself enjoying the company of his new co-workers and his meal, which was delicious. That it was cheap just added to the enjoyment.

As he dug into his roast beef, he glanced around. Rocks and foliage were everywhere. They sat in the third tier of the restaurant, next to a row of fake ferns and a redwood tree, not far from a waterfall and gurgling stream. Suddenly, he wished Gary hadn't chosen that particular spot for lunch. It reminded him of where the production assistant from *Beyond the Passage* had been found murdered a couple of days before.

His thoughts soon drifted to Catalina Montez. Detective Cagle must have released her by now. He hoped to God that Cagle had honored his promise of anonymity and didn't rat him out to Catalina. Now that a third young man had turned up dead, while their suspect was behind bars, Cagle might be so annoyed with him the detective could forget his promise.

Someone was saying his name. He looked up guiltily. The birthday boy deserved his full attention, but he'd lost track of the conversation, so lost was he in his own thoughts. But it wasn't Gary.

A police officer he recognized from Central Division was standing next to the table.

"You're that reporter from *The Express*?" he asked. His voice was surprisingly low for such a young skinny guy. Gary and the other two reporters eyed the officer with interest.

Robert wiped the corner of his mouth and set down his napkin. "I am," he said warily. He hoped the guy wouldn't give him the business about Catalina Montez.

"Sorry to interrupt your supper. Just came over to say I'm a little surprised to see you here. They must have someone else covering the story up in that Mexican neighborhood."

Robert sat back in his chair. He shot an inquiring glance at his friends, who shrugged. "What story?" he asked.

The officer blinked at him in surprise. "You haven't heard? That so-called Mexican witch you wrote about is dead. Murdered. They got the guy, but that's all I know."

His stomach lurched, and for one awful moment, he thought he was in danger of losing his lunch. Dear God. Someone had killed Catalina Montez.

"Jesus Christ," he whispered. He got up, nearly turning over the table in the process, and stumbled out of the cafeteria.

The street where Catalina had lived was blocked off by police cars, so he chose the next best option and parked in front of Espy Gaten's house a few doors down.

Robert jumped out of his jalopy and surveyed the scene. Most of the activity centered around the garden, but he could see a few police officers milling around the front of her house further down the dirt road. He was wondering what to say to the burly officer standing on the other side of the blockade when he heard footsteps behind him.

When he turned, he saw it was Espy Gaten, a shawl wrapped around her delicate shoulders, tears streaking her face. "What happened?" he asked, before she could even greet him.

Espy shook her head, weeping. "Catalina is dead. Louie Bonda's brother killed her."

"But why?" Robert stared at her.

Espy let out a puff of breath and slumped against the fence. "Joe must have believed she killed Louie. He was drunk. Shouting. When I got there, I was too late. He'd already stabbed her so many times. So many times." She paused, her shoulders shaking with sobs. "We called the police. All they had to do was go to Joe's house in Loma and take him away." She gave a big sniff and wiped a trembling hand across her eyes. "Did Catalina talk to you yesterday?"

Robert's heart thumped in his chest. "No. Why?"

Espy gave a tight nod, then looked away. "I went to see her at her house, after the police brought her home. She was mad. About the story you wrote about her, and the rose."

Robert's eyes snapped open. "Did you tell her about the roses? Detective Cagle told me we weren't supposed to say anything about them, and I didn't print it in my stories, except for the one that ran this morning about Don Lange."

Espy bit her lip, a shadow crossing her face. "No, I mean about the rose you cut from her garden."

"She saw me?" he stammered.

"Yes. Catalina said she was near the shed, and that she saw you cut a rose and take it." Espy considered him with dark reproachful eyes.

Robert moaned and tipped his head back until he was staring at the cold, gray sky. "I took it to the police," he admitted. Then he looked down at Espy, eyes pleading. "You saw what happened to Louie Bonda. I saw it too. That damn rose. You have to admit, Espy, that those are some pretty unusual long stem red roses, and I saw your face when your boyfriend showed up with some of them in a vase. You looked as shocked as I was. You recognized them too. You can't blame me. I know Catalina was your friend, but I thought I ought to tell the police." He stopped, feeling dizzy. If there had been a curb around, he would have sat down, but there were no sidewalks, no curbs, just a stretch of dirt. Raking both hands through his hair, he groaned. "It's my fault she's dead. If I hadn't opened my mouth, they never would have questioned her, and I never would have had to write that story, and Louie's brother would never have got the wrong idea about Catalina."

The fact was, Espy didn't need to blame him. He blamed himself.

No matter how many times he told himself he'd just been doing his civic duty, the fact remained that Catalina Montez was dead, murdered after she'd been taken into questioning based on a tip he'd provided the police.

Espy slowly shook her head, another sob rising in her throat. "Joe Bonda did it. We went to school with him, Catalina and me. He's always been trouble. He used to be so mean to her when we were kids, about her mom being a bruja." She took a deep, quivery breath. "It won't be his first time in jail. About ten years ago, he and some other guy got into a fight in the park, mostly just fooling around, but when Joe started losing, he got mad, pulled out a knife, and stabbed the guy. He almost died, and they sent Joe to jail. But not long enough, if you ask me."

When he finally mustered the courage to look at Espy, her face was still white with shock.

"I'm going back inside," she said quietly. "There's some work I need to do."

"Can you work?" he asked in astonishment. "In your condition?"

Espy sniffled, then swiped at her red-rimmed eyes with the back of her hand. "I already took a day off after finding Louie. They've been real nice about it, but I can't keep saying I'm too upset to work. If I keep this up, they'll fire me, and they're shooting a big scene tomorrow, and there's no one else who can do what I do, not without taking the costumes all the way back to the studio."

Robert gave a sympathetic nod. Calling in sick didn't cut it in the newspaper business either. You had to be dying or the star reporter who'd been around for years before you even thought about that.

He waited until Espy was inside, wishing she didn't have to be alone after such a traumatic experience. When the door closed behind her, he straightened his shoulders and patted his pocket to make sure he'd not forgotten his notepad. He'd come straight to the murder scene from Clifton Cafeteria without even stopping at a pay phone to check in with Harry. Gary had promised to tell Harry about the murder of Catalina Montez and reassured him he was making the right choice by driving straight to Palo Verde.

"Better to ask forgiveness than permission," Gary reminded him before he drove off, full of misgivings.

Despite the sullen expression, the burly officer tasked with keeping people away from the murder scene let Robert past without comment when he explained who he was. Neighbors stood in their yards, watching, including Mercy Acevedo and her little girl Jane.

Several police cars were parked with their headlamps pointing at the garden, flooding the area with light. He opened the latch of the gate and stepped inside. The plants and flowers seemed to prefer the cooler weather, their bright colors appearing almost iridescent in the harsh artificial glow.

He opened the latch of the gate and stepped inside. His footsteps slowed the closer he got to the shed where a group of officers stood. It wasn't a story he wanted to cover. Just the idea of writing about Catalina's death made him feel sick, but he was compelled to be there. He had to know what happened. And his only ticket in was his credentials.

An officer spotted him and rushed over, frowning.

"I'm with *The Express*," he explained. "Is Detective Cagle around?"

"No," said the tawny-haired man with matching mustache. "I'm in charge. Detective Niles." He pointed at Robert's camera and frowned. "No pictures, I'm afraid."

Robert swallowed. He'd brought the camera out of habit. Harry would be disappointed, but he wasn't about to argue, not that it would do any good. He had no desire to see Catalina's body. "That's fine," he said faintly, looking past his shoulder at the other officers. He didn't recognize anyone, though, so maybe he'd avoid being identified as the reporter who'd tipped off Cagle.

"I'll talk to you," said Niles. "But let's make it quick. The victim is Catalina Montez, thirty-one years old. We're told she made her living as a local healer and…"—he stopped and wagged his finger in Robert's face while keeping his own expressionless—"according to a reporter at *The Express*, a witch."

Robert's heart sank as the man continued.

"Her body was found at approximately 5:20 p.m. by several neighbors who heard screams. The man who later confessed to killing her was arrested promptly at his home in La Loma, where he was taken into custody without incident. The man's name is Joe Bonda, thirty-two years of age, with a history of criminal conduct."

Niles stopped again, pursing his lips as he watched Robert's pencil jerk its away across the notepad, something that was beyond Robert's control. His hand felt like it belonged to someone else, and it was simply not cooperating. His eyes didn't seem to work right either.

"Sorry," he said, swiping his hand across his clammy forehead.

"Bonda said he killed Catalina as revenge for killing his youngest brother, Louie Bonda, who was discovered earlier this week at a well in La Loma, the second victim in three related murders in this general vicinity…"

Robert interrupted. "Was Miss Montez still a suspect at the time of her release?"

"I do not believe our department ever referred to her as such," Niles answered briskly. "She was a witness, and when she was done answering our questions, she was allowed to go home." A scowl formed on the detective's face like a fast-developing storm, warning Robert that to continue would risk crossing into dangerous territory.

As punishment for his question, Niles fell silent, then looked around the garden as if for something better to do.

There were a few more details to get, none of which he wanted to hear, but he had no choice. He cleared his throat. "What was the cause of death?" he asked, as if Catalina had died of natural causes instead of at the hands of a vengeful brother.

"We won't know exactly until we get the postmortem back, but she took a good beating. Joe Bonda admitted to hitting her a few times, then he threw her against the wall. And when she was on the ground, he pushed her so hard she broke through the wall of the shed. And when she was on the ground, he stabbed her with some garden shears, but it's entirely possible she suffered a fatal head wound."

The color drained from Robert's face. It was worse than anything he'd imagined. If Catalina had magical powers, they hadn't been enough to save her from such a savage attack.

"Is there anything else?" he asked automatically. His first editor had taught him to always ask, and he was often surprised at how often the interview subject would offer something more, sometimes a fact or anecdote that made the story come alive or took it in a whole new direction.

The question seemed to catch Niles by surprise because the detective stared at him blankly for a moment before shaking his head. "No. That's it. It's tragic, but it's pretty straight forward, I'm afraid." He hesitated. "Oh, Catalina Montez is survived by two brothers currently residing in Arizona and a father, Gustavo Montez, resident of the neighborhood the locals call La Loma."

With his right hand still putting up a fight, he struggled to make one final note and thanked Detective Niles. He made it to the car before he began hyperventilating.

Chapter 22

It was the last thing Espy wanted to do—visit old man Montez in La Loma to offer her condolences. She'd never wanted to see Catalina's father again. He had treated his daughter so badly during her short lifetime. But she had another reason for going, to ask about the funeral services for her old friend. Gustavo Montez hadn't attended Palo Verde Church in years. It was possible he was like some of the old people around who went to Queen of Angels on Main Street, but she didn't think so because her mother said Gustavo rarely left Loma.

Getting through the day on the movie set had required every ounce of her concentration. For one thing, everyone had been in a tizzy after learning about Catalina's murder. She supposed it had to do with the air of mystery Catalina radiated, and her beauty, of course. The newspaper story that called her a witch on the front page had just added to the intrigue. But the director wasn't about to delay the action scene he'd already put off once when the police interviewed everyone about the killing of the production assistant, Don Lange.

When Mitchell Wood strode onto the set, bullhorn in hand, Espy hadn't been able to look at him. Not now that she knew what he'd done to Catalina. She'd told Bruce the awful story. He'd had been shocked and angry, but when Espy had suggested they tell the police, the color had drained from his face.

He'd shaken his head, a lock of black hair falling into his eyes, and he'd taken both her hands in his hands. "That would be the right thing to do, Espy, but we can't. Mitch knows people. If he finds out we're the ones who ratted on him, the best thing that could happen to us would be getting fired."

She hadn't understood. Not at first. "What do you mean?"

Bruce gave her a pleading look. "He's got connections," he said, his voice dropping to a whisper even though they'd been alone. When she'd shaken her head, still confused, those dark thick eyebrows she loved so much had shot up and his forehead creased with new lines. "The mob, Espy. Anybody who crosses him comes in for some unexpected trouble. No, no, no. We both need to stay quiet about this because you know how it is on a set. Everybody talks." When she opened her mouth to protest, he pressed on. "Espy, you need to listen to me. What happened to Catalina is terrible, but she's dead, and no good will come out of us talking to the police. There's no way we can prove it. And what's more, if the studio finds out we're accusing Mitch Wood of something like that, they'll fire us, and we won't be able to find another job in this town. They're banking big on Mitch. They expect him to be a real moneymaker. Think about it for a second. How do you think they'll react when they hear a couple of nobodies are spreading rumors about their favorite director?"

The truth of what Bruce said hit her with the force of a punch to the gut, leaving her breathless and her heart pounding. "Okay," she'd agreed.

"Good," Bruce answered. "But Espy, I've seen Mitch looking at you. Stay away from him. Never go into that trailer. Ever. Find an excuse. Any excuse. And I'll make sure Bruno knows we're an item. Bruno tells Mitch everything. He'll know not to mess with you." Then he'd hugged her tightly and kissed her tears of frustration away.

She only vaguely remembered the Montez house. She hadn't seen Mr. Montez since the beginning of ninth grade, which was the last time she'd visited Catalina at her house in La Loma. Mr. Montez had yelled at them when he found them in the kitchen, boiling the reed-like stems of the horsetail plants that grew on the side of the house. Catalina had invited her over, offering to make something that would help with Espy's bad, heavy period. Horsetail grew all over the neighborhoods, and she remembered plucking them from the ground as a child and shoving tiny pebbles into the hollow reeds, pretending she was blowing poison darts. She hadn't known they had medicinal uses until Catalina explained they could be used as a lotion to heal sores and as a tea to help control bleeding.

When Mr. Montez appeared in the doorway, asking what they were up to in an angry voice, she'd cowered behind Catalina, who remained at the stove, unperturbed, and calmly replied, "I'm making tea."

Maybe it was the way she'd looked at her father, with cold and unblinking eyes, or maybe it was the way her lip curled up on one side, the faint hint of a sneer, that had set the man off. The next thing Espy knew, he'd grabbed Catalina by her long hair and was dragging her away from the stove, shouting at Espy to get out, because he would not tolerate brujeria in his house. Catalina's older brothers had heard the shouting and came into the kitchen. They stood by with wide eyes and clenched fists but did nothing to intervene. Gustavo Montez was a big man with big muscles who worked putting tar on the streets, so Espy hadn't blamed them for standing back.

The next day, Catalina had shown up to school with bruises on her arms and a black eye but had refused to talk about her injuries. Not long after that, Mrs. Montez and Catalina moved into the small, dilapidated house in Palo Verde and, over the years, had gradually fixed it up with the help of their neighbors.

183

Her brothers had come, too, but went back to stay with their father after he'd threatened them.

The old Montez house was nearly unchanged over the years. Located in a remote spot off of a long, snaking dirt path that led into La Loma, the small house squatted among the rolling hills as if it was trying to hide from the other nearby houses, which were larger and tidier.

The steps to the porch creaked and groaned beneath her feet, and as she crossed to the front door, she could feel the alarming softness of the old wooden floorboards through her shoes.

Despite the fluttery feeling in her chest, she pushed her shoulders back and knocked on the door with a firm rap. She was a grown woman with a good job, and she wasn't about to let Gustavo Montez get under her skin. White paint peeled away from the house in long strips, revealing dark green paint beneath, the same color she remembered from years before.

It took a long time for Gustavo to come to the door. When he did, she could hear his shuffling footsteps coming from the back of the house along with a strange whistling sound, which resolved into a distinct wheeze.

A shadowy figure appeared behind the screen, much smaller than the man she remembered.

"Mr. Montez?"

"Who are you?" The voice dripped with suspicion.

She took a deep, calming breath and said, "I'm Espy Gaten from Palo Verde. That's my married name. I used to go by Espy Ortega when I lived in Bishop. I'm an old friend of Catalina's." She lifted her chin. "Maybe you remember me?"

"No," the man said, then coughed, a horrible, wet, rattling sound. When he recovered, he said, "What do you want?"

"I want to talk to you about Catalina," she said firmly.

There was a long silence, and finally, the door opened. "You can come in if you want," Gustavo said grudgingly, then unlatched the screen.

Espy swallowed as she stepped inside and squeezed past him into the living room. She turned to face him and got a good look at the old man. Gustavo Montez was so stooped it looked like he was in the process of bending over to pick a dime off the floor. The brawny, intimidating man she remembered was gone. Years of hard work and, by the sound of his lungs, years of smoking—who knows what else—had reduced the man to the scrawny, sickly figure who had to lean against the wall to keep from falling down. But his suffering had done nothing to soften the hard, straight line of his lips.

He waved at a sagging sofa. Espy sat and sank so far down her feet came up off the floor. She got herself into a straight sitting position with some difficulty and perched on its hard frame instead.

Mr. Montez lowered himself onto a chair. The effort sent him into another coughing fit, and it was at least a minute before he'd recovered enough to speak. "The girl is dead, if you haven't heard. I don't see what there is to talk about."

Espy pursed her lips and folded her hands in her lap. "That girl was your only daughter, Mr. Montez. And she was killed. Murdered. But she deserves a wake and a funeral, and you're her father. Have you talked to the Palo Verde church yet?"

Mr. Montez shook his head. "No. The police still got her body, and they haven't told me how long they're going to keep it." He leaned forward, gripping the sides of the chair to keep from pitching forward. "And I'll tell you something else. The church doesn't bury witches, and that girl was a witch, just like her mother." He shut his eyes and crossed himself.

185

Espy didn't answer. There had been some trouble about the funeral arrangements for Mrs. Montez, but she couldn't remember what. Only that there had been no wake, no funeral service in the church, just a short graveside ceremony at Evergreen Cemetery in Boyle Heights. Of course, her own mother had been outraged, but she didn't recall whether Mrs. Montez being a bruja had anything to do with such a scandalous departure from Catholic tradition. If a priest had refused to perform the rites for Mrs. Montez, maybe Gustavo feared the same for Catalina.

"But you will talk to the church?" she forced herself to ask.

Gustavo Montez gave a shrug, like she'd just asked him if he planned to paint his house soon.

It was time to try getting at the answer a different way. "Are your sons still living in Arizona? They must have been shocked to hear what happened to their little sister. Are they coming home soon?"

Gustavo gave a hoot of laughter, as if she'd just said something very funny. "Those ingrates haven't stepped foot in this house since the day they left."

Espy's fingers tightened on the edge of the sofa. "But they know, don't they? That their sister was killed?"

"I don't know, unless they read about it in the papers wherever they live," Gustavo admitted, grunting as he shifted positions in his chair. When he saw her shocked expression, he said, "It's not my fault. I haven't heard from them in years. They went off gallivanting to Arizona, and they never even bothered to send a postcard. So, how the hell am I supposed to let them know? I don't even have an address for those so-called sons of mine."

If Gustavo Montez wasn't such a hateful man, she'd feel sorry for him because he was all alone in the world, and she couldn't imagine he had any friends.

At that rate, even when the police finally released Catalina's body, she'd end up with the same sad little service at the cemetery with hardly anyone there because her father couldn't be bothered to tell anyone.

"Would you like me to go and see the priest?" she offered.

Gustavo snorted and flapped his hand at her. "Don't bother."

Espy had to resist the urge to shove him off his chair and smack him across the side of his dry, wrinkled face. "If you don't go see him, I will," she threatened, getting to her feet.

The living room didn't have much furniture, but what was there was covered in a thick layer of dust, and the floor felt sticky under her shoes. It would take a hard sweep to loosen the dirt, two more to brush it out the door, and at least six buckets of hot water to get it clean enough to suit her. She didn't want to imagine what the kitchen was like, or the outhouse which was still where she remembered it—off to the right of the property, so close to the edge of a hill that when you went inside, you thought it was possible it might tip over with your bare butt still over the black, yawning hole.

Gustavo didn't bother moving, but he did give a dismissive snort. "You go ahead and try it and see where it gets you, young lady. Some poor girls she'd put a hex on when she was fifteen years old went to the nuns, begging for their help, and the next thing I knew, the father—I don't remember his name now—was in my house telling me I had to get control of the girl because, if I didn't, she was going straight to hell. And when I said I'd tried everything, but she wouldn't listen, and neither would that witch of a mother of hers, the priest said, 'You bring her to me.' So, I had to take her, kicking and screaming, to the church. Not the little one in Palo Verde, but all the way in town. He gave her a good talking to about the things she'd gotten up to. Oh, she cried and everything, and said she was just trying to help people with her cures, but the priest was no dummy. He knew she was a witch."

As much as Espy hated to encourage the man, she hesitated by the door. "Was this priest a gringo?"

Gustavo shot her a look full of scorn. "What does that have to do with it?"

Espy sighed. The man was as ignorant as he was cruel. "He didn't understand our ways," she said. Then she pushed through the screen door, crossed the porch in two big steps, launched herself past the dilapidated steps, and landed on the ground so hard it hurt her feet, and a pain shot up her ankles. *Ouch.* As she hobbled away, relieved to no longer be inside with that hateful man, she heard the screen open behind her.

"I blame Catalina," Gustavo shouted after her.

Espy stopped mid-stride, then slowly turned to face the old man. All stooped and his face twisted with fury, he looked like a distorted image in a fun house mirror.

"For what?" she shouted back.

"She put a hex on me," he sputtered, hands on either side of the door for support. "I lost my job after that, and I was never able to keep another one. She admitted it. Said she was glad she did it."

"Catalina was just a teenager," she yelled, so angry now she was shaking. "Your own daughter was afraid of you. If you got fired, it was your fault. Not Catalina's."

Gustavo stomped his foot. "You go to hell. That girl was evil, and you're fooling yourself. She killed those men, and she got what was coming to her."

Espy stood still and stared at the man, unable to believe he would say such a thing about his own flesh and blood.

He disappeared inside, then the door slammed behind him.

Chapter 23

The night before Catalina's funeral, Jane's parents had a fight. Her father couldn't take the day off but wanted Jane's mother to take her, out of respect for the curandera who'd been their neighbor. Her mother said she wouldn't go because she'd never forgive Catalina for putting a hex on her that made her cry and sleep all the time. When Jane's father insisted, her mother said she had no intention of letting their daughter go to the funeral of a killer—because everybody knew Catalina murdered Angel and Louie even if the police were too dumb to have figured it out—and that had made her father even angrier. He said she was no better than Espy's mother, who was the biggest gossip in all of Palo Verde and Bishop.

In her heart, Jane knew Catalina could never have done such terrible things, and she had begged to go. Finally, her mother agreed—but only after lots of shouting—that she could go with Espy.

Which suited Jane just fine. Espy had made a new dress for Jane to wear on her sewing machine. Not black like the grownups would wear, but a dress made of soft gray that reminded her of the dove that made a nest above her porch.

Shoes were a problem. Her mother refused to spend money on new ones, so she had to wear her black and white saddle shoes. Espy said not to worry, that since she looked so pretty, no one would notice them. But Jane did. All the way from the car—driven by the nice man named Bruce—across the dry, crunchy brown grass, past the scary statue of an angel with enormous wings carrying away a naked lady, to the hole in the ground where Catalina's coffin would go.

Jane knew it was selfish, but she was disappointed to see just some old people from the neighborhoods. She'd imagined people from the movie would be there, too, and they would have noticed the pretty dress Espy had made with a swirly skirt and puffy sleeves. But no movie people were there. No one paid any attention to her, and it was hot and boring, waiting for the priest to say something.

All the waiting gave her plenty of time to look around as she stood between Espy and Bruce. It was her second time at a cemetery, but she couldn't remember what it was like the first time, two years before, when her brother died. He was buried at a different cemetery—Calvary. She did remember her mother had thrown herself on top of the casket, and when her father and uncles had finally pulled her away, they had to carry her all the way to the car, crying and screaming.

Finally, the priest started talking. He had one of those droning voices that made her feel sleepy. She wished she could sit down, but there weren't any chairs. Soon, she felt herself slumping against Bruce, who gave her a sympathetic pat on the back.

"Me, too, kid," he whispered with a roll of the eyes.

Espy began to cry. Jane scooted over so Bruce could comfort her, too, and soon, Espy had her head on Bruce's shoulder and was sniffling. Her mother said Espy had no business seeing another man, not so soon after her husband died in the war. Her mother also said Espy thought she was too good for the guys in their neighborhood, and that Bruce was just using her and would throw her aside when the movie was over. Her mother made Espy sound like a tissue she used to take off her cold cream. But she liked Bruce, no matter what her mother said about him or Espy.

When all the prayers were said and done—and there were a lot of them—the priest handed Espy a big bunch of flowers, and Espy stared at them for a long time, her mouth slightly open. For one terrible moment, Jane thought Espy might scream, but then Bruce took them from her hands and gently put them on Catalina's casket. With one hand on the back of Jane's neck and the other around Espy's waist, he guided them to his car.

Jane didn't know why Espy was so upset. She kept saying, "Those roses." Jane didn't know what that meant, but the red roses had been so pretty.

All the crying Espy had done had ruined her makeup, so now there was smeary black stuff under her eyes. Her hair still looked fluffy and pretty, and Jane thought her bangs looked nice too. She was wondering if Espy could cut some for her when she noticed her companions had gotten far ahead of her, so she ran to catch up, and for the last stretch, she decided to give her new dress an experimental twirl. Because she was so pleased with the way the light fabric lifted into the air and swirled, she tiptoed like a ballerina the rest of the way. She hadn't gone far when her right foot plunged straight into the ground, and she pitched forward onto her hands and knees. Panting with fear, she tried to yank her foot free, but it wouldn't budge. Something in the ground was holding onto it and wouldn't let go. She screamed.

Bruce was running toward her, Espy on his heels, as Jane stretched out her hand, praying he'd get to her before the skeleton in the ground pulled her under. And then Bruce was reaching down where the grass was eating her foot, and suddenly, she was free. Sobbing, terrified, but free. Espy collapsed next to her and pulled Jane onto her lap, making baby sounds while brushing the hair away from her face.

"It's okay, Jane," Bruce said, crouching next to her. "It was just a flower vase in the ground."

When she blinked at him, confused, he pulled something out of the grass and held it up for her inspection. She stared at it, then understood. It was a vase. A deep one, and just wide enough to catch her pointy foot as she tiptoed over it. When she glanced around, she saw the ground was full of holes she hadn't noticed and flowers sticking up here and there.

Jane slumped and gave a shaky laugh. "It scared me," she said.

When Bruce pulled her to her feet, her legs were so wobbly she stumbled. Espy whispered something to Bruce, and then he scooped her up like she was two and not eight. Jane felt so tired she let her head rest on Bruce's chest all the way to the car, where he announced he was taking them out to lunch.

The tapping noise grew louder. Jane couldn't ignore it anymore. She'd tried calling for her father, but she could hear him snoring from the next room. When he snored, she could stand next to the bed and scream into his ear, and he wouldn't hear it. Her mother was staying at her grandmother's house in Lincoln Heights because *abuela* got sick. So, for the first time in as long as she could remember, it was just her and Papa alone in the house. It wasn't the relief Jane thought it would be. There had been no Mama to fix dinner, or to tell her to go to bed, or to yell at her to put the book away and turn off the light.

So, Jane was free to read as long as she liked. It was a good book. A lady who came to paint in Palo Verde had asked Jane if she liked to read, and Jane had said yes. The next time she'd come, she pulled a book from her basket, *The Middle Moffat*. Jane was delighted the girl in the book was named Janey, except she was ten years old and not eight, and she was allowed to walk around by herself, even to the library, and Jane had never gone to a library.

Jane read so late into the night she was awake when the wind started to blow outside. Her bedroom was at the front of the house. Dry leaves flew against the windows, and she could hear them skittering across the porch, but that didn't explain the tapping coming from somewhere at the front of the house. Maybe someone was at the door. Maybe a chicken got loose from the coop and wanted to come inside to escape the wind.

There was nothing else to do but investigate. She threw back the covers and crept along the short hallway into the living room. The door was solid wood, not like at Espy's house with a piece of glass at the top you could look through and see who was there. The tapping sounded much closer, and if she wanted to see what was causing it, she had to go to the window, but the notion of standing in front of the glass so whatever was out there could see her was too scary. So, she dropped to her hands and knees and crawled across the wood floor, popping up next to the window. Then, very slowly, she pushed herself up high enough so her eyes were just above the windowsill and peeked through a gap in the curtains.

Nothing.

No skeleton from the cemetery. No scary looming shadow. Not even the tall man with the skull face from the city to give them another paper that would make her mother upset again.

Feeling a bit braver now, Jane stood, holding her breath, and stuck her head through the curtains, pulling them just under her chin. She scanned the porch, starting at the left where her mother kept a small altar to La Virgin de Guadelupe, to the right with its two chairs where her father liked to sit and talk to his friend Martin from Loma. It didn't take long to spot the problem. The sticking out branch from the small tree—she thought it was more like a bush—was hitting the railing, making a *tap, tap, tap*. And all because of the wind. The wind made unusual sounds, but it wasn't scary, so she went back to bed. She let all the air out she'd been holding and was about to yank the curtains closed when a movement across the road caught her eye, and she froze.

It was a white light. In Catalina's garden.

Was someone walking around over there? Maybe they were carrying a flashlight, and that's what the light was. But it didn't look like that. The light was too big, and it wasn't shiny bright like a beam from a flashlight. No, it was something else, and it made the hair on the back of Jane's neck stand up. The whiteness cast an eerie glow as it slowly moved from the back of the garden where the enormous cactus was to the middle section with all the herbs. Whatever it was seemed to be sticking to the skinny little path that ran from the back of the property to the front. The white thing seemed to be growing, stretching, until it was the shape of a person. She was trying to find her voice, to call for her father, when a great gust of wind rattled the windows and made the telephone wires hum so loudly they sounded like they were singing.

The white thing across the road was coming closer. Now that it was almost to the fence, she could see the top part had begun to take on the shape of a head, a head with long hair that swirled into the air as if lifted by the wind.

She knew she should be scared.

She knew she should run and wake up her father. Instead, she was filled with sadness, even sadder than when her brother died. Because that floating white thing was the ghost of Catalina. She was sure of it.

Her wrist tingled, and something tightened on it. When she looked down with a little gasp, she saw the red protection bracelet Catalina had made her was rippling slightly. She gave it

194

a little pinch to get it to stop, and it did, but as soon as she lifted her fingers, the strange rippling continued. When she looked up at the ghost, it seemed to be watching her. She knew it wasn't Catalina anymore. Not like she was when she was alive.

Jane raised a hand and gave a tentative little wave.

The Night Lady faded into the darkness.

Chapter 24

Espy suddenly found life in Palo Verde unsettling. Young men rarely went anywhere alone and disappeared from the streets after dusk. Mothers and wives issued stern warnings. *Go ahead and flirt, drink too much. See what happens. Wind up dead like Angel Ramirez and Louie Bonda.* Salvio Duran complained his liquor sales had dried up. On weekends, the neighborhoods in the ravine went quiet. Espy heard the whispered rumors—that a killer might be living among them. Suspicion turned toward the rental shacks in La Loma where Angel had been found. The cabins were filled with gringo bachelors, some of them transients. *It could be one of them*, people whispered. The house parties, with music blaring into the canyons, stopped. Even the tough guys stayed close to home on the weekends, avoiding the bars and nightclubs in the city below, afraid of who they might meet.

Filming had stopped, a break Espy had expected from the start. The lead actor had a commitment to star in a big New York play, and the director of *Beyond the Passage* had agreed to a break in the filming while he was out. That had worked out for that pervert of a director Mitch Wood too. It gave him a chance to get started on his circus movie in Florida.

Still, without the distraction of *Beyond the Passage* filming in the next canyon over—and the constant visits to her house for fittings and repairs—she was left with more time to think about her future, a future made uncertain by the eviction notice, which she'd shoved into the junk drawer in the kitchen where it belonged. Bruce was gone, reassigned as prop master to another Western filming in a remote area of Southern Utah. Before he'd left, he'd pulled her into his arms and told her to stop worrying—the solution was simple. She could move in with him. When she'd reacted with disbelief, he'd laughed and told her they'd talk more about it when he returned.

That had thrown her into an even deeper state of limbo. Had he been serious? Even if he were, would she consider such a thing?

Bruce's assignment had surprised them both. He'd taken to sometimes staying overnight, an arrangement that seemed somewhat scandalous, yet oddly natural.

When Mercy Acevedo had the nerve to say she was going to tell Espy's mother, she'd snapped, "Go ahead. I'm a grown woman if you haven't noticed."

When Mercy had carried out her promise, Espy's mother showed up while she was doing her morning sweep and began calling her names, including the inevitable "hussy." Espy, forced to breathe through her nose because her teeth were clenched so tight, used the straw edge of the broom to brush her mother out the door.

At the gate, her mother had stopped and shouted, "Catalina was a bad influence on you, Espy Gaten," before stomping off toward Bishop.

Her mother hadn't been totally wrong. Catalina had influenced her thinking but in a way Espy had come to appreciate. Their talks about men and sex had helped her shake the last of the clinging notions that had kept her from fully enjoying her time with Bruce, which included "marital relations" outside of marriage. Still, it was impossible not to feel a bit guilty about the whole thing. Her strict Catholic upbringing made sure of that. But what bothered her most was the knowledge she'd never enjoyed the act with Felix as much as she did with Bruce, maybe because Felix had been as shy in bed as in the rest of his life. With Bruce, sex was a fun and wild romp that left her breathless and giggling, and with the windows and all the curtains closed, she'd felt free to do something she'd never have done while Felix was alive—walk around her own home naked, pottering around the kitchen making coffee, and making the bed once they were finally out of it.

The truth was, she missed Bruce terribly and looked forward to their weekly phone call, which she took at Rose Delgado's house, sitting on the front porch with the long extension cord snaking through the living room, the black phone sitting on her lap. Once a week, Bruce and his friends from the crew would drive to Salt Lake City, and he'd call her at Rose's number on Saturdays at three o'clock. So far, he hadn't missed an appointment once, and the sound of his voice carried her through the lonely weeks.

Another reason for Espy's unease: Palo Verde felt emptier without Catalina Montez in it.

Sometimes, even though she'd seen Catalina's dead body, just for the briefest of moments, she couldn't believe she was gone. And it didn't feel right either because she was sure that, if she looked up, she'd spot her walking up the road, headed toward her garden.

One evening after work, she wasn't hungry enough yet for dinner, and she was too tired to take a walk, so she decided to take advantage of the warm October evening and the light that still remained. She sat on the front porch to drink a glass of red wine—poured into a coffee mug so that nosy Mercy Acevedo wouldn't tell people she'd started drinking. She started to sew the Halloween costume she was making for Jane as a surprise.

It was simple enough—a short red pinafore dress and a high-necked white blouse like the character wore on the cover of Jane's favorite book, *The Middle Moffatt*, which she must have read dozens of times.

She was hand-stitching the collar when a movement down the road made her look up. The light was dim, and she was forced to squint, but it seemed to be coming from Catalina's garden. The tops of the trees fluttered, except it wasn't windy out, so maybe it was birds or squirrels. And then the tallest trees seemed to bend over, as if a great gust had come along and was blowing them sideways.

Espy set down her sewing and hurried down the road for a closer look. When she got there, hands on the gate, she was overcome with a strange reluctance to go any further. She felt a tugging on the sleeve of her blouse. When she glanced down, she saw it was Jane, an anxious look on her face. Jane was often anxious now that school had started again. Her new teacher wouldn't let her read fifth grade books because she was in the third grade. Jane was bored, and the teacher had taken against her, calling her a show-off, so now the other kids did too.

"Everything okay at school?" Espy ventured.

Jane shrugged but didn't answer. She stared straight ahead, eyes fixed on the trees. Jane looked up at Espy. "It's too early for the Night Lady to come out," she whispered.

Espy felt her body go cold, and an awful tickling like a hundred tiny spiders raced up her spine. When she dragged her eyes back to the garden, she had the sense of a presence there, as if there was something just out of sight.

"Jane?" she said quietly.

Jane scrunched up her face.

"Jane, who is the Night Lady?"

"She's not anybody anymore," Jane said sadly, staring back at her with dark, solemn eyes.

Chapter 25

Espy started a list of people who swore they'd seen the Night Lady in Palo Verde, and within a week, it was so long it filled an entire page.

The Night Lady's name was whispered wherever she went with a mixture of fear and wonder. At first, the sightings were confined to Catalina's garden and only in the darkest of hours. But eventually people said they'd seen her ghostly figure wandering down the road, lingering on a porch, drifting past a window. She was often spotted in gardens, and once, a herd of goats followed her down an alley and up a hill where they had to be fetched in the morning.

Then, Espy started hearing much more frightening stories. Stories about the Night Lady paying nighttime visits to families on the verge of leaving. And someone always got hurt. People tumbled down steps, fell off porches, tripped and hit their heads on the corners of tubs or the sharp edges of furniture. Espy knew things had taken an even darker turn when she heard about an old friend named Rudy in Bishop. He'd sold his home of thirty years, and the night before he was due to leave, Rudy was so filled with regret he drank a whole bottle of cheap red wine while cleaning his hunting rifles. He was working on an old single shot Browning when a woman seemed to drop down from the ceiling right in front of him. His body jerked so violently the gun went off, he shot his oldest son in the leg. Later, Rudy had trouble describing the lady, only that she had a cloud of black hair like a swarm of gnats and black holes for eyes, and he hoped never in his life to see her again.

Lencha was called on to create protection amuletos and spells, and not just to protect them against what the Night Lady might do, but the way she made them feel when she was around—sad and depressed. And as if that wasn't enough, an encounter with the Night Lady would fill them with a terrible dread that would last for days.

"I feel doomed," Salvio Duran said as Espy shopped for groceries at Duran Market & Liquor. His daughter, Trini, had rolled her eyes and went back to reading her book behind the counter where she sat, manning the cash register.

On Saturday afternoon, while Espy waited for Bruce's call from Salt Lake City, Rose Delgado said, "I have this feeling that something horrible is going to happen."

When Espy asked if it could be the looming evictions, Rose had shaken her head, sending her tower of platinum hair quivering. "*Ai* no. I can't really explain it, but suddenly, I'm all cold, and I can't warm up, and then I'm feeling real low. Like everything is hopeless."

That summed up the way Espy felt whenever her path crossed with the Night Lady, which she did her best to make sure was as seldom as possible. No more walks after it got dark out, even to her parent's house in Bishop. No more sitting on the porch—front or back—having wine in a mug. She pulled the curtains closed, locked the doors, and latched the windows. Luckily, the Night Lady stayed outside and showed no interest in rattling doorknobs or materializing at the foot of her bed.

There was no question now—in her mind or anyone else's—who the Night Lady was.

It was the ghost of Catalina Montez, plain and simple.

How it came to be, and what it wanted, had people talking. Salvio Duran said people who died young and unexpectedly had

202

trouble leaving the earth behind and resisted going to the next place. Mercy Acevedo said Catalina knew what was waiting for her in the afterlife—the flames of hell for murdering three young men—and was too afraid to meet her maker. Whenever Espy pointed out Catalina couldn't have killed the third man because she'd been in jail at the time, Mercy said anything was possible when a witch was in cahoots with the devil. Espy believed it had more to do with Catalina's nature; she'd been mysterious and restless in life, and now the mystery had just deepened, and she was more restless than ever.

Some people muttered that Lencha, the curandera from La Loma, should do something about the ghost. Make it go away. But when Espy asked if they'd talked to Lencha about it, they'd shaken their heads and said, "*Ai*, no," and slinked away. Not that Espy blamed them. There was always something a bit odd about the woman. In many ways, Lencha was even more unknowable than Catalina, having become more taciturn with the arrival of the spirit.

One day, Espy had been surprised to see a line of people forming in the alley behind Bertita's house and, when she'd stopped to investigate, found that Lencha had set up a curanderia in a shed in the old lady's big backyard.

"Lencha felt bad that everyone who used to go to Catalina for their problems had to go all the way to Loma to see her, so I told her to use the shack out back. In the mornings, she works in Loma, then she's here almost every afternoon. One of my nephews fixed up the shack. He built a table and some shelves. And we're paying him two dollars a week to water Catalina's garden and to pick whatever Lencha wants because she won't step foot in there. I tell her she's being silly, but she won't listen."

"Has your nephew seen anything? The ghost, I mean?" Espy had asked.

203

Bertita threw her head back and laughed, exposing her scrawny, lined neck. Somehow, her wool cap stayed on. "He's no dummy. He only goes during the day." The woman turned serious. "But I'll tell you one thing. Catalina may be dead and gone, but she's keeping that garden of hers going because things are growing like crazy in there." She paused. "It's just not natural."

"What do you mean 'not natural'," Espy asked uneasily. She'd been avoiding that part of the street, but from her porch, she could see the trees in Catalina's garden seemed to be growing taller, and the morning glory vines had spread from the fence to the street light and along the wires that crisscrossed the dirt road.

Bertita frowned, thinking. "Well, everything is going like gangbusters in there. The yerba buena has taken over the whole lot. The aloe vera is as tall as you are. Mercy swears Catalina is haunting them."

Espy sighed. "Is that why Mercy put newspaper in all the windows?"

Bertita's eyebrows lifted so high they disappeared under the brim of her wool cap. "Yes. You know, I don't think much of the woman, but in this case, I don't blame her. I wouldn't want that garden across from me, either."

"What does Lencha say?" Espy asked. "About the Night Lady?"

"Not much," Bertita said with a little shrug. "She says she doesn't want to talk ill of the dead, but it's more than that. She doesn't even like to say her name out loud."

Soon, Espy heard there were sightings of the Night Lady even in the farthest reaches of La Loma. Several of the old gringo bachelors living in the rental shacks where Angel Ramirez had been killed had told Salvio Duran about their encounters when they came to spend their dimes at his store. As far as she knew, the ghost had never drifted outside the neighborhoods of La Loma, Palo Verde, and Bishop, although word had trickled out to the people living in nearby Solano Canyon that something funny was going on up in the ravine.

The strange appearances of the Night Lady cemented Catalina's reputation as a bruja. It didn't take long for Espy to notice her neighbors had stopped referring to Catalina as a curandera and started calling her "the witch" and "la bruja," seeming to forget overnight the woman had done more healing than magic. The line between the two had always been slightly fuzzy to Espy, and she'd begun to understand why Lencha had always been coy about how much magic she knew herself. Probably because Lencha was smart enough to understand how quickly the community could turn against a woman who practiced witchcraft, even after showing up at her door asking for cures for whatever ailed them.

Espy couldn't remember Catalina ever saying anything about casting spells on her garden that would account for the things Bertita had described, so after a few days of wondering if the old woman had been exaggerating, she decided it was time to see the garden for herself.

She set out on a sunny fall morning at eleven o'clock, wearing dungarees and a light sweater. The newspapers covering the windows of the Acevedo house seemed like an overreaction because the house did have curtains, and all Mercy had to do was keep them closed if she didn't want to chance seeing the Night Lady from the sanctity of her living room.

The papers did have one advantage. Mercy couldn't see her hesitating at the front gate of the garden, trying to gather up the courage to go in. Even where she stood, she could see Bertita hadn't been exaggerating. In fact, her description didn't do the garden justice because it was even more wild and overgrown than she remembered, and it was a riot of color. Purple. Yellow.

Pink. And the green. There was every shade imaginable, from greens as light as a honeydew, to leaves so dark they looked nearly black. Had it always been like that? She didn't think so.

Heart beating faster in her chest, she unlatched the gate. The purple morning glories were still in full bloom, while those clinging to her own fence had already closed for the day. She looked around for the skinny dirt path that cut through the center of the lot and had to rely on her memory to locate it because it was hidden beneath the oleander. It had always been showy, with its bright pink flowers, but Catalina had trimmed it so it resembled a tree. Now, it seemed to have doubled in size, as wide as it was tall, and seemed to be in the process of eating into the space where the angel's trumpet grew with its pendulous orange blooms. The oleander and angel's trumpet were both poisonous, she vaguely remembered being told, and she wished she had asked why Catalina included them in her garden. Maybe simply because they were pretty.

As she pushed her way through the growth, she saw stems of flowers that had grown so thick it would take an axe to cut them down. The garden was beautiful, but it was strange, a place more likely to give her nightmares than dreams when night finally came.

The prickly pear cactus towered above the metal roof of the shed. She had no intention of going back there. That's where she had seen Catalina's beaten and bloodied body.

When she was not much older than Jane, she read and reread the book *The Secret Garden*. This garden had its secrets, too, but darker and deeper ones. Despite the warmth of the sun, she shivered. It had nothing to do with her imagination and everything to do with the tangle of plants and vines that caught at her sweater as she advanced toward her destination.

The roses. Taller and straighter than before, their stems as thick and woody as a tree. At least two times the height of a man, maybe more. The red blooms, as wide and round as the dinner plates she had at home.

It was as unreal as a fairytale and far more unsettling.

She'd seen enough. The garden seemed to be pressing in around her. She knew the road was not far away. All she had to do was run in either direction to the street or the alley, and she would be free of the place, but as her muscles tightened, she found she was rooted to the spot. Her breath was fast and ragged, and her heart thumped in her chest.

Something rustled in the overgrowth. It was coming from the direction of the alley. A scream was rising in her throat when a long stick poked out of a bush and Bertita emerged, cursing. "What the hell are you doing here?" she demanded.

Espy's hand fluttered to her chest as the old woman hobbled up, using her cane to whack aside the heavy brush. "You scared me," she said accusingly. "I just wanted to have a look for myself." She sighed, looking around. "You were right. Something strange is happening to this garden. Why are you here?"

"Checking on you. Jane came running over saying she saw you come in here, and we got worried," Bertita said, scowling up at the red roses. "Those things are obscene. Come on, let's get out of here. This place isn't right. I'm not sure what's going on, but it's safe to say it's haunted, and we have no business being here."

Espy followed Bertita, who moved faster than she'd ever seen her, and soon they were standing in the alleyway where Lencha and Jane were looking anxious and wringing their hands.

Jane gave a little cry and came running over to Espy, then threw both hands around her waist, mashing her face against Espy's hip. She was wearing the red pinafore dress Espy had made her for Halloween, which she wore every day after school and every weekend. Espy glanced at Lencha, who was staring at her reproachfully, and she reached down and tweaked one of Jane's braids.

"I'm fine, Jane," she said.

"I can feel you shaking," Jane answered, voice muffled. After a moment, she looked up and blinked. "Did you see her?" she whispered. "The Night Lady?"

Espy gave the little girl's braid a playful tug. "No, Jane. She only comes out at night, remember?"

Bertita thumped her cane on the hard packed dirt of the alley. "Well, she's certainly been busy, that's for damn sure," she said, then gave a grim laugh. "You should see what else she's got up to in other people's gardens."

Espy's eyes snapped open. "What do you mean?"

Lencha shot Bertita a swift warning glance, then nodded pointedly at Jane. Bertita scowled and bit her lip but said nothing. Espy escorted Jane home, then walked briskly to Bertita's house, where both women were waiting for her in the kitchen.

Pan dulce already sat waiting on a plate, and Lencha had a fresh pot of coffee brewing. Espy chose a concha.

"Here's your *cafecito*," Lencha said, putting a mug in front of her. "I put a little extra milk and sugar in it for your *susto*."

She looked up at Lencha in surprise. The garden had scared her, but she thought she'd done a good job of hiding it. Then again, Lencha had a certain way about her, like she could see straight through people. She was doing that now, studying Espy with narrowed eyes.

Bertita dipped her pastry into her coffee and said, "You know the Flores family on Reposa Street?"

Espy nodded. "With the five kids?"

"That's them. Benny took a buyout from the city, and they moved out on Wednesday."

"Traitors," Lencha muttered, joining them at the table.

208

"Well, what's happening to Catalina's garden is beginning to happen to their front yard too," Bertita said. "The rose vines they had growing on the porch are all over the house."

"They've climbed on top of the roof too," Lencha put in.

Espy opened her mouth to speak, then closed it.

Bertita set aside her pastry on the brim of her saucer and continued, "And the Camachos on Bolyston? Same thing with them. Old man Camacho wouldn't listen to his son who wanted to see if they could get more money out of the city. He just took whatever measly amount they offered him. Then they moved out, and now that little patch of grass that had the fence around it is higher than the house. And you can't tell me that's natural because it isn't. And you know the birds of paradise Old Man Camacho used to make such a fuss over? Well, the heads on those things are the size of King Kong."

"They've only been gone five days," Lencha added, then shook her head.

Espy stared into her coffee cup. The eviction notice had sat in her kitchen drawer for months, and while she knew some residents would choose to move before the city made them, now that it was actually happening, it still came as a blow. Once families started to move out, more would follow.

Her throat suddenly felt so dry she coughed on a bite of pan dulce. Bertita thumped her on the back, then turned to Lencha and said, "And you think the Night Lady is making the gardens go crazy like that?"

Lencha pulled her long black braid and inspected the ends, frowning. Without looking at Espy she said, "I don't *think* it. I know it. Because I've been watching for her, and wherever I've seen her, the next morning the gardens don't look the same."

Back home, washing her clothes on the back porch, Espy's thoughts wandered back to her conversation with Catalina about the eviction notices. How Catalina had said she planned on resisting. In the middle of scrubbing a stain from a blouse, she froze, and closed her eyes. She understood only too well.

The ghost of Catalina, the Night Lady, was doing awful things to gardens that were now officially owned by the city.

Chapter 26

Robert didn't recognize Espy Gaten at first, not all dressed up in a black dress and bright red lipstick. She was stepping off a bus on Melrose Avenue in Hollywood, and he nearly bumped into her on the busy sidewalk.

"Espy?" he said, stopping mid-stride.

She hesitated, then her eyes lit up in recognition. The smile was the same, and so were the dark brown bangs.

"Robert!" she said in a friendly way, which came as a relief. At least she didn't seem to hold a grudge against him for the stories he'd written about Catalina Montez, something he still thought about almost daily, even though it had been months since she was murdered.

"I'm on my way to work," she explained. When she noted his confused expression, she added. "*Beyond the Passage* is on break, so I have to go down to the studio every day."

"Ah," he said nodding. The famous studio lot was just down the street, so when the crew wasn't on location, they went to work there, just like he was expected to show up at the newspaper office when he wasn't in the field reporting. He wondered what happened to the prop master, Bruce, but he wasn't about to ask. They were standing in the middle of the busy sidewalk, and a man brushed past and shot him a disapproving frown. He could take a hint. He glanced at his watch. He didn't have to be at his next interview for another forty-five minutes. "Do you have time for a cup of coffee?" he asked.

Espy gave a wistful little sigh. "I'm sorry, I need to get to work, and I still have a bit of a walk."

He nodded, disappointed. "Maybe another time." He hesitated. It wasn't the best time to ask such a sensitive question, but he had to know. "Have you decided what to do? About the notice you got from the city?"

She scrunched up her nose. "Not really. It's complicated, at least for me." Her dark eyes widened. "Maybe you can do another story about it. I haven't seen one in the papers for a long time. There's a meeting tonight at Bertita's house. Can you come?" She paused, then gave another smile. "She's making tamales."

He chuckled. "You know how to bribe a guy. I'll be there, but I can't promise anything. My editor might not go for it, so don't get your hopes up." In fact, he was sure Harry wouldn't be interested in a small community gathering without the fireworks of a contentious public meeting, but it would be worth attending. Maybe get a jump on something interesting, like the residents planning a protest.

Espy studied him for a moment, then nodded. "Thank you for being honest. It starts at seven o'clock."

Robert tipped his hat. "I'll see you there." As she was turning around to leave, he said, "Do you think the others will be okay with me being there? Not all of them were happy about my paper calling Catalina Montez a witch."

"I don't think that's going to be a problem, Robert."

"What do you mean?"

She sighed, then looked away, biting her lip. Finally, she said, "A lot has happened since you've been up there. Almost everybody calls Catalina a bruja now, but that's not your fault." Then she hurried away, leaving Robert to stare after her, wondering what he was getting himself into by returning to Palo Verde.

Robert sat perched on a hard-backed chair, balancing a plate of tamales, rice, and beans on his lap. He was on his fourth tamale, thanks to the stern-faced curandera named Lencha who kept whisking away the used husks and plopping a fresh tamale whenever he wasn't looking.

He looked around Bertita's good-sized living room. Her house was by far the biggest he'd seen in the neighborhood. Espy had mentioned Bertita bought it with money she was paid after a fatal accident involving her husband and children but hadn't elaborated. He recognized most of the faces, but there were a few new people too.

As expected, most of the conversation dealt with the looming evictions and how to fight them, and by the end of dinner, the group had decided to rally as many residents as they could to make protest signs and join in a letter-writing campaign to city officials but nothing newsworthy enough to merit pitching a story to his boss.

Also, as he expected, people had questions about the murders of the three young men, focusing on the two they knew: Angel Ramirez and Louie Bonda.

"What do you mean they have no suspects?" Salvio Duran wanted to know. The owner of the little market in Palo Verde pounded the table with his fist. "What the hell have the police been doing all this time? They might be working a little harder if they weren't two Mexican kids."

Espy shifted in her chair. "There were three men, Salvio, and Don Lange was a gringo."

Salvio ignored this and pounded the table again. "And here's something else. Has anyone thought to point out that the movie you've been working on stops, and suddenly, there aren't any more murders around here? You can't tell me that's a coincidence. If you ask me, Espy Gaten, that pretty-boy boyfriend of yours better watch out when he comes back because he could be next." Espy fell back in her chair and gasped.

Robert eyed Salvio Duran with newfound respect. That there hadn't been a fourth murder while the entire movie crew had disbanded was more than just a little intriguing.

During dessert—a fried tortilla dusted with sugar and cinnamon—Robert asked Espy for her thoughts on the matter. Her eyebrows nearly disappeared under her brown fringe of bangs. "You think someone on the movie crew is a killer?"

"It's possible," he admitted. "You've got all kinds of people on the crew. I mean, not just the actors and actresses, but all those men doing the behind-the-scenes work. Not that I've been around the set too much, but there were a lot of people coming and going. Who keeps track of them all?" He brushed sugar from his lips and shrugged. "What does anybody really know about their backgrounds?"

Espy swallowed. "They do hire a lot of temps."

"Have you ever noticed anyone…a little off?"

A shadow crossed her face, and she lowered her gaze. "If you ask me, most of the people working on the movie are a little off. Except for Bruce."

"What do you mean?"

Espy broke off a piece of her pastry, popped it into her mouth, and chewed thoughtfully. "They're just a funny bunch. Creative. Hard-working. But most everyone I've met is constantly worried about something or the other. It's a hard business. I didn't really mean anything by it." Her brown eyes

214

flickered in the lamp light. "But I can't imagine anyone that I've met is a *killer.*" Her mouth fell open, and a moment later, she'd clamped it shut.

He leaned toward her. "Espy? Did you just think of something? Someone?"

She didn't answer. Not for the longest time. They finished their *banuelos* in silence. He'd given up hope of getting Espy to say anymore when she looked around to make sure no one was listening, then scooted her chair closer. "What's that the thing you mentioned where someone tells you something, and you swear not to write about it?"

Alarm bells started ringing in his head, and his mouth dried up. "It's called off the record."

Espy nodded. "Then that's what I want."

"Of course. It's off the record. My lips are sealed."

Espy took a deep breath. "It's not my secret to tell, and Bruce made me promise not to say anything. But I trust you. Remember the bruises on Catalina's face? And the cuts? Mitch Wood did it. He tricked her into going to his trailer, forced himself on her, and beat her up."

This wasn't what he was expecting. The news made him feel dizzy, and sick to his stomach. "Did she go to the police?"

Espy looked down at her hands. "No. She wouldn't go. And it's a long story, but Bruce would kill me if he knew I told you. He says it's not safe for us to talk about it." Then she looked up at him, eyes wide with fear. "Do you understand, Robert? You can't tell anyone about this. Not a single person."

"Sure," he promised. Bruce was a good guy. A reasonable guy. If Bruce said it wasn't safe, the man had good reason. "Do you think it could be Wood? Killing those guys?"

"If it were *women,* I'd say maybe. But it doesn't make any sense that he would do that to *men.*" The conversation seemed to have tired out Espy because her face appeared drawn, and he noticed dark circles under eyes. He had to agree with her assessment. It didn't make any sense to him either. Then again, he wasn't a criminal expert.

Robert was putting on his hat when Salvio came over to him and said, somewhat nervously, "Can you please walk Espy home, young man?"

"Of course," he replied with surprise. He lowered his voice. "I understand. It sounds like everyone is still on edge about the murders up here."

Now it was Salvio's turn to look surprised. He walked out onto the front porch, motioning for Robert to follow him. The others were too busy talking amongst themselves to notice. There was no light on the porch, so the two stood in the darkness of the October night. It was much quieter in Palo Verde than the streets below with their traffic noise.

"Haven't you heard?" Salvio asked.

"Heard what?"

Salvio sniffed. "About the Night Lady."

"The Night Lady?" echoed Robert. "Who's that?"

"The ghost of Catalina Montez, that's who," Salvio said, as if he couldn't believe Robert's ignorance. "Jane Acevedo was the first to see her, and now, just about everybody has. Lencha won't do a damn thing about it, although I don't see why not, but she says she doesn't have the power to get rid of her. And now people who don't want to leave are thinking about it because that ghost is scaring them away."

Salvio Duran talked as if everyone believed ghosts were real. As if Robert did too. Maybe the people around there did believe in ghosts, like they believed in brujas and magic spells for love and success. The owner of the store had seemed like a sensible man, even if he was excitable. "This isn't some kind of joke, is it?" he asked, unable to keep the suspicion out of his voice.

The screen door opened and Espy appeared, wearing her coat. "Salvio isn't joking, Robert," she said quietly. "If you walk me home, I'll tell you all about it."

Together, they walked down the steps, Robert's hands shoved as far as they would go into the pockets of his trousers. Espy insisted on taking the long way to her house, explaining she didn't walk in front of Catalina's garden anymore. The detour was even longer than Robert expected because she also refused to walk past a house the city had just taken over. At first, he thought it was some strange sort of moral objection. It wasn't until they were in her small living room with all the curtains closed and she'd opened a bottle of red wine that she began to tell him about the Night Lady.

By the time she was finished, they'd finished the bottle, and in his tipsy condition, he insisted on seeing Catalina's garden for himself.

Espy refused to accompany him, so he went alone, borrowing a flashlight.

The Acevedo house was strangely dark, and then he remembered what Espy had said about the newspaper in the windows.

There was no reason to turn on the flashlight. The moon was full and bright, the garden made luminous in its silver glow. What he saw took his breath away, made his heart beat faster, and made his mouth fall open. The garden was so changed he hardly recognized it. It was strangely beautiful in its grotesque abundance, the blooms of the flowers still open as if it were the middle of the day and not nearly ten o'clock at night. Even from that distance, he could smell the roses, which meant it was exactly as Espy had said. The roses had shot up, bigger and even more luscious than before. Their overpowering fragrance filled him with disgust.

And fear.

It was ridiculous to be afraid of a garden. But he was.

As his hands gripped the fence, he felt something on his knuckles. When he looked down, he stopped breathing and saw a vine slithering across his pale skin, nearly silver in the moonlight.

There was no one around to see him run.

Chapter 27

Los Angeles, 1951

November and December flew by, a blur of story assignments and long days. Robert worked Thanksgiving, Christmas, New Year's Eve, and a quick turnaround to New Year's Day, just what he expected as a single man and the newest reporter. His parents and sister had been disappointed, of course, but there'd been no chance of making the thousand-mile journey to Denver and get back in time for his scheduled shifts.

Every day, Robert would wake up expecting a call from Harry, saying the body of another dead young man had been found, but the call never came. He made inquiries into Mitchell Wood and understood why Bruce had warned Espy not to talk about what the man had done to Catalina. Mob ties. And he was known to attend wild parties where nobody asked questions, and the women hired to entertain were later hushed up with money or threats. But none of the information he managed to learn led him to suspect Mitch had killed Angel, Louie, and Dan and stuck roses where the sun didn't shine.

At the same time, he'd had no luck convincing Harry to cover the numerous city council meetings involving the looming evictions in Palo Verde, La Loma, and Bishop. He was surprised to see some of the other papers jump in, although the stories had taken a decidedly pro-public housing stance, saying the development was necessary to reduce poverty and crime, and described the neighborhoods as "slums."

So, it was a big surprise when Harry summoned him to his office.

"Guess where I want you to go?" he asked, slamming down the phone.

"Surprise me," Robert said. He was in a good mood. *Beyond the Passage* was back filming in the canyon beyond Palo Verde, and he'd just happened to run into the actress with the pretty legs when he was out having a drink with Gary. Darla Diamond had flirted with him, and he'd had a witness, so he knew he wasn't imagining things.

"Ask her out, for God's sakes," Gary had said.

He hadn't. The way she stared at him with her golden eyes unnerved him and set his loins on fire. He couldn't get the simple words out. But when Darla brushed past him on her way out, she'd whispered into his ear, "Why don't you stop by the set sometime and see me?" Which was something he definitely would do as soon as he could find the time.

"You finally get to cover that story you've been yakking my ear off about," Harry said.

Robert stared at him blankly.

Harry threw up his hands in exasperation. "The evictions, Robert. The evictions! I just got a call that the city is beginning demolition in the Bishop neighborhood this morning. They've got bulldozers and everything." Harry's frown deepened. "What are you standing around for? You don't want to miss the drama, do you?"

Robert knew some residents had accepted the city's buyouts and left their homes empty. But he was shocked the city would begin demolition while so many people still lived in the neighborhoods. An intimidation tactic, he guessed.

Once he'd recovered from his surprise, he cleared his throat. "No, sir. Don't want to miss any drama," he said, then scooted out the door.

He was grabbing his camera from the bottom drawer of his desk when Gary looked up and said, "While you're up there, don't forget to go by and see that hot little number who was all over you the other night."

"Darla Diamond," Robert said automatically.

Gary wriggled his eyebrows. "Darla was *definitely* in the mood for love."

Robert smiled as he remembered the song by five-year-old actress Darla Hood in the *Our Gang* series.

He strode through the bullpen, the camera bumping his chest.

When he arrived in Bishop, the smallest neighborhood in the ravines, the bulldozers were already there, and a crowd of people had gathered. A few women he didn't recognize stood by, looking anguished. They carried protest signs that read, *Save our Homes*, while a sheriff's deputy stood by, eying them warily, as if he expected them to erupt into violence at any moment.

It was mid-morning, when most of the locals were at work or school, and there were few people to witness what was about to happen.

The houses chosen for demolition were in the lowest part of the canyon, closest to town, and marked with red tags tied to the porch beams. The fences were already gone, and the vines that had covered them lay in heaps on the ground.

As Robert got closer, he stopped and stared.

The transformation that had taken place at Catalina's garden had happened there, too, just not to the same fantastic degree. Climbing roses covered the porch, nearly hiding the windows from view. They carpeted the roof and stretched between the houses, so all three appeared linked in unison by the vines drooping with white tea roses.

The fallen morning glory vines ripped from the fences had begun to creep along the road, so thick it would be easy to mistake it for a bed of ivy if it weren't for the profusion of purple blooms that shimmered with dew in the soft morning light.

Robert approached the Sheriff's deputy, holding out his press card. "Robert Cleary from *The Express*. Is there anyone here from the city that I can talk to?"

The deputy was around the same age, pink-cheeked and baby-faced. He shook his head. "No. I don't think they planned on sending anyone out."

"How many houses they taking down today?" he asked.

"Four," the deputy answered readily.

Robert lifted his eyebrows. "Is there another one someplace else? I'm only counting three red-tagged houses."

The deputy grimaced. "The fourth one is tucked way back there. That's the one that's got them worried."

"What's the problem?"

With a sidelong look, the deputy said, "If you walk on over, you can see it for yourself."

It was an invitation he wasn't about to refuse. Robert hurried away before the deputy could change his mind. He found a small group of men in work clothes, huddled together, arms folded across their chests. The property in question was on a deep lot. He assumed a house was back there, somewhere, but it was hidden by the most enormous plant he'd ever seen. As his eyes made their upward journey to take it all in, he gasped. The thing stood about fifty feet tall, with long leaves that twisted and curled, giving it the appearance of growing underwater, pushed and pulled by the currents.

Other similar plants grew around it, some taller than Robert, but they were dwarfed by the monstrosity at the center.

Eyes never leaving the plant, he walked up to the group and introduced himself.

The men looked worried. The one with a weathered tan face and a silver-tipped crew cut said, "I'm Dave, the foreman. No one told us about that thing when we got the job."

"What is it?" Robert asked.

Dave sighed. "Some kind of agave plant from what we heard. One of the ladies holding the signs said it wasn't anywhere near as big as this a week ago, but she was talking a whole lot of nonsense, so I'm not sure I trust her. But it doesn't matter. It's there, and we're trying to decide whether we should ask for another crew to chop it down first. Our equipment can run it down, no problem, but it's the spikes on the leaves that I worry about. Also, another crew has to clear all of that away, and they're going to need heavy gloves to avoid getting all cut up, so I'm thinking we might as well let them get this garden cleared out before we tackle the house."

Robert squinted at the agave. If a house was back there, the massive plant was doing an excellent job of hiding it. "Mind if I take a few pictures?"

Dave shook his head. "Be my guest."

Robert snapped a few, then went in search of the women holding the protest signs. "Good morning," he said, "I'm a reporter with *The Express*. Robert Cleary. Did any of those houses they're about to demolish belong to you?"

Both women were middle-aged, wearing floral dresses topped with pinafore style aprons, as if they'd just stepped away from the kitchen. And maybe they had. They shook their heads.

"No," one said, wrinkling her nose in disgust. "We live in La Loma, and we're not about to give in to the city like those people did. A friend who lives on Paducah Street down here ran all the way up to see us and told us about the bulldozers, so we came and brought our signs. My name is Elma Lopez." She nodded at her friend. "That's Mary Fonseca."

Robert slipped his notepad out of his pocket and jotted down their names. "Thank you for talking to me. Are you familiar with the house that has the giant plant in front?"

The women exchanged uneasy glances. "Yes," Elma said, then pursed her lips.

"Was it always so big?" His hands were suddenly so clammy he had trouble holding his pencil.

"*Ai*, no. Of course not," Elma replied, as if she'd never heard such a ridiculous question.

Mary eyed his notepad with suspicion. "We don't want anything we say about that plant in the paper, do we Elma?"

Elma dropped her protest sign and shook her head. "No, we don't."

With a barely perceptible sigh of resignation, Robert shoved his notepad and pencil back in his pocket. "Okay. We are officially off the record now. So, tell me what you know about the agave."

Elma shivered and made the sign of a cross. "I'd be careful if I were those men."

"That's for darn sure," Mary interrupted.

"The Garcia's owned that house. When they got their notice, they couldn't wait to sell up. Ruben couldn't even wait for the city agents to come see him. He went running down to the housing authority, begging for a deal, so they were the first in Bishop to move out. They left…" Her words trailed off, and she glanced at Mary for help.

"Two and a half weeks ago," Mary said. "They're my second cousins, and I visited them while they were packing up to say goodbye and—"

"And the yard wasn't like that, was it Mary?" Elma interrupted and shivered again.

Mary shook her head slowly. "No, it was not. The agave was there. It's been there for as long as I can remember, but it was only as tall as me. Not like it is now."

Robert rubbed the side of his face. It was one thing to see Catalina's garden by night, to imagine that his eyes had deceived him in the moonlight after several glasses of red wine, but it was another to see a plant so large it defied belief in the light of day.

He knew the answer, dreaded the answer, but he had to ask. "And how do you account for it getting so big so fast?"

Elma picked up her protest sign from the ground and rested the wooden handle across a shoulder. "You know that poor woman who was beaten and stabbed in Palo Verde by that no-good Joe Bonda?"

Robert nodded. "Yes."

"Well, when she was alive, she was a witch." She paused. "I don't know how else to say it. And she's come back, except now she's a ghost, and lots of our friends have seen it with their own eyes. We haven't, and I thank the Lord he's spared us, because once you see her, you feel so sick and tired of life you just want to die, and it can take days before you start getting better. Everyone is calling her the Night Lady. She just wanders around, lost and sad-like, but if you sell up? Well, watch out because the Night Lady doesn't like that. And people say something isn't right at Catalina's old garden, and the man who owns it took one look at it and got so scared he fell down and hit his head. He was screaming so loud someone finally came to help him. Then he got in his car, and he hasn't been back since. Isn't that right, Mary?"

Mary's eyes widened. "That's what I heard too. And whenever somebody gives in to the city and moves out, the Night Lady shows up in the yard, and then stuff begins to grow all big and crazy like." Her lips flattened into a straight line, and her nostrils flared. "But nobody listens to us. Nobody cares

225

about what happens up here. Heck, we still don't have paved roads or sidewalks. When I tried telling those workmen over there to be real careful, they thought I was nutsy cuckoo, didn't they Elma?"

Elma rolled her eyes. "She was just trying to do them a favor. Those plants aren't normal. Who knows what's wrong with them. They could be poisonous or something."

Mary Fonseca held up a wrist. She was wearing the same type of bracelet little Jane Acevedo wore. "See this?" she asked. "It's for protection. I never take it off. Ever. A curandera who lives in Loma made it. These things are selling like hotcakes."

As if to prove it, Elma showed off her red bracelet too.

"You mean Lencha?" he asked.

The women stared up at him in surprise. "You know her?" asked Elma.

"I've met her a few times," he admitted.

"Isn't that something," Mary asked.

The woman had been more forthcoming about the Night Lady than he could have hoped, considering he was a stranger and their warning to the men with the bulldozers had been met with ridicule. But he still had a job to do, and it was time to shift gears. He pulled out his notepad again and interviewed the two women about the families who'd owned the soon-to-be-razed homes and their thoughts on the city's plan to build a low-income housing project. They had plenty of choice words for that. When he was done, he thanked them and found the foreman, who was sitting on a low stone wall, scowling as he inspected his right forearm. His sleeve was rolled up, and the skin between his wrist and elbow was covered in deep scratches.

"What happened?" Robert asked in alarm.

"I tripped on a fucking vine, that's what," Dave snarled. "I fell into that god damned plant and got all scratched up. One of my guys went into town to call the office and tell them to send a crew to cut those monsters down. The last thing I need is for one of us to fall off the bulldozer and have this happen, except worst. The other guy went to a drug store to find some bandages."

Robert peered at the expanse of wounds and swallowed. The skin around the scratches was red and puffy. "Looks like it hurts," he said sympathetically.

"You better believe it," Dave said, squeezing his eyes shut. "Hurts like the devil. It's beginning to itch real bad too. I hope that stuff isn't like poison oak."

Robert studied the scratches. He was no expert, but they looked worse than they ought to be. "Maybe you should go to a doctor."

The man's head jerked back. "You think so?"

"Just to be on the safe side," Robert said evenly. No use scaring the man, but the wounds looked pretty nasty to him, and given what he knew about their otherworldly origin, he wondered if the agave plants had undergone a more sinister change than just their size.

Robert offered to drive Dave to the closest hospital, the French Hospital in Chinatown. He waited around until a nurse appeared, who explained the doctor was admitting Dave because the wounds seemed to be infected, and Dave was having trouble breathing. The doctor also sent instructions the plant was not to be touched until they could determine the nature of the toxin. So, Robert hurried back to Bishop and relayed the information to the two stunned workmen, who reluctantly agreed to tape off the property and post a "No Trespassing" sign until the doctor could send an expert to collect samples from the plant.

Mary and Elma had left, no doubt tired of waiting for the demolition to begin.

The other three houses were old and made of wood. It didn't take long for the digger to smash the first one down. Robert's arms felt heavy as he lifted the camera to his eye and framed the shot. When he'd taken several pictures of the powerful tractor running over the broken roof, he saw the bulldozer grind to a halt. Then he noticed something bright green caught in its giant wheels. Vines had wrapped around the tires and undercarriage, jamming the gears.

Chapter 28

With everything he knew and couldn't say, it had to be the hardest story he'd ever written in his career. He'd finished the article an hour before and was reading it over yet again. It was still giving him fits.

LOS ANGELES- A recent spate of accidents involving houses red-tagged for demolition in a semi-rural community known as Bishop in Northeast Los Angeles has prompted a stern warning from city officials.

The latest mishap on January 18 involved fire department training exercises on two houses scheduled for demolition. One firefighter suffered severe burns and was transported to the hospital. There are conflicting reports about what happened. A fire official said the rear part of the house was unstable and collapsed around the man, trapping him inside. Witnesses standing in the alley behind the property claimed they saw the firefighter enter through the back door, but when the fire exercise began and flames and smoke became visible, the firefighter was prevented from exiting through a window due to the heavy growth of vines and foliage surrounding the house.

"We suspect the instability of the property was caused by a criminal element living in one of the sub-barrios where a low-income housing project is planned," said Chris Sanford, a spokesman for the city. "If the residents refuse to sell their properties at fair market value, then the city will proceed to the

next step, which is forcible eviction through eminent domain. What happened to the firefighter in Bishop is just the latest example of violent resistance, and we will not be intimidated by these tactics."

On January 8, the day of the first scheduled demolition in Bishop, the foreman of a bulldozer crew tripped and fell into an agave americana variegata, a succulent perennial, cutting his arm. Within twenty-four hours, the man had died of respiratory distress caused by unknown toxins believed to have come from the plant, though agave plants are known to be harmless. Tests are ongoing. On January 11, a member of a demolition crew entered another property on Garibaldi Street, also in Bishop, to do a walk-through without notifying the crew of his whereabouts. The demolition began on schedule, and later, his body was discovered. Sanford called it a horrific, unfortunate accident. On January 16, on a hill leading toward the community of Palo Verde, the driver of a bulldozer was killed when the tractor overturned as it climbed a steep embankment. The crew reported that a sudden gust of wind sent leaves and branches flying, and they are believed to have temporarily blinded the man.

The unusual nature of the accidents has alarmed work crews, and anonymous sources said workers are refusing assignments in the neighborhoods of Bishop, La Loma, and Palo Verde. Sanford confirmed the city has temporarily halted scheduled demolition while it investigates. An official with the fire department said it's ceasing training exercises in the area.

The article was the best he could do, but the story had as many holes as Swiss cheese.

The eyewitnesses were none other than Rose Delgado, the Spanish translator who lived in Palo Verde, and her friend Martin, who'd gone to Bishop to complain about all the smoke from the training exercises blowing up into their neighborhoods.

They hadn't intended to stick around long enough to see another condemned house go up in flames. It was just too upsetting. But when the sympathetic young firefighter promised to talk to the chief and see what he could do, they'd stayed on, mostly out of curiosity. And when he'd busted out the window and swung himself inside, they'd watched in horror as a thorny bougainvillea vine started sending out shoots. Within minutes, it had covered up the entire window, trapping the fireman.

The city had another interpretation of the events and was using it as ammunition in its ongoing eviction campaign.

Sanford, a weak-chinned, shifty bureaucrat, would not provide any more specific information about the so-called "criminal element," and when Robert called Detective Cagle to elaborate, Cagle said, "Let me get back to you on that," then slammed down the phone. He hadn't returned any of Robert's calls since. In the end, Harry said they'd have to run the quote without more details, and even he hadn't been too happy about it.

There was no firm evidence, no witnesses, no explanation of how some poor folks from a "poverty-stricken slum" had suddenly become experts on sophisticated sabotage. Even his boss, Harry Barkin, thought it smelled fishy.

Pointing the finger at the "criminal element" just infuriated the residents even more, mostly because they were powerless to defend themselves. Who would believe a ghost called the Night Lady was behind all the accidents?

Robert did.

He'd seen enough of what she'd done to the abandoned gardens. The Night Lady was out for vengeance. But he couldn't include that in the paper, not unless he wanted to be fired and hauled off to the looney bin. Harry would say he'd been spending too much time with the locals. Guilty.

He'd taken to driving to Palo Verde on Thursday nights to have dinner with Espy and Bruce, the prop master. Bruce was a nice, cheerful guy who was easy to talk to, and when he'd asked about Darla Diamond, Bruce had lifted his eyebrows and said, "What do you want to know?"

"Does she have a boyfriend?" Robert asked while Espy was busy in the kitchen.

"I don't think Darla is the boyfriend type," Bruce said with a wink.

Each time he left, Bruce walked him to his car, and Robert wasn't too proud to object. The streets were awfully quiet and lonely at night in Palo Verde, and Catalina's haunted garden was just down the street. Bruce had surprised him by admitting he'd seen her, just once, but refused to say any more. When he'd asked Espy about it, she said Bruce had seen the Night Lady wandering around the movie set late at night and afterwards had stumbled to her place and stayed in bed for two days. In that time, he'd refused to eat or bathe, saying he had no energy, no will to live.

"I had to call Lencha," Espy said, shaking her head. "I'm not sure what she did because she wouldn't let me watch, but it worked, and he finally snapped out of it."

"How's Jane?" Robert asked. He hadn't thought of the little girl in a long time.

Espy shrugged, disappearing into her oversized sweater. "Fine." She hesitated. "Her father came over the other day. He said he can't take it anymore. Mercy wants him to board up all the windows, and she keeps asking Lencha to put a protection spell on her house to keep away the ghost. He's so worried he's sent Jane to stay with Mercy's sister in Boyle Heights."

"Mercy seemed a little high-strung," Robert said.

Espy bit the top of her lip, a reluctant smile curling around her mouth. "And mean. But we're being a little unfair. I don't like the idea of living so close to a ghost either."

They stood together on the porch as Robert pulled on his sports jacket. The night was cold. Cold for Los Angeles. It sobered him up after his two glasses of red wine. "Is Jane's dad going to sell?"

"I think so, yes," Espy said, looking down at her socked feet. "Jane's lonely here. Her mother is real strict and doesn't let her play with the other kids. If they move, they'll probably go to Boyle Heights with the rest of the family, and she'd have cousins to play with."

Robert nodded. "And how about you?"

Espy looked over her shoulder through the screen door where Bruce was stretched out on the sofa, eyes closed, a magazine resting on his chest. "I was born here, and I don't want to leave, but I don't think I have a choice."

Robert didn't think anyone did. As he drove past the empty lots in Bishop where houses once stood, through the yellow glow cast by the lone streetlight, he shivered. The whole place felt doomed.

Chapter 29

When he got to Espy's house in Palo Verde for his usual Thursday night dinner, Robert found Espy and Bruce waiting for him on the porch.

"We've been invited to Bertita's," Espy said.

Robert grinned. "Tamales?"

"Of course," she said with a laugh. "I hate making them myself. Too much work, but I love eating them."

Bruce threw his arm around Espy and knocked his hip into hers. "She's not telling you the whole reason we're going, though," he said, then wiggled his eyebrows suggestively.

"And what would that be?" he asked uncertainly. Whatever it was, he hoped it wasn't another community meeting they wanted him to write about for the paper.

Bruce winked. "A certain actress by the name of Darla Diamond is expected to be there."

At the mere mention of her name, Robert felt himself flush.

"Bertita is fixing dinner for some of the crew, but other people will be there too," Espy rushed to add.

"Great," he said, hardly able to get the word out because he was suddenly breathless.

Bruce gave one of his hearty infectious laughs and pulled them down the steps. At the gate, they made a right, even though the shortest way to Bertita's house was straight down the street. But that would take them past Catalina's garden, and no discussion about avoiding that was required. The walk took twice as long, but it was worth the extra steps if it meant not having to look at the garden, which now resembled a jungle, according to what Jane Acevedo's father had told Espy.

Bertita welcomed him inside with a clap on the back and a puff of cigar smoke in his face. He was glad when Lencha came along, said a quick hello, then plucked the cigar from the old woman's mouth and carried it off through the swinging double doors into the kitchen. All the living room furniture had been moved into other parts of the house, and several outside picnic tables had been brought in. Winter in Los Angeles was nothing compared to the cold temperatures in Denver where he'd grown up, but it was still a bit too chilly to sit outside and eat.

He found himself sitting across from Rose and Martin, who always seemed to be together, flanked between Henry Loya, the bespectacled owner of a market in Boyle Heights, and Carlos Vasquez, the trim, mustached man from La Loma he'd met while waiting in line to see Catalina for a headache cure. He hadn't seen him since, and he was a bit surprised to see him there.

When Carlos went into the kitchen in search of a saltshaker, Rose leaned over and whispered, "Carlos's mother is Bertita's cousin, and he comes around every once in a while to check on Bertita." She batted her eyes. "But the real reason he's here is Espy. He's been carrying a torch for that girl for as long as I can remember." Which explained why Carlos looked so hangdog every time he glanced over at Espy, who was sitting at the next table with Bruce.

There was still no sign of Darla Diamond or the other members of the movie crew. Bruce said they'd been shooting a scene with dogs, and anything with animals or children tended to run into complications. Robert felt himself twitch every time the front door opened.

Of course, Bruce noticed, and when he walked by to load up on seconds, he'd whispered, "Get a hold of yourself, lover boy."

Robert tried to take his mind off Darla by catching up on the neighborhood news, which was as plentiful as it was disturbing. Rose said she'd lost count of the number of residents who'd taken buyouts from the city since the first of the year but suspected there were more because some people were reluctant to share the news, fearing they'd be called traitors. And not long after they did move, the Night Lady would appear, and then it was just a matter of time before the morning glories, climbing roses, and yerba buena started taking over. And if there were agave plants, they multiplied faster than rabbits.

Children were told to stay out of the abandoned yards after what happened to the demolition foreman who'd died after falling into the giant agave in Bishop. To make sure they listened, parents now threatened them with the Night Lady in addition to the Llorona, the crying lady who'd killed her children, and the boogeyman known as the cucuy. But there was one main difference. The Night Lady was real.

Halfway through dinner, Lencha disappeared, and when Robert went into the kitchen for a fifth tamale, he saw a line of people standing outside a shed, waiting to see the curandera.

Bertita caught him peering through the window and said, "She's so busy! She's even got me helping her make those red bracelets." She held her hands up in the air. The knuckles were swollen and slightly deformed, making Robert wince. "And me, with this awful arthritis." She chuckled. "I'm terrible at making the little knots, but nobody has complained yet, and I don't think anyone is about to because they're desperate for protection. That's what they want these days. Anything she can give them to keep the Night Lady away." Bertita took Robert's plate, went to a giant pot on the stove, and added another tamale next to

237

the one he'd already served himself. "You're too skinny, young man," she said sternly. Then, with a sidelong look, she added, "And women don't like their men *too* skinny."

This he ignored. His grandmother said the same thing every time she saw him.

"Can't Lencha do something about the ghost? If she's making those bracelets and things, isn't that a form of magic? And if she's got enough magic to do that, can't she..." He struggled for the right word. "Banish her or something?"

Bertita blinked in surprise. "Banish? What the hell is that?"

"Send her away for good," Robert explained.

Bertita thought for a moment, then slowly shook her head. "No. Believe me, I've asked. Begged. We can't keep on like this with the gardens going *loco* and people crying for days after they see the Night Lady, but Lencha says Catalina was more powerful a bruja than we gave her credit for, and her own powers can't compare. She's afraid to try. She says it can backfire, and it's too dangerous." She leaned closer to him, enough so that the smell of stale cigar wafted into his face. "But whatever you do, don't say anything to Lencha because she doesn't like talking about it and especially not to you, after what you wrote about Catalina in the paper."

Robert sighed. That was one story he'd always regret. And one story he'd never live down in Palo Verde. "I promise," he mumbled, then slinked into the living room to rejoin the others.

Everyone was listening to Henry Loya with wide eyes. Rose Delgado's eyes were brimming with tears. "But you were born in Loma, Henry," she said, sniffling. "And didn't your father build the house you're in?"

Henry gave a sad smile. "Yes, but my wife wants to go. With an eviction hanging over our heads and with Catalina being killed and those unsolved murder cases, her nerves are a wreck, and because her nerves are a wreck, so are mine." He looked down at his empty plate and sighed. "I went to the housing authority last week and signed the papers, and this morning, we put a down payment on a place in Boyle Heights. No view to speak of, but it's bigger, and there's even a little cottage in the back we can rent out. And I'll be just a few blocks from the market."

In between wistful looks at Espy and frowns at Bruce, Carlos Vasquez had been listening intently. He said, "Catalina's father left. We heard they offered him just five thousand dollars for that falling down house of his, but he took it. Before he left, he told my mother he was going to live in Mexico."

"Good riddance," Rose muttered. "That man was hateful."

Carlos's jaw hardened. "He used to beat the hell out of Catalina. But she got him back."

Robert's head snapped up. "What do you mean?"

"She showed up in his yard one night. Our house is up the hill, and from there, we can see everything. My mom was up late one night, and she saw the Night Lady wandering around his yard. The next morning, he was in the middle of the road, walking in circles. Mom went down to talk to him, and he kept saying he forgot what he was doing, and then he started crying like a baby and couldn't stop, so she took him back to his house. She wanted to call a doctor, but he said he'd seen Catalina's spirit, and that she'd cursed him, and there was nothing a regular doctor could do. So Lencha came."

Bertita had been standing nearby, listening. "Lencha?" she exclaimed.

"You didn't know?" Carlos asked, glancing over at her in surprise.

Bertita scowled. "I did not." Then she turned on her heel and disappeared into the kitchen, muttering.

"What about his garden?" Espy asked from the neighboring table, tipping back in her chair so she could see Carlos.

Carlos touched the corner of his black mustache and gave it a little twirl. "The usual." His eyebrows shot up, and he gave a bitter laugh. "Or the unusual. Remember that nopales cactus in the front yard? It's three times the size it was before he left, and the horsetail has got under the house. The stems are so big and strong they're busting through the floorboards."

Espy gasped and clapped a hand over her mouth. Rose blessed herself.

Carlos's eyes narrowed as he watched Bruce rub Espy's back. When he'd finally managed to look away, he said, "I never knew if I should believe all those stories about Catalina being a witch, that she put a hex on people, but I don't doubt it now. Because only the ghost of a witch can do the stuff that's happening around here." He looked around the table. "If you want my two cents, everyone ought to be real careful because she might just be getting started."

Chapter 30

Footsteps thundered on the wooden porch, and seconds later, the front door of Bertita's house flew open. Suddenly, the living room was filled with a dozen members of the movie crew. Robert's heart hammered in his chest as he watched them head straight for the kitchen and the food, complaining loudly about how late they'd had to work and how hungry they were. He felt a crushing disappointment that Darla wasn't among them, but moments later, she sauntered in, hair loose around her shoulders, wearing a red dress.

The last time he'd seen her, he'd been in a crowded, dark bar, so he hadn't been able to get a good look at her without her movie makeup, wig, and costume. Her hair was the shade of winter wheat. He was terrible at ages, but he guessed around thirty. She seemed older due to the confidence she exuded. She was staring at him without seeming to care who noticed.

Darla stopped behind his chair and in a low, husky voice that tickled his ear said, "Don't tell me I'm too late," which made him choke on the water he'd sipped to cover his nervousness.

Bruce leaned over Espy and gave him a look of exasperation. Robert took a deep breath and gripped the sides of his chair, wishing he didn't feel as nervous as he did. Moving back in with his family after graduating from college meant saving money but sacrificing certain experiences, which included unexplained lengths of time away from home with women.

When Darla had finished dinner, she went into the kitchen and came back carrying two bottles of beer. Then she stopped next to his chair and nodded at the front door.

"Join me," she said.

Bruce had to jab him in the ribs to get him moving.

Darla was already seated on the squashy couch in a dark corner of the porch, her legs tucked under her. She patted the space next to her. "Come on, sit down."

He did, sinking into the couch, feeling the warmth from her body in the cool night air. There were no street lights on the road, just the glow from the living room lamps on the other side of the curtains. Stars winked in the sky above the hills of Elysian Park.

Darla retrieved a beer from the porch railing and handed it to him. "Tell me about yourself, Robert Cleary."

"You know my last name," he said in surprise.

Darla sipped her beer and said, "Of course I do. I've read every word you've written since that story you did on that first awful murder at those shacks. I knew Angel a bit. I can't imagine what he was doing over there. It doesn't make any sense. It's tragic. I don't know what kind of person could do such terrible things. I saw those photos." She shuddered. "How do you stand it? It must take an awful toll on you, seeing mutilated bodies like that."

This wasn't the conversation he'd been expecting, but it wasn't unusual either. Most people asked the same sorts of questions when they learned he reported on violent crime.

"It's rough sometimes," he said.

Darla shifted, trying to get comfortable on the lumpy sofa. "You're a very good writer. Clever. I can tell by the way you word things there's more to the story than you're letting on."

"You can?" he asked. Even to his own ears, he sounded alarmed.

She shrugged, chuckling. "It's probably just my woman's intuition. Or my imagination. My roommates say I read too much."

He welcomed the subject change. "What do you like to read? I can use a good book."

Darla reached over and pushed the bottle of beer to his lips. "Let's see. *Lady Chatterly's Lover. Moll Flanders. Nana* by Zola, just to name a few." She paused. "I like my reading with a little spice. It helps make up for my boring life."

When his sister was in high school, he remembered her sneaking *Lady Chatterly* into the house, but his mother had found it and had raised a fuss, saying no daughter of hers would be reading such filth in her home. He guessed *Moll Flanders* and *Nana* were similar titles.

It was a bit like riding a horse for the first time, and someone handed you the reins to a thoroughbred. He had no idea what to do. "So, you like your literature naughty?" he asked.

Darla gave a delighted laugh. "The naughtier the better." He could feel her staring at him. "How about you?" she asked, giving a playful tap on his arm.

"Hemingway. But my favorite author is Nevil Shute. He's English." He paused, silently cursing himself. He asked strangers questions for a living, so why did he feel so awkward around Darla? Probably because he wasn't on the job, and he'd had little experience with women, at least none who had been anywhere nearly as sophisticated.

"Did you always want to be an actress?" he asked.

"Not always," she said bitterly. "But since I come from a poor family, and I didn't get to go to college like I wanted, and I can't type or take dictation to save my life, there aren't a lot of options for gals like me who aren't cut out for office work." She sipped her beer. "I'm not sure I have much in the way of acting ability, but I seem to keep getting parts, even if they are small, but I can pay the bills, and books are free at the library, so I have all I need." She paused. "Or almost. This life gets lonely sometimes." Her words hung on the night air.

Robert felt himself touched by her story, told in such a matter-of-fact way. He'd never given much thought to the plight of single women and their lack of choices.

"A reporter's life can get that way too," he said, then felt himself blush at the unspoken suggestion that together they could solve their mutual problem. He cleared his throat. "Are you from Los Angeles?"

Darla gave a low, throaty laugh. "Is anybody from here?"

"The people here sure are. Most have lived here all their lives, and now, it looks like they're going to have to leave."

"I've been hearing about that," Darla said. "It's a raw deal, if ever I saw one. I like it up here. It's peaceful. If the city didn't have other plans for the place, I'd try and move up here. It's got to be less expensive, and I'm tired of having roommates."

"Aren't you afraid of the Night Lady?" he asked.

Darla stiffened beside him. "What do you mean?"

"The ghost of Catalina Montez. Plenty of the locals swear they've seen her."

There was a long silence. "I haven't heard that," she said slowly.

Robert glanced over at her in surprise. "I thought word traveled fast on the set."

"I'm a little surprised myself," Darla said in a quiet voice. "But one of the locals would have had to tell someone. Angel and Louie were big talkers, but they're not around anymore, and Espy keeps herself to herself. Well, except for Bruce Knox, something the single ladies can't get over, that he's fallen for a Mexican girl, even if she is real pretty. Bertita and the lady with the braid are polite enough, but they don't really talk to us. So no, this is the first I'm hearing there's a ghost." A long silence followed. "Is it a scary ghost or a sex symbol ghost? Because if it's the latter, I can think of a few fellows who'd love to see it. Like the director. You should have seen his face when he saw her walk onto the set. Like he'd been hit by lightning."

"I'm sure it was the same reaction when he saw you," he said lightly.

Darla turned to face him. "Do you think so?"

That time, the words came easily. "Of course," he said firmly. "You're a knockout."

"Then what are you doing sitting all the way over there?"

Who made the first move, Robert couldn't say, but suddenly her arms were around his neck, and his lips were pressing against hers. Her hand pressed into his thigh, and he ran a hand over her knee and up her silken thigh.

She pulled away. "Now that's more like it, Robert," she said, her voice husky. With a tantalizing flick of her tongue in his mouth, she stood up and smoothed her dress. "I think we deserve a special top up." Then she disappeared inside.

A window behind him creaked open. Bruce stuck his head through a gap between the curtains. "How's it going out there?" he asked in a conspiratorial whisper.

"Fine," Robert stammered.

"I'm telling everyone to leave out the back, so you're not disturbed. And you're welcome."

Robert managed a weak, "Thank you." He couldn't have been more grateful. If anyone came out now, they'd spot his overly excited condition, even in the low light conditions of the porch.

When Darla finally came out, she stood between his knees, looking down at him, and held a glass to his lips. Tequila. From his evenings with Espy and Bruce, he knew it hit him fast and hard, but that night, maybe that wasn't a bad thing. When he hesitated, she dipped a finger in a glass, then pushed it between his lips, and he felt his knees go weak. He drank what she'd poured.

"Good," she murmured, rubbing her knee against his groin, lighting it on fire. "Now you sit there and enjoy your drink while I pop into the ladies."

His eyelids were so heavy he could hardly pry them open. It was as if they'd been glued shut. His limbs felt heavy too, but he hadn't lost all sensation because someone was sitting on his lower back, rocking back and forth. A hand reached around under him, massaging, and if it didn't stop soon, he'd lose all control.

Something covered both sides of his face, tickling his nose, but he was powerless to move it aside. Slowly, he forced his eyes open. At first, it was too dark to distinguish shapes, but there was enough light to see a rough wooden wall and the bars of a cell. He was face down on a cot in a jail.

Hair. Long hair. And for one awful moment, he thought of Catalina. The ghost of Catalina, come back in human form, to have her revenge against him. Her neighbor Mercy Acevedo claimed Catalina had put a hex on her, one that made her sleep for days. If that was true, then maybe it was Catalina behind him now, and the stupor he found himself in was the result of a hex. But as the hand reached around and spread his buttocks, and the gyrating on his back continued, panic struck him.

It was no ghost. He'd been with someone. Someone at Bertita's house. The memory slipped from his bleary mind. Espy. And Bruce. He'd arrived with them, and then…

Darla. Darla Diamond. She was the last person he'd been with. After Bertita's, they'd walked into the night, arms wrapped around each other's waists. But before that, she'd given him something to drink. Tequila. But the liquor didn't completely account for what was happening to him now. While the naked flesh pushing into his back was responsible for the unbearable, hot urgency, he was powerless to resist. Something more sinister than Tequila had put him into a drugged-like state.

Curare.

That's what the toxicology reports had found in the bodies of Angel, Louie, and Don. But Darla didn't have long straight hair. It must have been someone else behind him.

He moaned, caught in a misery of fear and desire. He had to turn around. Had to see the face of his tormentor. And he had to do it quickly, suddenly, because he desperately needed surprise to work in his favor.

Tensing all his muscles, willing his bleary brain to obey, he rolled over with a grunt. The woman yelped and fell to the floor. Then she was crawling away on her hands and knees, grabbing her clothes as she went, the globes of her naked bottom the last thing he saw as she stumbled through the open doors of the tiny jail cell and disappeared.

He sat on the edge of the cot and buried his face in his trembling hands. It took a while for the shaking to subside. His body knew what his mind was unwilling to admit. If he hadn't startled the woman who had done that to him, he would have ended up dead, just like Angel, Louie, and Don.

A sob rose in his throat. When he'd choked it back, a laugh came up to replace it.

It wasn't at all like he'd imagined his first time.

Chapter 31

"Darla is too fast for him," Espy complained to Bruce as she watched him dress. She wished he didn't have to leave, but he had a 6:00 a.m. call with a stop to make at the studio in Hollywood before that, so he decided not to spend the night.

"Robert could use some speeding up," Bruce laughed, buttoning his shirt. "And Darla is just the woman to help him out. She's had her eye on him for a while. She's been asking lots of questions about him." Bruce put his hands under his chin and batted his eyes. "Is he married? No! A nice good-looking guy like him? Well then, he must have a girlfriend. He doesn't! He's new to the city? Oh, he must be lonely without family or friends around!"

Espy brought her knees up to her chin. "I think she lies about her age. She told me she's thirty-two, but I've seen her without makeup. She looks more like—I don't know—thirty-five, thirty-six." She knew she sounded catty but didn't care.

Bruce ran his hands through his dark hair. It was so glossy and smooth it settled right into place. In the time she'd known him, she'd never seen him take a comb to it. If only her thick hair cooperated like that.

Bruce came over and pulled her to her feet. Her robe opened, and she didn't bother to close it. "Here's another thing I've heard," he said, running a finger between her breasts. "Actresses lie about their age. All the time. They're either pretending to be older, or they're pretending to be younger.

That's the way it is in Hollywood. And don't think men don't do it either because they do." And with a kiss and a promise to see her in the morning, he was gone.

She knew she ought to get back in bed and go to sleep, but she was too restless for that. Sex had that effect on her. Plus, she'd received a visit from a city agent reminding her of the deadline to accept a buyout and move. When she asked what would happen if she didn't, he said the city would forcibly evict her.

"Don't be surprised if a sheriff's deputy shows up one day, and you find all your belongings out front," he said before leaving.

She thought the man was lying. A few neighbors said they heard the same thing weeks ago, but nothing ever happened. Still, the threat was enough for those already on the verge of selling up. All they'd needed was another push. And every time someone moved and abandoned their property, the Night Lady was happy to take over.

With all her energy, she should get some work done. The director, Mitchell Wood, had insisted on new, even skimpier, saloon dresses for Shirley and Darla for an upcoming scene, so she might as well start on those. She'd finished cutting the first pattern when she remembered she'd forgotten to bring home the bolts of fabric from a small trailer on the set. It was never locked, and the set was just up and over the hill. She decided to walk over and pick them up. Palo Verde was a safe place to walk, even at that hour.

Except for the Night Lady.

But she was mostly seen in Bishop those days because of the fast-growing number of vacant homes, and the set was in the opposite direction.

Even a ghost couldn't be in two places at once.

Still, she knew better than to leave without protection. Espy slipped a red bracelet over her wrist, stuck the *bolsitas* in the pocket of her coat along with an *amuleto* for good measure, then left, walking quickly up the dirt road, clutching a flashlight, the cold night air brushing her face.

When she reached the top of the hill, she stood for a moment and scanned the set. She didn't like Mitchell Wood, the crooked-nose creep, but she had to give him credit for creating such a wonder in the canyon. In the light of day, the set looked real enough—if you could ignore the lights, cameras, and wooden braces that were everywhere—but in the light of the moon, it was like discovering an old western town time had forgotten. All was silent and lonely without the crew. She hurried down the steep road and was crossing the square to the trailer when she heard a noise and froze.

It seemed to be coming from the jail. Heart pounding, ears straining, she listened as the wooden floorboards creaked and groaned. Someone was walking inside. She aimed her flashlight at the jail. The door swung open, and a tall figure stumbled out.

"Robert!" she cried and rushed toward him. He lurched sideways, holding out his hands as if to keep her away. He was shirtless and barefoot, his pants barely up around his waist.

"Espy?" he said, blinking as he stared past her, then all around. "I'm at the set. This is the set."

"Yes," she said, newly alarmed. He was so unsteady on his feet he looked ready to fall over. "What are you doing here? Where's Darla?"

He looked around, hands clenching convulsively. "Darla. I'm not sure."

"Are you drunk? You're talking funny."

He wiped his mouth and shook his head. "Maybe," he said faintly, then wobbled. When she reached out to steady him, he yanked his arm away and lurched again. "Don't," he said.

251

There was no question. He was slurring his words. She needed to get him home and sober him up.

"What time is it?" he asked, looking around again.

"Around eleven," she answered, staring pointedly at his chest. "What are you doing here?"

"I don't know," he said, visibly shaken. He nodded at the jail. "When I woke up, I was in there." He was doing his best to steady his voice, his eyes pinned on the stars above.

"What's the last thing you remember?" she asked.

"I was having a drink with Darla on Bertita's porch. We were…" His voice trailed off, and he grimaced.

She held up a hand. "I get the picture. And then what?"

"And then we were walking somewhere. And then. You know. I thought we ended back at her place, or maybe some motel. And then I was awake, but I couldn't move, and someone was on top of me, someone with long hair, longer than Darla's, and then I finally managed to shove her off, and she ran. And now I'm feeling sick, but I honestly don't think I drank that much. A beer and a little Tequila, not enough to make me feel like this."

The reporter was usually a neat and tidy dresser, but now he was disheveled. The man had suffered a terrible shock. And whatever had happened, Darla Diamond was somehow involved. That's the only thing that made sense, because the two had been together, and now she was nowhere to be seen.

"You wait here," she said firmly, so he wouldn't argue.

Without waiting for his reply, she strode into the jail, the beam of her flashlight sweeping across the battered wooden desk and chair and into the cell. The jail had four complete walls, unlike some of the buildings on the set. The fake iron door was open. A dark shadow splayed across the floor in the far corner. Hand trembling, she aimed the flashlight at it. Whatever it was, it wasn't moving. As she crept closer, she saw the shape for what it was. A wig. And not far from it, a scarf. She stared down at them, licking her lips, heart pounding in her ears.

She was alone in the room, but still, she moved cautiously, as if expecting the mass of hair to come alive. Dropping to her knees, holding her breath, she lowered her head until she could peer under the cot. The hand holding the flashlight was shaking so badly the beam bounced up and down. At the furthest reaches, against the wall, was a long stem rose, the bloom still attached but limp and slightly flattened. Before she scrambled to her feet, the last thing she noticed were its sharp thorns, so close together they resembled teeth.

Espy hovered outside the bathroom. Robert had been inside for half an hour, soaking in the tub. She was worried. On their walk back to Palo Verde, her supporting him the entire way, he'd stopped three times to retch on the road and twice since they'd reached her house. She'd almost insisted on taking him to the French Hospital in Chinatown.

"I'm fine. I'm fine," he'd insisted.

Fine was the last word she'd use to describe his wild-eyed condition.

Now, she could hear him breathing on the other side of the door and the occasional splash of water as he moved around. She walked down the hallway and made several circuits around the table in the living room, frowning at the wig, scarf, and long-stem red rose she'd taken from the jail. Espy knew she should have left them right where she found them, but she hadn't been thinking straight.

She went back to the bathroom and leaned her forehead against the door. "Can you hear me, Robert?"

"Yes," he said, then made an irritated sound.

"It's not too late. We need to tell the police. I can call them from Rose's house."

"No! No police. I mean it." She could hear him struggling to get up, and then a splash as he sat back in the water.

"Are you alright?"

"No. Yes. I'm fine. Can you please, please just leave me alone for a few minutes. I'm trying to think."

Espy backed away from the door. She wished Bruce was with them. He'd know what to do. When she'd helped Robert take off his shirt, his back was covered in scratches. Did Darla Diamond have long nails? She couldn't remember. And there had been something else too. The unmistakable musky smell of sex had wafted into the air as he'd dropped his trousers.

Finally, Robert came out, wearing a pair of Bruce's pants and a robe. She was sitting on a straight-backed chair next to the table.

"Are you feeling better?" she asked, frowning as she looked him over. His normally bright blue eyes were dull, and his face was so pale. She noticed for the first time he had a splash of freckles across his nose. She should have made him go to the hospital. If he keeled over and died, she'd never forgive herself.

Robert nodded weakly, then perched on the edge of the couch, holding the robe shut. "Better," he murmured. "Thank you." His eyes wandered over to the items next to her, and he squeezed his eyes shut.

He didn't want to talk, but they had to. They couldn't pretend something horrible hadn't happened back there at the jail. "Robert," she said, sounding sterner than she'd intended. He flinched. "I think we both know who did this. We can't kid ourselves. It had to be Darla. You were with her at Bertita's. She went inside and brought you Tequila. She probably put something in your drink while no one was looking, but maybe

254

she didn't put in enough, and that's why you were able to snap out of it."

Robert pressed his fingers into the side of his head. "Curare. That's what the toxicology reports said had been given to Angel, Louie, and Don. But how would Darla get a hold of something like that?" His voice rose. "And how do we know it was really Darla?"

When she folded her arms in front of her chest and returned his stare, he said, "I guess, maybe Darla had something to do with it. Maybe she lured me."

"Of course, she had something to do with it," she snapped. "She had everything to do with it. Open your eyes, Robert. We had three murders while they were making *Beyond the Passage*, and then not one while everyone was away. That is not a coincidence. Darla went to Florida with Shirley for another movie, and now she's back. Bruce said she'd been asking questions about you. Personal questions." She hesitated. "If I were a man, would you tell me what happened to you?"

Robert stared down at his bare feet, refusing to meet her eyes. His toes were long and skinny. "No," he finally said. "It's nobody's business."

She sympathized with his anxiety, but she had to ask. "Is there any chance it was a man?"

His head snapped up. "No!" he practically shouted. His face had turned a bright and angry red.

"You said you couldn't be sure it was Darla," she said with a little shrug. "I'm sorry, but it's something to think about, isn't it?"

Robert's shoulders slumped, and he fell back on the couch with a groan of frustration. "It was a woman, Espy. I know it was. I'm not about to explain exactly how I know that, but you're going to have to trust me."

Restless again, she got up and paced around the small living room, taking stock of the situation. He didn't want her to call the police. He didn't seem ready to face the obvious. Darla Diamond had sneaked a drug into his drink, then had led him to the empty set where she could kill him. She hadn't had to look far for a long-stem red rose because a big bouquet had been delivered earlier in the day. She'd seen them arrive with her own eyes. Most of the crew had.

When Darla had sashayed into Bertita's house earlier that evening, wearing her man-catching red dress, the old lady managed a polite hello but eyed the two-bit actress with suspicion. And now she remembered what happened after that.

She said, "On the day Louie Bonda died, he and Darla were here. Just the usual costume stuff. They left together to eat at Bertita's house. I asked Bertita if she'd seen them, and she said she had. They sat at the same table, and Darla was flirting up a storm, and poor Louie looked like he'd died and gone to heaven. They left together, and Darla had a hand stuck in his back pocket."

Robert gave her a bleak stare. "Oh," he finally said.

"Oh is right," Espy replied, her hands on her hips. "And there's something else. Bertita said she was really surprised that the police never showed up to ask her any questions because, as far as she can figure, she was one of the last people to see Louie Bonda alive. She would have been more than happy to tell them what she'd seen."

That finally seemed to get through to Robert. He was nodding, slowly, and he seemed to have made a decision.

She crossed the room and took both of his cold hands in hers.

"Espy," he said. "Do you think you can help me?"

Other than the city telling her she could stay in her house, she couldn't think of more welcome words.

256

Chapter 32

For the first time in his career as a newspaper reporter, Robert called in sick, paying Rose the Spanish translator who lived in Palo Verde five cents for borrowing her phone.

"A touch of the flu," he'd told Harry.

"Sorry to hear that kid," Harry said sympathetically. "Hope you feel better soon. It's no fun being sick."

While he'd lied about the flu, the fact was, he felt like hell. When he'd pried his eyes open after a rough night on Espy's couch, he had a throbbing headache, a dry mouth, and a case of loose bowels that confined him to the bathroom for an hour. No ordinary sickness had caused all that.

Darla Diamond had.

With the dawn had come the certainty he'd lacked the night before. The worst of the drug he'd been given had lifted from his brain, leaving frightening and shameful memories and the knowledge he'd narrowly escaped the same fate as Angel, Louie, and Don. Memories began to return—the walk with the actress from Bertita's house to the set, the way she'd ripped off his clothes, the light from the moon illuminating the length of her neck, the fullness of her hips. His recollection of the things he'd done with Darla, some eagerly, willingly, and others with reluctant submission, settled into his bones like a chill. He erupted in uncontrollable shivers for most of the morning.

Now that he'd recovered a bit, he felt shattered and desperate but determined.

He believed Darla Diamond had tried to kill him. But now, he needed to prove it. Nothing Espy had said could convince him to go to the police, not after what he'd done to Catalina Montez. The guilt he felt was even worse, knowing that Darla was the killer and the curandera from Palo Verde never was. If there was the smallest chance he was wrong about Darla, he would not make the same mistake twice. There was also the strong possibility Detective Cagle wouldn't believe him anyway after he led the police to arrest Catalina, only to release her when Don had turned up dead while Catalina was behind bars.

And he had suffered no consequences. Falling out of favor with the police detective didn't count, and the ribbing his fellow reporters had doled out was annoying but short-lived. Catalina Montez paid the ultimate price, and there were some in the communities she'd called home who continued to believe she was the killer, even after her death. He owed it to the woman to clear her name, and not just out of fear of what she'd become. The ghostly figure of the Night Lady was beyond his comprehension, but her motivation might be as simple as needing justice to be done. If that was the case, it was something he could give her.

He just needed evidence.

Despite feeling rattled, he began to formulate a plan.

Sitting in Espy's kitchen, drinking coffee with the seamstress and Bruce, he said, "We need to find out more about Darla. Can you help? Can you ask around, carefully? Where she's from. Where she lives. Anything and everything you can find out."

"Of course," Bruce muttered. The prop master still looked dumbfounded about Robert's encounter with Darla.

Espy frowned. "And then what?"

Robert sighed. "And then I do some investigating on my own, with whatever you two manage to dig up."

258

"Is that even her real name?" Espy asked, her frown deepening. "It sounds made up to me. And silly."

Bruce reached over and gave Espy's hair an affectionate tug. "Most actresses don't use their real names, and most actors don't either. Lauren Bacall used to be Betty Joan Perske, and Ernest Borgnine was born Ermes Borgino, the son of Italian immigrants. So, we have our work cut out for us. If Darla has immigrant roots, too, she wouldn't want to admit that to movie people. But she might have told her friends."

Espy turned to Bruce, eyes widening. "Does she have any friends? On the movie, I mean. Sometimes I'd see her gossiping with one of the other actresses, but most of the time, she'd either be flirting with men or on her own."

Bruce nodded thoughtfully. "Not that I know of. Maybe you can ask Shirley about her?"

"Sure," Espy agreed readily. "And I know a lady in accounting at the studio. The one who does the paychecks. She lives in Loma. Sometimes we have lunch together."

"Jenny Hoover," Bruce chimed in, snapping his fingers. "I forgot she lives up here. She's the reason we've been shooting in the ravine, actually. Jenny was talking to Bruno one day, and she told him how this would be the perfect place to build a set, so he came and scouted the area, and the next thing we knew, Mitch had made a deal with the city."

Robert scowled. "You're going to need to talk to Jenny in person. And she's going to want to know why you're asking about Darla. Even if you come up with a good cover story, she might not tell you because it's personal information." Suddenly, the whole enterprise seemed impossible, and he slumped in his chair, feeling defeated even before they'd started.

Espy jumped up from her chair, went down the hallway, and emerged a few seconds later, wearing red lipstick and a green coat.

"Where are you going?" Bruce asked, reaching out and taking one of her hands.

"To go see Jenny," Espy answered with a grim smile. "I need to pick some things up at the studio anyway." Then she winked and left.

Robert stared after her. He had no idea what she planned on saying to the accountant, but if he was a betting man, he'd put ten bucks on Espy Gaten.

At Espy's behest, Robert stayed at her house in Palo Verde for the rest of the day. He'd agreed, glad not to make the drive back to Hollywood in his state, but also because he dreaded being alone with his dark thoughts.

Darla's nails had scratched his back, her cruel touch etched into his skin and his memory. He wondered how long it would take to trust a woman again. Maybe never.

When Espy and Bruce finally returned, it was dusk. When he heard the front gate creak open, he greeted them at the door. Down the street, the giant cactus in Catalina's garden towered above the trees. It was the hour when thoughts too easily turned to the Night Lady.

Espy went straight into the kitchen and reached for the bottle of Tequila on top of the refrigerator.

His stomach tightened as he reluctantly accepted the glass she offered. He didn't think he could ever drink Tequila again. "Any luck?" he asked.

Espy sipped her drink and nodded. The red lipstick had faded, and there were dark circles under her eyes after the long night they'd had, but the seamstress was obviously pleased with herself, and Robert felt a flicker of hope.

"We got lucky," she said, a faint smile playing around her lips.

Robert stared at her. When it came to getting answers out of people, smarts and persistence were more important than luck. "What did you learn?" he asked, then held his breath.

"Darla's real name is Judith Saenz," Espy said, setting down her glass. "She's thirty-five, and she lives in Hollywood." She reached into the pocket of her coat and pushed a scrap of paper across the table. When he looked down at it, two addresses were scribbled there. One in Hollywood, the other in Oklahoma City.

He looked up, eyes widening. "Are these what I think they are?"

Espy tapped the paper. "This is where she lives now. That's her last known address. Jenny said when Darla—I mean Judith—was hired and came in to fill out the forms, they got to talking, and Judith said she'd never been this far west before, and she'd never seen the beach." This was more than Robert could have hoped for, and it made his job much, much easier.

Espy went on. "I talked to Shirley and some of the other extras too. They said Judith didn't talk about herself much. Just said that she'd grown up in the South but never mentioned where, and that she'd only started acting a few years ago after Mitch Wood spotted her at a diner in San Antonio."

Bruce lifted his eyebrows. "Guess who else called in sick today?"

Robert's mouth fell open. "Judith?" he said. The name felt strange on his lips, but now that he knew about Darla's dark nature, it seemed fitting. He realized he hadn't given any thought to Darla's whereabouts, or how she would react, knowing he'd thwarted her plans. He'd assumed she'd pretend nothing had happened and would show up to work as usual, feigning wide-eyed innocence if confronted. The truth was, he'd focused on himself and what she'd done to him, not what might happen next. Just more evidence he wasn't yet thinking straight.

"Yep, she did," Bruce said. "And Bruno confirmed her story, said he'd been with Mitch Wood on location in San Antonio when they stopped for a bite to eat. Judith had been at the counter. Mitch couldn't stop staring at her, so he told Bruno to ask her to join them, and she did, of course. Mitch even gave her a screen test, but it was pretty clear she didn't have much potential. But the camera loved her, and she could manage a couple of lines of dialogue as long as the dress was tight enough and she got to show off those legs of hers." Bruce paused long enough to throw up his hands. "Bruno's words. Not mine. This is my first movie with Mitch Wood, but Bruno says Darla has worked on every one of his since then."

Robert's pounding heart jolted in his chest. "Were there any—"

Bruce was already shaking his head. "Murders in the same area where they filmed in the past? Not according to Bruno. He said it was something he'd thought about, too, and so did the police, but as far as he knew, nothing like that had happened. And by the way, whatever else we can say about Darla—and there's plenty—this is the first time she's ever not shown up for work." The prop master drank his Tequila, then sniffed. "Bruno was actually worried about her."

Espy nodded. "I talked to Shirley on the set. She was real surprised too. She said Darla is a real trooper and even showed up to work when she had a terrible cold, and they had to use lots of makeup to cover up her blotchy nose. Shirley wanted to take her some soup, but she didn't know where Darla lived, and none of the other girls did either."

Robert leaned forward and stared down at the paper with the addresses written in Espy's spidery longhand. Judith Saenz lived less than ten blocks away from his apartment in Hollywood.

Chapter 33

Robert needed a plan. As twilight turned to night, he walked to Rose Delgado's house.

The Spanish translator opened the door willingly enough after she'd peeked through a gap in the curtains, then scolded him for walking alone after dark when the Night Lady was out. "My friend Martin just called to say she was on Yolo Drive, so I guess you're okay for now. But hurry up before she comes back."

"I will." He handed Rose two nickels, then dialed the first number. He left a message with the newspaper operator to tell Harry he'd be out sick the next day too. Then he dialed the second number.

He didn't dare show up at the address of the woman whose real name was Judith Saenz. If she was home, she'd recognize him immediately, and who knew how she might react. She was, after all, a killer. Correction—suspected killer. So far, he'd only been able to confirm two things: Judith was a bad actress, and she'd changed her name. Neither was a crime. He had nothing on her yet that could connect her to the deaths of Angel, Louie, or Don and only hazy memories about his own assault.

Instead, Robert opted for the next best thing. He asked his friend Gary from *The Express* to pay her a visit and see what he could find out. That had meant telling Gary a bit of the truth and agreeing to share the byline if a story came out of it. Gary had been shocked and, in the end, had readily agreed, promising to keep the whole thing quiet.

The next day, Robert sat hunkered down in Gary's car several blocks away, waiting nervously. That Judith lived in the same neighborhood was unsettling. He must have driven past her place dozens of times on his way to and from work, but not once had he seen her around.

Like him, Judith lived in a small, nondescript apartment building, except it looked untended, the grass overgrown with weeds and roses running tall and wild.

Long stemmed red roses. The kind he'd seen sticking out of Louie Bonda. The kind Espy had found under the cot in the jail on the set.

When the redheaded reporter finally appeared, hands shoved into his pocket, whistling, he knew Gary was onto something. He forced himself to wait until Gary had stuck his head through the open window on the driver's side.

"You really can pick 'em," Gary said without preamble. "Darla, AKA Judith, is also known here as Colleen Webb. The landlady had no idea who I was talking about when I mentioned Darla Diamond, and she'd never heard of Judith. So, I described her, and the landlady said, 'Oh, you mean Colleen,' and I say, 'Oh, sorry, I must have got the names mixed up, silly me.'"

Breathing through gritted teeth, Robert said, "Was she there?"

Gary rolled his eyes. "Can I please tell this my way?" He climbed into the car and settled into the driver's seat, then began ticking off his fingers.

"Number one. She's single and lives alone, no roommates. Number two. No visitors. Ever. Three, she comes and goes at all hours. Four, doesn't take kindly to landladies who ask nosy questions. Five. Colleen, also known as Darla Diamond and Judith Saenz, moved out this morning. No notice. The landlady

266

says another tenant saw her loading things into a car. She didn't bother to say goodbye. The rent was paid through the end of the month." With that, he wiggled his five fingers and made a fist.

Robert opened his door and was half out of the car. "Can we…"

Gary grabbed his shirt and pulled him back inside. "Don't bother. I already had a look. The place is cleaned out. It was a furnished apartment. Not a single bobby pin left behind, and she must have taken her trash, too, because I looked in the dumpster at the back of the building, and it's empty. It seems your girl thought of everything."

Robert ignored this and stared straight ahead, thinking. Darla had lied about having roommates. She lived alone, and obviously, that had suited her just fine because, by all accounts, she was a loner. She hadn't brought men home. Probably because she liked it rough and didn't want anyone coming around to complain about the noise. If her dates even survived. He wondered how Judith came to choose her victims. Did she carry that rare sedative around in her purse, just in case the opportunity arose? And how about those long-stemmed roses? Did she keep them wrapped in freezer paper in the trunk of her car? Or was everything carefully planned?

Gary waved a hand in his face. "I was thinking," he said loudly.

Startled, Robert flinched and said, "Sorry. What was that?"

"I guess I'll have to repeat myself," Gary said with a martyred sigh. "I was thinking I could call an old buddy of mine in San Antonio. He works at the paper there."

Robert shot him a blank stare. Gary rolled his eyes again and pretended to knock on the side of his head.

"Anyone in there? You need to get hold of yourself, Robert. Come on, come on. Think for a moment. What does Judith Saenz have in common with San Antonio, Texas? Do I need to spell it out for you?" Then he drummed his fingers on the steering wheel.

Robert slumped in his seat and buried his face in his hands, shocked at his own stupidity. He couldn't afford to be so slow at a time like that. Just a few hours into his plan, he'd lost focus, lost track of what he'd set out to do. It wasn't anything extraordinary or complicated. Just basic journalism, the stuff he did every day without thinking twice. Gather information, confirm it, follow up, and see what else he could find out. Repeat until he had enough to write a story or, in this case, go to Detective Cagle with enough certainty that he wasn't blowing the whistle on an innocent woman.

Again.

It didn't matter that he knew in his heart and his soul that Judith Saenz was his attacker, almost his killer. And he needed to hurry because there was no telling what else she would do, and to whom, while she was still free.

He tried to get a hold of himself. He sat up and pushed his shoulders back. Then he turned to face Gary and that time squarely met his gaze. "Can you call your buddy from my place?" he asked. "I don't want to show up at the newsroom, since I'm supposed to be sick."

Gary thumped his shoulder. "That's more like it," he said, then started the car.

Two hours later, Robert was sitting in the Los Angeles Public library, pouring through old copies of the largest newspaper in Oklahoma City. The library had a collection of newspapers from around the country, going back a few years, and the librarian, a pretty young woman with short curly hair, had been more than happy to help. He was alone. Gary had gone back to work after calling his old college friend who worked in San Antonio. No one at the paper could recall a Judith Saenz in the news, nor any murders involving young men, unsolved or otherwise. It was only then that Robert remembered a friend from his first job in Salt Lake City had taken a job at an Oklahoma paper. Robert managed to get hold of him and asked him if there had been any murders of young men.

Bingo.

"You mean the Edward Hunter case?" asked Joe.

"I'm not sure," Robert admitted, fingers tingling as he pressed the receiver against his ear. "Who's Edward Hunter?"

"Well, you were just asking if we'd had any murders of young men, and we did. Young women too. Five in total. It was a few years back, but it was a very big story at the time. The murders were brutal, and some of the bodies were mutilated. They caught the guy. Edward Hunter. But if you ask me, the police made a big mistake letting his wife go because she had to be in on it."

"His wife?" Robert asked faintly.

"Yes. Judy Hunter." There was a long pause. "I heard she changed her name after she was released. Went back to her maiden name, Judith Sands or Saints or something. Don't ask me what happened to her because she left town. Why you asking?"

Robert squeezed his eyes shut so hard he felt the cords in his neck bulge. "Just following up on some leads," he replied vaguely. "If I were to look up that case, what would those dates be?"

"Summer of 1947. That's a year I'll never forget. Now listen, Rob, if those leads lead to something, you be sure to let me know," Joe said sternly before hanging up.

It had taken less than fifteen minutes to find what he was looking for.

The date: June 20, 1947. The body of a twenty-five-year-old female was found in a park. She'd been raped and had suffered a cracked skull. The murder weapon, a bloodied brick, was found nearby. Three days later, another young woman, age twenty-three, was found, strangled to death in an alley behind a popular nightclub. Police suspected she was tortured and murdered elsewhere, then dumped. The detective in charge of the case refused to describe the nature of her injuries and would only say they were numerous and of a sexual nature. He would repeat himself less than a week later when the body of a third woman, age twenty-six, was found in a vacant lot near the same park where the first victim had been discovered.

Robert read on. He felt drained but determined.

Two more bodies were found in the second week of July. That time, men aged twenty-three and twenty-five. They, too, showed signs of sexual abuse and torture. Both had been strangled with a length of rope. After they had been identified, the police discovered a link between all five victims. All were described as exceptionally attractive and outgoing, and all had frequented the same popular nightclub. Eventually, a witness stepped forward identifying Edward Hunter, the thirty-five-year-old bartender, as the man seen leaving the club with the female victims. Later, another witness told police a lovely young woman had lured him to her apartment where Edward Hunter awaited, and it was only after a prolonged assault he had been able to escape. The woman was identified as Edward's wife, Judy Hunter, and she was arrested and questioned. Judy hired a lawyer and claimed she'd acted under duress, that if she had refused to obey, Edward would have killed her too. That was vehemently denied by the witness, who told police Judy was complicit. When she was released, he'd spoken on the record to every reporter who showed up to interview him, saying Judy Hunter was a liar and a menace to society.

The story included the only photo he could find of Judy Hunter.

Darla Diamond stared back at him. Younger. Even prettier. Slightly rounder in the face. But unmistakably Darla.

He pushed back from the table as if a snake had slithered across the page, his heart bumping in his chest. Reality felt like it was slipping away. Both he and Judith had traveled thousands of miles from home, taken jobs in the vast city of Los Angeles, and their paths had crossed in a semi-rural neighborhood destined for destruction. The odds of meeting Judy Hunter—then Darla Diamond—were staggeringly small. Yet, somehow, it had happened.

When he was finally able to breathe normally, and his legs stopped feeling like they were made of noodles, he looked around for the pretty librarian. He was alone in the room. Good. He didn't have time to waste, and he wasn't sure she would let him check out a newspaper anyway. With a final, furtive look over his shoulder, he tore out the articles he needed, including the one with the photo of Judy Hunter, folded them neatly with trembling hands, and stuck them inside his reporter's notebook.

He just hoped Detective Cagle would be in his office when he got there.

Chapter 34

After finding a place to park around the block from the Los Angeles Police Department's Central Division in downtown, Robert sprinted to Detective Cagle's office. He'd been called out on a case but wasn't expected back anytime soon, the desk sergeant said. Robert sagged against the wall and stared blankly at the young officer, who was looking him over with a wary eye. He knew it had been a longshot, but all the same, the disappointment was crushing.

"Would you like to talk to someone else?" the officer asked. He was fresh-faced and chisel-jawed, straight out of central casting.

That's the last thing he wanted to do. Explaining everything to someone new would take hours. Robert shoved his hands in his pockets, feeling the folded newspaper article, reminding him of what was at stake. The longer he waited, the more likely Judith Saenz would get away. If Cagle wasn't back by the afternoon, he'd have no choice but to pass along the information to another detective. "Is there any chance you can tell me where Detective Cagle went?" he asked hopefully. "Maybe I can have a quick chat with him there."

The young officer shot him a disapproving look. "You know I can't do that. Why don't you give a call in a few hours? If Cagle's around, I promise to let you know. Save you the trip over here." He gave the phone a fond pat. "That's what this thing is for."

Robert felt his face go tight and his toes curl in his shoes. He opened his mouth to say something he was sure to regret, then thought the better of it, gave a curt nod, and hurried out of the building.

Frustrated, he sat in his car, wondering what to do next. He could go to his apartment and get a jump on the story. A first-person account from the perspective of a survivor of Judith Saenz, nearly her fourth victim in Los Angeles. He wouldn't mention everything, of course, not the sexual assault he'd endured, but enough to get the point across that Judith was an evil woman and a deviant. When the time came, he'd write it. But for now, what he really wanted was to talk, to try to make sense of what he'd learned. He decided to head back to Chavez Ravine. He owed Espy and Bruce the truth because he couldn't have found out what he had without them. That's where he would go.

He hadn't eaten lunch, but he wasn't hungry, hadn't fully recovered from the sedative Judith had given him. It was mid-afternoon, and the traffic was still light, so he made it to Palo Verde in twenty minutes.

When he pulled up to Espy's house, he saw Bruce's car parked out front, which was unusual because he normally parked closer to the movie set. His heart began to beat faster. He hoped nothing had happened to Espy.

The screen door was open, and he could hear voices inside. One, a man's voice, was vaguely familiar, but he couldn't quite place it. He knocked, and Espy came to the door wearing red pants, a checked shirt, and her hair pulled back in a high pony tail. With her signature bangs, she looked like a teenager.

She peered at him through the screen, eyes widening. "Is everything okay?" she asked anxiously, pulling him inside.

As soon as he entered, the unmistakable smell of Phillipe's French dip sandwiches reached his nose, and his stomach grumbled. "Fine," he murmured. "More than fine."

Bruce looked up and waved a wrapped sandwich in the air. "I brought extras. Come on. Sit down. You look like you could use something to eat."

His stomach rumbled again, and as he made his way to the table, he hoped it wouldn't betray him. There was too much to do, and he couldn't afford to spend the rest of the day bent over a toilet.

The other man in the room was Carlos Vasquez, the fellow he'd met while waiting in line to see Catalina Montez outside her curandera shack, the same fellow who had looked decidedly unhappy to find Espy and Bruce on such cozy terms at Bertita's house.

While Espy brought him a plate and a glass of water, Carlos greeted him with "Hey, lover boy," which made Robert cringe.

Espy shot Carlos a swift warning glance. "Leave him alone, Carlos."

"Me?" Carlos held out both hands, palms up. "I just want to know this kid's secret, that's all. Maybe it's the blue eyes, but whatever she saw in him, she didn't see in me because she wouldn't give me the time of day."

Espy and Bruce exchanged glances. "I think you would have been too much to handle," Bruce said slowly.

Knowing the meaning behind that vague statement, Robert felt the blood drain from his face. Carlos Vasquez radiated a confidence and swagger he lacked, with the tightly coiled muscles of a boxer, while he was a lightweight, in body if not in mind. Both Angel and Louie had more impressive physiques, but Judith had ten years on them, and no doubt had used her experience against them.

Robert unwrapped his sandwich. He saw with relief that it was turkey. He didn't think his stomach could handle anything as heavy as lamb or beef.

Espy cleared her throat. "Carlos stopped by to tell us what happened in La Loma today," she explained.

Carlos nodded, mouth full, and swallowed. "I picked the right time too. I haven't had Phillipe's in a long time." He shot a somewhat stiff smile at Bruce. It seemed he hadn't quite gotten over his resentment that the prop master had ruined his romantic intentions toward the seamstress.

Robert's thoughts drifted as he took small bites of his sandwich, wondering how long Detective Cagle would be out, and what he would say when they finally spoke. In his mind, the story still came out in a jumble, not the well-ordered sequence that came so naturally when he wrote a news story.

"Do you want to come and take some pictures?" Carlos was asking. "There's still blood all over the porch."

That jolted Robert back into the conversation. "Blood?" he asked, looking around.

Espy gave him a sympathetic look and said, "The city sent a demolition crew to Catalina's father's house this morning."

"I thought they were taking a break," Robert said, blue eyes widening. "Because of all the accidents."

Carlos smirked. "You mean because of the Night Lady. Didn't I tell you she was just getting started?"

"You did," Robert acknowledged. "So, what happened?"

Carlos crumpled the sandwich wrapper and dropped it onto his plate. "I'll say it again." When Robert nodded, he continued. "My house is up on a hill, and we can see the old Montez place. This morning, here comes the damn bulldozer and a truck with three men. So, I went down there to watch. I could tell they were real nervous because, well, you should see the place. The horsetail is taller than the house, and it busted up through the floorboards of the porch. And the bulldozer driver says no way, he's not going to drive over all those plants after what's happened to the other guys. And then they start fighting about what to do, and finally, one guy, who starts acting all tough, says he'll start cutting down the damn horsetail if they're such scaredy cats. He goes to the truck and gets this big machete, I swear, then he starts whacking his way up the falling-down steps. He's on the porch when he starts screaming. So, we all run over there to see what's wrong, except we can't really see the guy because he's in the middle of a bunch of that reedy stuff, and it's like he's fighting in there. Finally, he just sort of falls out and goes off the side of the porch, and he's all cut up and bleeding." Carlos stopped and took a deep breath.

Robert stared at him, aghast. "And then what?"

Carlos' eyes flicked toward the ceiling and he crossed himself. "And then we had to call for an ambulance from my house, that's what, and by the time it came, the guy was in such bad shape, I'm not sure he made it." Carlos pushed back from the table and rose to his feet. For the first time, Robert noticed the man was wearing an orderly's uniform. White short-sleeved shirt, white pants, black belt. It suited him. "I'll check on him when I start my shift." He nodded at Robert. "You want to get some pictures, or not?"

Robert thought for a moment. With two days off from work, he could use a good story to make up for his absence, one that would tide him over until he was ready to work on his Judith Saenz exposé.

"Sure," he said, getting to his feet. To Espy, he whispered. "I'll be back as soon as I can. I have something to tell you."

Espy bit her lip but said nothing as she walked them to the door.

Carlos climbed into Robert's car, and they drove to La Loma. Most of the homes were still occupied in the hilly neighborhood. The few that weren't had gardens so wild the roof lines were barely visible above the wayward growth. The Night Lady had been very busy.

When they'd reached the Montez house, the property was deserted. Only the bulldozer remained. A trail of blood led from the porch to the dirt road. They stood at the edge of the property, Carlos clutching the sleeve of his shirt. "I wouldn't get any closer if I were you," he said in a quiet voice. He pointed at the porch. "The horsetail the guy chopped down has grown back already. I've only been gone a few hours."

"I won't," Robert reassured him, then removed the cap from the camera lens and slipped it into a pocket.

Harry would be intrigued by the photos when he saw them. He'd also have lots of questions Robert wouldn't be able to answer. It would be yet another biological mystery for city officials. They'd scratch their heads, promise to investigate, and then issue cautions to avoid the area until they'd determined the cause of the problem, which never seemed to happen.

A gust of wind blew over the hill, making the crisscross of wires whistle above their heads. The wind ruffled their hair, as if trying to urge them back toward the car.

"Take your pictures and let's get out of here," Carlos urged. When Robert glanced at him, he shrugged and gave a sheepish smile. "This place gives me the creeps," he admitted, then turned and went to wait by the car.

It took Robert just a few minutes to take the photos, and when he was done, he drove Carlos to the French Hospital for his shift. It was the least he could do. And then he headed back to Espy's house. Espy and Bruce were cleaning up after lunch, so they gathered in the kitchen, drinking coffee, and listened to a full accounting of Robert's day, from the visit to Judith Saenz's apartment in Hollywood, to the calls to the newspaper offices in

San Antonio and Oklahoma City, and finally to his fruitful hour at the library.

As Espy and Bruce stared, he carefully unfolded the articles he'd ripped from the archives and smoothed them out with slightly trembling fingers.

"I can't believe it," Espy said, then clapped a hand over her mouth.

Bruce leaned forward, peering at the photo of the woman who had, at the very least, been complicit in the deaths of five young people. He kept his hands in his lap, as if touching the photo would contaminate them. "It's her all right." He gave a low whistle. "You got lucky, Robert. She would have killed you if she could."

Robert rubbed the side of his face, suddenly exhausted, but remained upright in his chair. His day wasn't over yet. Espy and Bruce walked with him to Rose's house to borrow her phone. Rose wasn't there, so they let themselves in and put a nickel on the counter. Detective Cagle still wasn't back and wouldn't be until around seven that evening, the chisel-jawed officer said. Robert slammed the receiver down so hard the phone bounced off the dark wood cabinet and fell to the floor.

"Wait at my house," Espy said. "You shouldn't be alone."

Bruce gave him an encouraging slap on the back, then drove off to the set. Espy settled down behind her sewing machine and cast furtive, worried glances in his direction. Robert sat at the kitchen table, organizing his notes on the story he dreaded writing, the one that detailed his personal involvement with the actress known as Darla Diamond in Hollywood.

As the light faded, he grew more and more restless until he could not sit still a moment longer. He announced he was going for a walk. Espy nodded absently. She was absorbed in hand-sewing tiny cloth-covered buttons on the front of a red satin dress.

The wind had picked up in Palo Verde, lifting dry dirt from the road. Murky clouds of dust swirled in the air around his head, making him cough. He hurried past them, listening to the rattle of rickety gates, wishing he'd brought his jacket. The evening was unusually cool for Los Angeles, even for that time of year. He walked aimlessly, too preoccupied with Judith Saenz to pay attention to his route.

When he finally glanced up, suddenly aware of his surroundings, he was taken aback. He was standing in front of the garden that once belonged to Catalina Montez—the haunted birthplace of the Night Lady. He recoiled at the stretch of monstrous vegetation before him, strangely luminous.

In the twilight, as the wind rose around him, a flash of red darted among the untamed growth. For a moment, Robert imagined it was the dress Catalina had worn the day he'd sent her to jail and, ultimately, to her death.

Chapter 35

Her mother was in such a good mood she let Jane tear off the newspaper from the front windows of the house. Jane was happy, too, because the next day they were moving to their new house in Boyle Heights, just around the block from her cousins. Her mother hadn't let her tell anyone, though, not even Espy. She said she didn't want anyone to stick their nose in their business and try to make them change their mind. Once her mother decided she'd had enough of the Night Lady and the tall man with the scary skeleton face from the city, they'd started packing up, and that was that.

Her mother was on the back porch, folding sheets and blankets and putting them into boxes.

While Jane was stuffing strips of yellowed newsprint into a garbage bag, she noticed she'd missed a patch in the corner and was scratching it off with her thumbnail when a movement across the street caught her attention.

It was the nice reporter man, Robert.

She hadn't seen him on her street in a long time, but nobody else came by because the Night Lady scared them. She hadn't seen the ghost of Catalina in a long time either, but sometimes after her parents were asleep, she could *sense* her nearby. It wasn't too scary. Not like the boogeyman or the Llorona. The Night Lady didn't make noises, but sometimes a scream would reach her ears, and she knew a neighbor had the bad luck of seeing the Night Lady. Lencha, the curandera with the long braid and dark-rimmed eyes, would visit her mother, and she'd heard her say she had come up with a special remedy for *susto*. Her mother asked for some, just in case she or Jane saw the ghost and suffered a bad fright, so Lencha had come back with a small bottle. Jane's father said it was nothing more than sugar water, which had made her mother angry, so they started fighting. But now, her mother was in a good mood because they were moving.

She was about to knock on the window to get the reporter's attention when she saw him go into Catalina's garden. The gate had fallen off its hinges, and there was no one around to fix it. No one ever went in there, not even the teenage boy who used to cut things down and take them to Lencha. Everyone was too scared.

After making sure her mother was still on the back porch, she quietly opened the front door and slipped outside. She could still see Robert but just barely because it was almost dark out, and there were so many plants around. She crept past the gate.

It was a good thing he was wearing a white shirt. By the way he was looking around, she could tell something was wrong.

And something else too.

The Night Lady was in there. Somewhere.

She didn't think he should be in there.

Jane's head was beginning to feel funny, fuzzy, and her knees felt wobbly, just like the time she fell at the cemetery and thought a skeleton had grabbed her ankle.

"Mister Robert," she hissed.

But he was too far away, and he couldn't hear her.

Then the white shirt was gone, like something had yanked him into the plants. She clenched her fists so tightly her nails cut into the palms of her hands. She stood there, unsure what to do. If she went to her mother, she'd order Jane back into the house, slam the door behind them, and cover the windows again. But Jane knew something was wrong. Robert needed help.

And then she heard his muffled screams.

The night had seemed to swallow her up the moment she'd set foot inside the garden. She came to a sudden stop, not knowing which way to go. The little paths were gone. Vines tangled in her hair, and enormous blooms drooped in her face, making her gag with their strange scents.

"Robert!"

She was scared. More scared than she'd ever been. But she had to find the nice man, and she sprang forward, pushing through the heavy growth, hitting wildly at branches and thorn-covered stems. She felt them scratch her arms, but still, she continued.

Then there was another sound. Like someone being dragged across the ground, a horrible grunting, and then a terrified, "*No, no, no.*"

It was just ahead now and a little to her right. Rounding a giant cactus, staying as far away from it as she could, she nearly fell into a little clearing.

When she'd righted herself, panting, she froze.

The Night Lady was there. Not the white glowing figure she'd seen before, but a tall figure in a red dress with black hair that swirled in the air. More like the old Catalina, but scary, and Jane could sense the anger that surrounded her like a cloud, just like she could tell when her mother was angry. Jane wanted to run, but her legs wouldn't work. Her eyes jumped around like she couldn't control them either, and finally, they settled on the ground. What she saw made her whole body start to shake.

Robert was being sucked into a hole in the ground. He was half in, half out. Once, she'd watched a matinée movie where a lady got sucked under quicksand, and that's what was happening

283

to Robert. He was holding onto a vine. His face was all twisted, and his mouth was open wide, but no sound was coming out.

The figure in the red dress just stood there, not moving, black holes where her eyes would have been.

"Catalina, don't!" Jane screamed. She tried to jump in between the ghost and Robert, but she found herself flying backward, and she slammed against something hard. As she scrambled to her feet, she saw the red string bracelet on her wrist—the protection bracelet Catalina had made her while she was still alive, the bracelet Catalina promised would protect her from ghosts.

With a wail, she stepped in front of the ghostly figure in red and waved her hand with the bracelet in front of it. "Stop it, Catalina. Stop it! You have to stop," she cried. Then she fell to her knees, sobbing.

The muddy earth around Robert stopped churning, and he was desperately trying to pull himself out of the hole. He was shouting too. "I'm sorry, Catalina. I'm sorry. It wasn't you. It wasn't you. It was never you. And I have the proof. I have the proof, I swear. Just let me take it to the police, please."

Jane didn't understand what he was talking about, but she sensed his desperation. His desperation to live. With a trembling hand, she ripped the red string from her wrist and flung it at Robert. For a moment, she thought he'd drop it, but he caught it with the same ease she'd seen boys catch baseballs in the street, his fingers closing neatly around it.

One elbow propped on the edge of the hole, he waved the red string in the air. And then someone was rushing toward him. Someone in a dress and an apron with a long, dark braid rushed past the ghost, fearless like it was just a statue in a park. Lencha. The curandera from La Loma. And then Lencha was dragging Robert out of the hole in the ground. When Jane turned to the Night Lady, she could feel the ghost's anger fade, and then she was overcome with all sorts of feelings: shame, regret, hopelessness, and sadness. A sadness that gripped her heart and made it hard to breathe.

Robert was on his hands and knees, panting. Jane watched the Night Lady rise into the air and begin to twist. Lencha reached into a pocket, pulled out a bottle, and used her teeth to tug off the cork. Then she splashed what looked like water on the ghostly figure. Jane could feel the air crackle, and there was an explosion of sounds—terrible screams from the Night Lady that made her heart freeze. She was watching a fight between the ghost of Catalina and the curandera from La Loma. But it was a one-sided fight. Only Lencha had come armed. A metal object appeared in her hand. A silver star with lots of points. Lencha held it high in the air and waved it back and forth. The Night Lady seemed to be losing all her color. The red was gone. Her black hair turned gray, the color of storm clouds, and she was all blurry around the edges now.

Lecha swayed from side to side, muttering. Jane couldn't understand what she was saying. Then, with a shocking suddenness, Lencha threw the star at the Night Lady. Jane didn't see what happened next because the curandera shouted at Jane and Robert to leave as the Night Lady began to howl. Robert pushed himself to his feet, grabbed Jane's hand, and pulled her through the tangled garden. When she looked over her shoulder, Lencha was staring up at the Night Lady, reaching back into the deep pockets of her apron, a terrible expression on her face.

Chapter 36

Bertita was waiting for them in the alley behind Catalina's garden. She shoved them along to her house, where Espy stood waiting on the porch, wringing her hands. Espy ran to meet them at the front gate and half-carried a limp Jane into the house.

"Thank God you're alright," she said to Robert. "When you didn't come back, I went around the neighborhood looking for you. Jane's mom was in panic, saying Jane was gone and that the Night Lady must have taken her."

"Lencha knew exactly where to look," Bertita chimed in.

Espy looked at Bertita in astonishment. "You left Lencha behind? By herself? All alone with the Night Lady?" Her black bangs seemed to quiver with alarm.

He'd been wondering the same thing after seeing what the ghost of Catalina Montez could do. "We need to go help her," he said. He stood there irresolutely. Going back to the garden was the last thing he wanted to do.

With a sniff, the old woman pushed up her sleeves. "This is something that Lencha has to do alone," she said bitterly. "At least that's what she said. That woman is as stubborn as a mule."

Then, dressed in a long, flannel robe and the same brimmed woolen cap she wore every day, Bertita hurried to the Acevedo house to fetch Jane's mother.

Robert sat between Espy and the stunned little girl, who remained silent as she obediently sipped her drink. Jane was covered in scratches and was bleeding, but she didn't seem to notice. She was in shock, he supposed.

Finally, Robert said, "You're one brave kid."

Jane took a quivering breath and replied, "Thank you. I'm glad the Night Lady let you go."

"Me too. It was a close call," he said with a sigh.

Jane sighed too. "Yeah."

"What do you think Lencha did back there?" he asked. He had no business talking to a kid that way, but he couldn't help himself, and she was the only one who'd seen what he had.

Jane set down her mug, then covered her face with her hands. "I don't know," she finally said between her fingers.

Espy shot him a warning look and shook her head as she pulled Jane onto her lap and began to stroke her hair.

When Bertita returned, carrying a paper bag, Mercy shoved past her, and began scolding Jane for sneaking out of the house and nearly giving her a heart attack, then threw herself at her daughter's feet and burst into tears.

"She's okay now," Bertita said gruffly. "I'm going to make some champurrado," she announced a moment later and shuffled into the kitchen. Robert could hear her muttering about Lencha, which told him how worried she was about her friend.

After they'd finished drinking the thick hot chocolate and cinnamon drink, Bertita hustled Jane and her mother into the bathroom where they stayed a long time.

When they finally came back, Jane was all cleaned up, wearing flannel pajamas, covered in bandages, and smelling of iodine tincture. Bertita had gone a bit overboard with the antiseptic, but Jane didn't seem to mind. Bertita served them each a pan dulce, then went out onto the porch to smoke a cigar and wait for Lencha.

Using a voice barely above a whisper and with a growing feeling of unreality, he told Espy everything he could remember.

288

She listened without interruption, her mouth slightly open, face pale.

"I don't think you can take anymore," she said, eyes full of sympathy.

After one supernatural attack and another human one, he didn't think so either. But his mind and body found a way of handling it—he could feel a numbness setting in.

Bertita and Lencha came through the front door. Lencha looked worn out, while Bertita hovered around her, firing off questions in Spanish. The curandera said nothing, then went into the hallway toward the bedrooms, Bertita close on her heels.

After several minutes, Robert heard a door slam, followed by something hard smacking wood—Bertita's cane, he guessed—then Bertita shuffled into the living room, a grim expression on her face. "Don't ask me what the hell happened because she won't say," she grumbled.

Jane set down her pastry. "Is the Night Lady gone?"

Bertita gave a pained smile. "Now that I can answer. Yes. At least, that's what Lencha says, and as much as she annoys me sometimes, I believe her. And so should you." Then she pointed at Robert and jerked her head in the general direction of the bathroom. "I think it's your turn to get cleaned up, young man."

Robert nodded and stood up. Something fluttered out of his pocket, and Jane jumped off her chair to retrieve it. It was the article he'd taken from the library, the one with Judith Saenz' photo. He stared at it in astonishment. Somehow, as the earth had opened up beneath his feet and tried to swallow him alive, the Night Lady looking on, he hadn't lost it. It was slightly damp and smeared with dirt around the edges, but it was still intact.

He felt tears stinging his eyes as he hurried to the bathroom. There, he found a pile of men's clothes neatly stacked on the toilet seat along with a fresh towel. The pants and shirt were worn but clean and roughly his size. They'd belonged to

Bertita's husband, he guessed. Her thoughtfulness touched him, and he had to blink back the unexpected rush of emotion as he washed himself in the bathtub. Most of Judith's scratches were on his back, so at least he didn't have to see them. It was enough knowing they were there.

When he emerged, there was still no sign of Lencha.

"I'm going to the police now," he whispered to Espy, who nodded solemnly and gave his arm a little squeeze.

He said goodbye to Bertita, telling her there was something he needed to do, and he felt small arms wrap around his waist. He didn't have young children in his family, so he did his best and gave Jane an awkward pat on her back. At the gate, he remembered something, and he doubled back.

"It sounds like you won't need this anymore, but thank you for letting me borrow it," he said to Jane, reaching into his shirt pocket and handing her the red protection bracelet.

Jane nodded solemnly. "I'm going to keep it anyway because Catalina made it. And the boogeyman could still be around."

Robert drove straight to Central Division, and that time, Detective Cagle sat behind his desk and waved him in. "Not you again," he snapped, scowling.

Robert was undeterred by the reception. He'd expected it and had come prepared to get him through the next hour, or longer, if that's what it took.

He pulled out a chair and sat opposite the detective, who studied him with frank curiosity. "This better be good, Cleary," he said, then tipped back in his chair, lacing his fingers behind his head.

"It's better than good," he replied calmly. "And I almost got killed, if that makes you feel any better."

The front two legs of the detective's chair hit the ground so suddenly Cagle was nearly launched across the desk. "What do you mean?" he asked, voice rising.

"I know who killed Angel Ramirez, Louie Bonda, and Don Lange. Because she tried to kill me too." He pulled the folded articles from the pocket of his borrowed flannel shirt and slapped them on the desk, then watched as the detective opened them one by one and read the stories with furrowed eyebrows.

Finally, Cagle looked up. "Who is she?" he asked in a flat voice.

"She goes by Darla Diamond. She's an actress with a small part on *Beyond the Passage*. I happened to meet her in one of the neighborhoods near the set." He'd begun to stammer as he got to the next, most difficult part. "She started flirting with me, and I, well, I kind of liked her."

Cagle's eyes narrowed as he tapped the photo of a younger Judith Saenz. "And no one would blame you," he said, his voice softening considerably.

"We had a drink together. Up at a house in Palo Verde. She must have spiked my drink because things got fuzzy after that, and when I came to, I didn't know where I was. She'd put on a wig, so at first I didn't recognize her. I don't think she expected me to wake up because, when I did, she ran off. The same woman who found Louie Bonda happened to come by, and she found me too."

"What happened to the wig?"

Robert stared at a splotch of damp on the wall above Cagle's head. "It's at Espy Gaten's house." After a moment, he added, "We found a scarf too. And a rose."

Cagle jumped up out of his chair. "What the fuck is wrong with you, Cleary?"

"I know, I know," he said weakly, closing his eyes. "In my defense, I didn't want to blow the whistle until I knew for sure. This time."

The detective tipped his head back and groaned. "Those three things weren't enough? Ah, come on. You should have known better. You had no business moving that stuff and destroying what little evidence was probably left behind. Was Darla wearing gloves?"

Robert's gaze fell to his shoes, which were still muddy from the Night Lady's garden. "No."

"Of course not," Cagle said, sounding disgusted. The detective began pacing the room, arms folded across his chest. "You should have come straight to us. We could have picked her up and tried to match whatever fingerprints you didn't manage to ruin. Jesus effing Christ." He cleared his throat and grimaced. "How far did she get with the rose?"

"I was spared," he replied.

Cagle clapped his hands, a noise so loud and sharp in the quiet office that Robert jumped. "Good," he said. "Now there's one bit of good news. Better for you than me, of course, but we'll take it." He hesitated. "What else did she do to you? And no holding back this time. I want to know everything."

Robert felt the room spin around. When it had stopped, he gripped the edge of the desk and said, "Okay. We did it. Or, at least, I'm pretty sure we did. But then things got a little rough the second time around, and that's when I woke up enough to realize what was happening. My back is a mess. I'm pretty sure they were her nails and not the rose."

Cagle stopped pacing and stared down at him. "Is all quiet on the western front?"

Robert frowned. "What's that supposed to mean?"

The detective rolled his eyes and pointed at his crotch. "Is everything okay down there. Is it...? Are you intact?"

292

"If you mean all parts are accounted for, yes," he replied through gritted teeth. "I'm fine."

"Unless she gave you the clap," Cagle said.

Robert's head snapped up. "Oh. I hadn't thought of that."

"Well, you should," Cagle replied glumly. "Let's just hope she didn't skip town. We need to find her." He reached into a drawer and slapped a notepad on the desk. "Write down her last known address for me, and everybody you've talked to about our nasty piece of work. And don't leave anything out this time."

At his apartment, Robert sat staring at the blank sheet of paper sticking out of the typewriter. His thoughts kept returning to the Night Lady as she stood before him in the garden, menacing in her red dress, the features of her face obscured by a ghostly shroud. But there was no question, then or now, that it was the spirit of Catalina Montez. He'd felt her turmoil as he'd been dragged backward into the yawning hole in the ground, with the dirt falling in around him. If Jane hadn't arrived when she did, and Lencha shortly after that, he'd be dead. Two attempts on his life made a pretty good excuse for writer's block, but it wasn't the time to dwell on them. He had to get cracking because he needed to get the story to his boss. They needed to be ready to publish as soon as Detective Cagle called.

He got started on the article, his fingers soon pounding on the keys. Within an hour, he'd written an account that gave him no pleasure but was accurate and straightforward enough to satisfy Harry. He hit the release lever of his Remington and rolled the paper out. Ripping was not an option, he'd learned the hard way, not unless he wanted to tear his hard work in half.

Harry was still in the office and looked up in surprise to see him. "I thought you were sick."

"I was," Robert replied, then fell into the closest chair. It was a relief to be in the brightly lit building. The familiar surroundings calmed his nerves after his terrifying encounters.

"You got something for me?" Harry asked hopefully. "It's been a real slow couple of news days."

Robert placed the manila file folder on the desk. It contained a single sheet of paper, single-spaced, and took Harry less than two minutes to read through it.

When he was done, he turned reproachful eyes on Robert and barked, "This is too short, Cleary." He paused long enough to point at the bullpen. "Get in there. It needs at least another thousand words. And this time, add some feeling to it, for god's sake. Some details. It reads like the world's most boring press release." Then his expression softened, and he came around the desk. "I'm sorry you had such a rough time, kid," he said, squeezing his arm, then giving him a gentle push toward his desk. "I just hope they get the bitch."

The lack of pity, counter-balanced with just the right amount of empathy. It was exactly the tonic he needed. The mention of "the bitch" also jolted him out of his reportorial complacency. There was another call he could make to add to the story and, if he was lucky, satisfy the burning questions that still consumed his thoughts: *Why? Why would a smart, beautiful woman like Judith Saenz kill?* Maybe the man who survived her assault in Oklahoma City had some idea, the fellow who'd raised a ruckus about her release and had called her a "menace to society."

The switchboard operator completed his call to his old friend Joe at the newspaper more than a thousand miles away, and he breathed a sigh of relief when he was put through to Joe's desk. Joe called back ten minutes later with the home phone number of Danny Hill, now age twenty-seven. Robert dialed.

After he'd introduced himself and explained what he was after, a long silence followed before Danny cleared his throat. "I'll talk to you."

Fingers tightening on the receiver, Robert began asking questions. They came in no particular order, and when he finally got around to admitting he'd fallen victim to Judith Saenz, Danny gasped. "You, too? She went after you too?

After this, Danny began to speak more freely, then eagerly. Robert listened, eyes closed, forgetting to take notes. Several minutes passed when he realized his mistake, and his pencil flew across the notepad, determined to catch every word.

Danny paused in his story, then moaned. "Now look, Robert. I'm no goody two-shoes, and I wasn't back then either. But Judy was something else. And yeah, I heard what she told the police. That she was a victim and all. But nothing could be further from the truth. She approached me at the bar, and after we got to talking, she's the one who made the first move. She stuck her hand down my pants and whispered all the right things in my ear to get me to go back to her place. *Their* place. I had no idea she was married. I had no idea the bartender was her husband. When I went to get us another drink, he winked and asked me what I was waiting for. 'Get out of here and have a little fun,' is what he said. I remember it like it was yesterday. And it *was* fun, until things started getting out of hand, and suddenly, Edward Hunter showed up, and he's a big guy, you know." Danny made a strangled noise on the other end of the line, then continued. "And he's holding me down, and I'm face down, and suddenly Judy is…" His voice trailed off. "I don't want you to print this."

Robert's hand trembled. The pencil fell from his fingers and rolled off the desk. "I won't. I promise."

"There are laws against what she did. And you're going to have to trust me. It was *her*, not him."

Robert had to unclench his jaw to get the words out. "Did she use something?"

"You bet she did," Danny said angrily. "But the police didn't care. Didn't even tell me to go to the doctor and get myself checked out, even though I was bleeding. One of the officers joked that a guy had to pay good money to get that sort of treatment. But I *never* asked her to do that to me. Never. And the more I told her to stop, the more excited she seemed to get, and then things got really weird because Edward Hunter started getting excited himself, and for a few minutes there, I was scared because he started touching me. But then he was all over Judith, and that's when I managed to get away. If I hadn't, I'm sure I would have ended up like those other guys." Danny exhaled loudly. "Okay. You can write this up now if you want to. I'm not going to talk about *that* stuff anymore. But here's what you've got to understand. If Edward Hunter hadn't been there, I would have ended up dead. Because she *liked* what she was doing. She liked me being afraid. She liked it when I begged her to stop. That woman may look normal, but she's not. She's anything but, and what happened at her place told me everything I needed to know. That Judith Saenz has a screw loose. She was no victim. She was every bit as violent as her husband, and I'll tell you something else. He didn't make her that way. She was Bonnie to his Clyde, and all those officers who told me a woman couldn't do such things? Well, they were wrong then, and they're wrong now, and you're lucky to be alive, Robert. The only difference between what she did back here in Oklahoma City and what she did in Los Angeles was she got a little more sophisticated and started using drugs to knock the fellows out because she couldn't rely on her husband any more to keep them down."

When they finally hung up, Robert stared at the notepad in stunned silence. Danny's story had shaken him. Badly. He went to the bathroom, splashed water on his face, and scrounged a cigarette from another reporter. But instead of calming his nerves like he'd hoped, the smoke gave him a coughing fit. He dropped the Camel in an ashtray in disgust. Sitting at his desk, he flexed his hands over the Remington and began typing. This time, with feeling.

Chapter 37

Robert was already on his second cup of coffee when the phone rang. Glancing at the clock, he saw it was 7:30 a.m.

"If you hurry and get over to the movie studio, you can get a photo of us arresting Judith Saenz," Detective Cagle said, sounding uncharacteristically breathless.

Nearly dropping his mug, Robert leaned against the counter for his support. "You're kidding?"

"I kid you not. We caught a break. That accountant at the studio? I sent an officer to see her, and she was working late, getting the paychecks ready. She said Darla Diamond had called her earlier in the day. Said she was out sick and wouldn't be going to the set but would pick up her check in person this morning. Sounds like our girl is a little short on cash."

Robert blinked. Darla must be confident that he hadn't gone to the police, counting on his embarrassment about their encounter to keep him quiet.

"I'll be there," he said. He jotted down the details on the notepad sitting next to the phone, grabbed a new roll of film, then quickly got dressed.

In the mirror, his face appeared haggard, his blue eyes dull. He felt as worn out as he looked, and the day was just getting started. He had no desire to see Darla Diamond again, to witness her hauled off in handcuffs. As he loaded the film into his camera, his hands began to shake. A bad sign. He was afraid he'd botch the photo, and they only had one shot at it. There was no reason why he had to be the one to take it. He had his limit, and he'd just reached it.

He called Harry Barkin and explained, fully expecting Harry to holler at him to pull himself together. Instead, Harry said, "Now listen, kid, you need to cut yourself a break. Gary's here. I'll send him over. Why don't you come on in and wait. Then we can put that story together."

Robert thought for a moment. "I'd like to go. Just to be there, you know. If that's all right with you."

Harry didn't hesitate. "That's fine. Just come straight in afterwards. See you soon." Before he hung up, Robert heard him shout, "Hey Gary, get in here."

On the short drive to the studio in Hollywood, Robert began feeling clammy, and when he checked himself in the rearview mirror, he saw sweat beading on his forehead. His stomach had started acting up too, rolling and churning. And by the time he'd flashed his press credential to the guard at the studio gate, he began to shiver. Maybe whatever drug Judith Saenz had given him was still working its way out of his system.

He put on a wide-brimmed hat and pulled it low down over his face. There was little chance Darla would spot him, but he couldn't be too careful.

He'd never set foot on a studio lot before. If it were any other time, he'd be looking around in excitement, but all he felt was a powerful urge to run back to the car and drive away. When he spotted Gary pacing in front of a low building with a long bank of windows, he gave him a little wave, then hid behind a wide, low palm tree. Several other men milled about in the bright morning sun. They wore gray suits, and to the casual eye, they looked like the other men he'd seen on the way in. But he knew they were police officers dressed in plain clothes. There was no sign of Detective Cagle. He had to be around somewhere. It was too big a case for him not to be.

He had a long and agonizing wait. An hour passed, and after all the coffee he drank, he had to go in search of a bathroom. His hand trembled as he pulled up his fly. The clothes he'd worn the night he'd been with Darla were now in the possession of the Los Angeles Police Department, along with the scarf and red rose Espy had found beneath the cot on the jail set. Cagle had sent an officer to collect them from Espy's house.

Robert was back in position behind the palm when he spotted a woman walking briskly toward the building. She had straight auburn hair and wore big sunglasses that hid most of her face, but he'd recognize those legs anywhere. The same shapely legs that had pressed against his hips and pinned him to the cot as he gradually became aware of his dire situation.

The woman who had reduced him to a vulnerable victim.

Heads turned as she sauntered by, swinging her hips.

Even at a time like that, taking such a risk, she couldn't help but strut her stuff. His blood ran cold in his veins, not from fear but from hatred. Hatred for this woman who had claimed to be the victim of an ex-husband she'd never mentioned. Who plotted and tortured and murdered. Whose personal taste was a bit more refined than Edward Hunter—instead of bludgeoning her victims, she preferred poison and sexual assault. She disappeared into the building.

Minutes later, the woman he'd known as Darla Diamond reappeared, head held high and hands behind her back, flanked by two officers in gray suits, Detective Cagle not far behind. The wig was gone, and her natural hair, the color of winter wheat, was disheveled.

He was so transfixed by her arrogant, unrepentant expression that he strayed from his hiding place behind the giant palm, and she stopped. Their eyes locked. His insides felt like they had melted, and he had to force himself to return her unwavering gaze, sweat beading on his forehead. She looked him over, a smile playing around the corner of her lips.

When Gary began taking photos from several angles, Darla stared straight at the camera, making sure to keep her jaw angled just right.

Robert was sure of one thing. When the newspapers hit the stands, Judith would manage to look her very best, even on her very worst day.

Chapter 38

Espy stood in her new kitchen, looking out the window, seeing the view that would take some getting used to. The modest cottage sat high on a hill on the backside of the Hollywood Hills, overlooking a canyon dotted with trees and houses. She'd taken hardly anything with her, throwing out most of the things that marked her short marriage to Felix. Her mother had made a fuss, of course, just as she had about Espy choosing a civil ceremony instead of a proper church wedding, but with her belly fluttering and expanding, getting married sooner rather than later was the best choice. And besides, Bruce wasn't Catholic, and that would have presented all sorts of complications.

After the movie wrapped, she'd gone alone to the city housing authority and sold her house for $9,500, then came home and told Bruce she wanted to spend some of it on an extra bedroom for the baby. He'd frowned, saying it wasn't necessary because he had enough money. And besides, he wanted to build the room himself. But Espy reminded him it wasn't just his house any longer. She wanted to make her new home her own, using some of her own money, and in the end, they compromised by buying new furniture and adding a small sun room she could use for her projects.

Some days, she couldn't believe her luck. When she'd finally got the courage to show her boss the designs she'd made for their next movie with lots of dance numbers, he'd made her his assistant. And when she admitted she was expecting a baby, he'd shrugged and said she could work at home until she was able to come in. Sometimes, she wondered if his acceptance had anything to do with her new name. She went by Espy Knox now, and with her light complexion, not many people knew she was of Mexican descent. While she didn't keep it a secret, it wasn't something she shouted from the roof tops either. Her heart broke a little each time she heard about a family from one of the old neighborhoods taking a buyout, only to discover they couldn't buy a house wherever they wanted, even with cash in hand. Some neighborhoods didn't want Mexicans or Blacks moving in and had laws to keep them out, so they were forced to buy in Boyle Heights, or Lincoln Heights, or as far away as Pico Rivera.

She'd visited the Acevedo family at their home in Boyle Heights, and she'd been happy to see Jane playing outside, surrounded by cousins her own age. The move had been good for Mercy, too, who now had plenty of new things to complain about, like how her sister let her children run loose in the streets and how Salvio Duran's daughter had abandoned her widowed father in Palo Verde, moved to Boyle Heights, and taken a job at Henry Loya's market. When she hugged Jane goodbye, Espy saw she'd mended the red protection bracelet Catalina Montez had made for her and still wore it around her thin, brown wrist.

After that, she drove the car Bruce had bought her to Evergreen Cemetery and visited Catalina's grave, cleaning the stone with a rag she'd brought, then sitting on the grass and talking quietly to her old friend.

"I'm sorry I had to leave Palo Verde, Catalina," she confessed. "But I just couldn't take it anymore. I was never like you. A fighter." Her eyes filled with tears. "I hope you're at peace now. You deserve it, after everything you've been through. And Robert forgives you, and Jane's so happy at her new home that she's forgotten all about what happened that night. More people are selling up and leaving. But you stay where you are and don't worry about all that. The place has got plenty of resisters, including Bertita and Lencha, and you know how stubborn they are."

Espy talked until her mouth was dry and the sun was straight overhead. She couldn't feel Catalina's presence—not like when Catalina roamed the neighborhoods as the Night Lady ghost—and she found it reassuring. After saying one final prayer, she left.

That night, she and Bruce drove to Palo Verde for their regular Thursday night dinner at Bertita's house. It was a warm, February evening, and when they arrived, they found everyone in the backyard, sitting around the picnic tables. Rose Delgado and Martin were making the rounds, pouring red wine.

Carlos was in the kitchen, an apron wrapped around his waist, as he dished out rice and beans while Bertita, leaning against the counter, supervised.

Espy left Bruce talking with Carlos about a boxing match and went in search of Lencha. She found her in the shed at the back of the property. It was much like the one in Catalina's garden, dried herbs hanging from the ceiling, worktable covered with tins and bottles.

Lencha eyed her midsection with a knowing little smile, then said, "When is the baby due?"

Espy thought the new dress she'd made covered it well. "Am I showing that much?" she asked in surprise.

Lencha shook her head. "No. But I can tell." Which was exactly like Lencha. The woman had always been tight-lipped and more than a bit mysterious. Lencha studied her through narrowed eyes. "Are you feeling sick? Do you need me to make you something?"

"I'm fine," she said hurriedly. The truth was, she did have morning sickness, but she had no intention of taking any cure Lencha concocted. She didn't quite trust the woman, but if anyone ever asked her why, it would be impossible to explain. Perhaps she just liked to keep her curanderas and brujas separate. But there was one thing Lencha deserved credit for, and that was making the Night Lady go away, once and for all. For that accomplishment, Lencha had earned the respect and gratitude of many of the residents who had once been Catalina's customers.

Espy swallowed, then met the woman's gaze. "Bertita used to say you were afraid of the Night Lady, but on that night, I saw you. I saw you run to the garden, and you told me to stay in the house. Why? Why wouldn't you let me come."

Lencha shrugged. "Because I knew you were expecting a baby, and I didn't want to take a chance that anything would happen to you. Catalina wasn't Catalina anymore. She was the Night Lady, and she had become this ugly, mean ghost. Jane helped, by being there. Catalina always loved that little girl. I'm not sure that what I did would have been enough. And yes, I was afraid. I'm not much of a bruja. Not like my mother, or Catalina's mother." She paused and gave a rueful smile. "But enough to deal with the Night Lady."

That nearly qualified as a speech for quiet Lencha, and Espy gazed at her in astonishment. "But how, Lencha? *How* did you make her go away?"

Lencha flicked her long black braid over her shoulder, then shoved her hands in the pockets of her pinafore-style apron. "With intention," she said, then turned on her heel and walked out of the shed.

Espy stared after her, pinching her lips together. She counted slowly to ten, then twenty, and when her irritation with the infuriating woman subsided, she went to rejoin the others.

Halfway across the yard, she spotted Robert Cleary and came to an abrupt stop. He'd missed the last Thursday's dinner, and she'd been unable to reach him at home. She'd even left a message for him at the newspaper but hadn't heard from him. At breakfast, she told Bruce she was getting worried, and Bruce had promised to drop by Robert's apartment if he didn't show up that night. And now, there he was, standing along the fence, looking just fine and dandy, talking with a pretty young woman.

She marched over to him and said, "Robert!" louder than she intended because he flinched.

Voice cracking, he said, "Oh hi, Espy." He shifted from one foot to the other, and a blush crept up his neck. "This is Carol Lansdale. Carol, this is Espy Gaten. I mean Knox. Espy Knox. She's a costume designer."

"*Assistant* to the costume designer," Espy rushed to say. "Nice to meet you, Carol."

Carol stuck out her hand. She had the type of effortless short curly hairstyle featured in magazines and almond shaped brown eyes. With her firm handshake and ready smile, Espy liked her immediately. Robert seemed to relax slightly, and suddenly, she understood. Carol was why she hadn't heard from him.

"How do you two know each other?" she asked, watching as Robert began to fidget again.

"Oh!" Carol said easily. "I'm a librarian, and Robert is a big reader. That's where we met. At the library."

Robert nodded, blushing again. "I'm glad you're here," he stammered. "I was going to stop by your new place and say hello." He cleared his throat. "And introduce you to Carol."

Carol took Robert's arm. "He's told me all about you, Espy. And Bruce too." She looked around. "I'd love to meet him."

They found Bruce in the kitchen, where he was drinking a beer with Bertita. After the introductions, Robert ushered her into the living room and closed the door behind him. Espy stared at him expectantly. The guy looked miserable. "You haven't told her, have you?" she asked.

Robert pressed a palm against his forehead. "No. Every time I'm about to do it, I chicken out. I mean, what am I supposed to say?"

"She didn't read it in the newspaper? It was such a big story. Everybody was talking about it."

Robert eyed the door to the kitchen nervously, as if he expected Carol to appear any moment. "Apparently not. She must be the only person in Los Angeles who didn't. I can't believe the fix I'm in. Carol doesn't like reading the news. She says it's too depressing. It's all books, books, books with her. Jane Austen. The Bronte sisters. Daphne du Maurier." He gave her a pleading look. "What am I supposed to say?"

"The truth," Espy said firmly. "It's not your fault, Robert. You didn't have a chance against someone like Judith. And here's another thing. You're a grown man." She dropped her voice to a whisper. "If you're worried that Carol will faint when you tell her you're not a virgin, believe me, she won't. Unless she's a dummy."

Robert coughed and stared down at his feet. Espy half expected him to say, *aw shucks*. "We've already…," he said, his voice drifting off.

Whatever she'd been expecting, it wasn't that. Espy threw her head back and laughed so hard she had to hold her stomach. "Then you have nothing to worry about," she gasped.

"That's what you say," he said glumly.

She gave his arm a shake. "Robert, if she doesn't understand, then she's the wrong girl for you. But I can tell she really likes you, so tell her, and soon, and I can guarantee you're going to feel a lot better when you do."

That time might eventually come, but it wasn't now, because her lanky friend continued to stand there, shoulders curled forward and looking miserable. Which reminded her. "What's the latest on Judith? I keep checking the paper to see if there's anything new, but there hasn't been. And I've haven't been able to get hold of you."

"The story is running tomorrow," Robert said, eyes glinting. He was teasing her, but she was glad to see the look of satisfaction that had come across his face. Anything was better than the haunted expression he'd worn since he'd stumbled, half-dressed, out of the jail on the set.

"And?"

"And they finally found the evidence they'd been looking for. Just yesterday, in fact. Judith had been renting a garage from an old man in the Miracle Mile neighborhood. They might never have heard about it if he hadn't happened to see her picture in the paper, so he contacted the police, and they went had a look. They found a second car, the one she planned on using to leave town before she was arrested, and in the trunk they found a suitcase with the clothes that had belonged to Angel, Louie, and Don, along with her stash of the drug she used to dope them. And me. Cagle says after that, she confessed. So, after a trial, and with any luck, she'll be on her way to The California Institution for Women in Tehachapi out near the Mojave Desert."

Maybe it was the unexpected bit of news, or the baby, but Espy suddenly felt light-headed and warm all over. When she'd recovered, she gave a barking laugh that startled Robert, which made her laugh even more. "Good. I'm glad they got her, and I hope she never gets out after what she did." She paused, carefully considering her words. "Were you ever able to find out more about Judith? About why she was…the way she was?"

Robert pressed his lips together, eyes turning inward. "Maybe. Her parents are dead. I tracked down some other family, but no one would talk to me, except for a younger brother. He said she ran away from home when she was fifteen, and he hadn't seen or heard from her since. He said their father had a mean streak, especially when he drank, and the night before Judith left, he saw his father coming out of Judith's room in the middle of the night, but he was only twelve at the time, so he hadn't thought much about it until he was older. But he said Judith had a mean streak herself, and he had a couple of scars to prove it. I told Detective Cagle all this, by the way, and he said sometimes you never really know what makes people do the things they do."

A pained look crossed Espy's face. She hated to see her friend suffer. And wonder. He'd probably wonder all his life why that awful woman had chosen him as her victim. But he was young and smart, and by the looks of it, he'd found a wonderful new girl to help him forget what he'd endured at the hands of Judith Saenz.

She gave him a quick hug, a slap on the back, then pulled him into the kitchen.

There was one more thing she wanted to do before they left Palo Verde.

"Can we please drive around a bit?" she asked Bruce after they reached the car. The light was fading, but there was still enough to see.

"Okay," Bruce said reluctantly, opening the door. Once inside, he put both hands on the steering wheel but made no motion to start the car. "Are you sure? It's a little depressing."

"I know. But they're supposed to start tearing down more houses tomorrow."

"Bertita's not selling," he mused. "And neither are most of the people who were there tonight. They said the city was going to have to drag them out, kicking and screaming, and I believe them. But I'm glad you sold." He reached over and stroked her hair. "Where do you want to go?"

She couldn't bear to look at her old house, having already said goodbye to it, so Bruce went another way, and they drove past Catalina's garden, now a dry, brown expanse that would have broken her old friend's heart. Across the street, the Acevedo house looked abandoned, the white painted windows like dark empty eyes. In La Loma, the house that Catalina had grown up in, had suffered in, was no more. It was just a pile of rubble. The abnormal vegetation that killed and injured workers on the city's demolition crews had withered, and after some nervous testing, the demolitions began again, leaving empty lots where houses filled with families once stood.

The Night Lady no longer stood in their way. It would be up to the resisters now.

They made their final circuit through Palo Verde, exiting through Bishop. Espy felt her belly flutter. A light-hearted feeling spread throughout her body as she thought of her new home and her new life, and she knew she could never set foot in the old neighborhoods again.

THE END

311

Keep reading for a preview of

THE CITY WANTS THEM GONE. THE DEMONS WANT THEM DEAD.

INTERNATIONAL AWARD WINNING AUTHOR LATINO BOOK AWARDS

THE MONSTERS OF CHAVEZ RAVINE

DEBRA CASTANEDA

Chapter 1

Los Angeles, Autumn 1952

Her father's messengers arrived one by one throughout the morning, leaving Trini Duran to conclude she had wasted her time nagging him to get a telephone. He didn't need one. Not when he had his friends to do his bidding.

By ten o'clock, she'd heard, "Ai, Trini, it's so sad your father is up there all alone."

By eleven, "If you want my honest opinion, Trini, he's not looking so good these days."

And by the time lunch rolled around, a comment so sharp it could have poked her in the eye. "God have mercy on your soul, Trini, for abandoning your father like you did."

When Trini overheard her boss talking on the phone, she escaped to the shed outside the back of the store where she could eat her lunch in peace. She sat down on a rickety chair and swatted away a fly. A bee appeared through a crack in the wooden slats, buzzing near her sandwich. Several ants crawled up her socked foot. She had dispatched the pests when the door flew open. Henry Loya stood there, regarding her solemnly.

"Your father says you need to go home," he said without preamble. Just one of the reasons Trini liked the man. He didn't beat around the bush.

She rose with a sigh. "Now what?"

Henry hesitated, looking troubled. "He said some weird stuff is going on, but he wouldn't say what. Said he needed to show you in person."

"What kind of stuff?" she asked, feeling a knot in her belly.

With her father, if it wasn't one thing, it was another. A new customer he thought was a spy from the California Housing Authority. Another visit from a city official threatening to kick him out of Chavez Ravine, once and for all.

It was Henry's turn to sigh. "You know how your father is. He wouldn't tell me." He paused. "Look, Trini. I've tried talking to him. Told him he didn't have to stay. That he could take the money, close up. Retire, or open a new market in the empty store in Lincoln Heights."

By this time, Trini had lost her appetite. She stuffed what remained of the sandwich in her apron pocket. "That's what I keep telling him, but he won't listen."

Henry gave an indulgent smile. "He's as stubborn as the rest of them. But, Trini, I think you should go. Something's not right. I can feel it."

Trini stared at him in surprise. She'd worked for Henry Loya for one year, and during that time, he'd never said a word about leaving her father behind. Which made him the only person she knew who hadn't tried to make her feel guilty. Not that she needed any help in that department. She felt lousy about it every single day.

"Okay, I'll go," she lied.

She didn't like to go against Henry, especially not after everything he'd done for her, giving her a job and a place to live. Making it possible for her to take classes at L.A. City College, which reminded her—she needed to study. Her father and his Chavez Ravine problems would have to wait. Besides, she and her brother had begged him to sell his properties to the city. Beto had even invited him to Pico Rivera, where he and his family had moved.

Salvio Duran would not budge. He'd been born in the Palo Verde neighborhood of Chavez Ravine, and he would die there, he announced to anyone who would listen, and to hell with the city and their stupid plan to build low-income housing.

"But it's eminent domain, viejo," Ripper had pleaded. "You don't have any choice. Nobody does."

Even former convicts like Ripper Cuevas knew about "eminent domain." Ripper managed Henry's second market in Boyle Heights. Trini liked him, even if some of the old people still held it against him that he did time in prison. But Ripper was a hard worker and didn't talk much, and he'd tried to convince her father it was useless to continue fighting against the city and its pinche plan to build cheap apartments for people who already had houses with yards.

Trini followed Henry back into the market, suddenly busy with women shopping for dinner. She took her place at the cash register. Of all the jobs she did at Loya Market, this was her favorite, even though she sometimes had to talk to the customers—it beat stocking the shelves or cleaning out the refrigerators, but she thought all that yakking was annoying. Which explained why the customers preferred talking to Henry. Often, they did more talking than buying, but Henry didn't seem to mind.

Late in the afternoon—another warm fall day in Los Angeles—a small group had gathered on the benches outside the entrance. She peered outside. By their angry faces and all the hand waving, she could guess what they were talking about—Chavez Ravine. No matter how hard she tried, she couldn't seem to escape the place.

She recognized Rose and Martin, friends of her father, and somebody new joined them. It couldn't be.

Yes, it was. Bobby Guerra.

What the hell was he doing here? She'd grown up with him in Palo Verde. He was a couple of years ahead of her in school. He'd disappeared for a while and later, she heard he'd gone to college. A few months ago, he turned up again, working as a community organizer. Precisely what that meant, Trini had no idea, but she was sure it involved talking people into stuff because the guy had always been a smooth talker.

She scurried to the bathroom and checked her hair. It was shiny and clean, at least. Good thing she'd washed it the night before. She dug out a tube of lipstick. A swipe of red did the trick, and just in time, too. She had resumed her place at the cash register, determined to ignore him when Bobby walked in. He grabbed a bunch of Cokes and set them down in front of her.

"You drinking all those?" she asked.

"Nice to see you, too, Trini," he said, lifting a single eyebrow.

She rang him up and held out her hand. He slapped a dollar into her palm, never taking his eyes off her face. "Has anyone ever told you it's rude to stare?" she snapped.

Bobby grinned. "Is this how you treat your customers?"

"Only the ones who get on my nerves," she replied, handing him his change.

"I can see you haven't changed a bit, Trini," Bobby said over his shoulder, smiling as he strode toward the door.

She watched as he handed out Cokes to the small group outside. Her heart was beating so hard she had to sit down for a few seconds to calm down. He'd become even better looking with those white teeth, smooth brown skin and strong jaw of his. Bits and pieces of their conversation drifted through the screen door—substandard housing, fair market value, holdouts.

When she wandered over to the window, pretending to straighten up the "Today's Sale" sign, he was still out there, talking. He caught her looking and waved for her to join them.

"No, thank you," she mouthed, shaking her head. After learning her lesson the hard way, she'd rather stick a needle in her eye. All those city people who made decisions about Chavez

Ravine were nothing but liars and tricksters, and no amount of meetings or protest signs would change things.

She picked up a duster and began swiping at the shelves, her back turned to the plate glass window. Didn't Bobby have more important things to do than hang around the market?

Henry walked back in, went to his tiny office at the back of the market, and returned, jacket in hand. He sighed. "Can you close up, Trini? Bobby's talked me into going to one of those damned city meetings. Wants me to give a speech." Trini blinked in surprise. Henry rarely cursed.

"Isn't it too late?" she asked. "I thought the city already decided."

Henry shrugged. "That's what I keep telling him, but he's like your father. Stubborn as they come. And speaking of your father, you said you'd go see him. Don't forget."

"I won't," she said, crossing her fingers behind her back.

The last thing she wanted to do was go all the way to Chavez Ravine and get an earful from her father. She'd see him in a few days and give him a chance to calm down. Bring him an apple pie and cook his favorite dinner when she got there, even get her good-for-nothing brother Beto to do his part and visit the man if he could drag himself away from Pico Rivera. In the meantime, she had plenty to keep her busy. Besides all the studying she needed to do, there was that new book she'd checked out from the library and the movie at the Vern Theater she'd meant to see. Tomorrow was her day off, and she deserved a treat. Already feeling better about things, Trini managed a smile at Rose when she ducked in to say hello. Bobby came in, too.

"I'll see you around, Trini," he said, looking her over again in that way of his.

"If you say so, Mister Community Organizer," she said, turning around and walking toward the back of the store.

319

Her face felt like it was on fire. When she looked over her shoulder, Bobby was still standing there, smirking. Then he winked, turned on his heel, and left.

Author's Note

When I was growing up, my mother and the rest of her family would often reminisce about their old neighborhood of Palo Verde, and the friends they had in La Loma and Bishop. Sometimes, later in life, they referred to it as Chavez Ravine.

The story of the fight to save the villages from destruction through eminent domain evictions is filled with brave people challenging injustice. Out of respect for their memories, I have not included them in this story. To get one small detail wrong would be to do them a great disservice.

While the battle over Chavez Ravine depicted in the story generally follows the sad trajectory that happened in real life, it fictionalizes the politicians, as it does the contentious public meeting in which the character Bobby Guerra speaks.

If you're interested in learning more about the history of the area, I've compiled a list of recommended reads on my website, debracastaneda.com. There, you'll also find an artistic illustration of the main character, Trini Duran, based on my mother at age twenty-two.

Thank you for choosing to read this story. For that, I'm extremely grateful! As an independent author, reviews can make all the difference in getting the word out. If you enjoyed *The Monsters of Chavez Ravine*, I hope you consider rating it and leaving a review on Amazon and/or Goodreads.

More Books By Debra Castaneda

The Monsters of Chavez Ravine
A 2021 International Latino Book Awards Gold Medal Winner!
Before Dodger Stadium, dark forces terrorized Chavez Ravine.

Dark Earth Rising
Themed novels that can be read in any order

The Root Witch
A beautiful forest. A terrifying legend. It's 1986. Two strangers, hundreds of miles apart, grapple with disturbing incidents in a one-of-a-kind quaking aspen forest.

The Devil's Shallows
A novel about a controversial housing development on a California slough, an urban legend caught on tape, and a series of horrifying events that have residents fighting for their lives.

Circus at Devil's Landing
Creatures that howl in the night, a mysterious circus, and a clash between a ringmaster and a woman determined to rescue her captured lover.

The Copper Man

Haunted tunnels. Unexplained deaths. Eerie sightings. Decades after The Copper Man killed her brother, Leah Shaw returns to the remote mining town of Tribulation Gulch where a lethal mystery awaits.

A Dark and Rising Tide

When a massive storm surge hits the central coast of California, the ferocious surf destroys buildings, floods streets, and washes up something sinister from the depths of the Monterey Bay.

About the Author

After a career as a journalist in radio and TV, Debra Castaneda now devotes her time to writing horror and dark fiction. She lives with her husband in Capitola, California.